ACCIDENTALLY FALLING FOR MY BEST FRIEND

CHICAGO AWAKENINGS
BOOK TWO

LEXI AMBER

CONTENTS

CONTENT WARNING:

This book contains mentions of

- chronic illness (Type 1 diabetes)
- healthy eating discussions in the context of diabetes
- medical emergencies and hospital stays
- death of a parent in road accident with drunk driver
- a homophobic, racist background character
- the risk of being cut off for being LGBTQIA+ for a secondary character
- There is also mention of pregnancy, adoption, fostering, egg donation and surrogacy (mainly in the epilogue)

This is a romance with explicit content that is inappropriate for anyone who is under the age of 18, or is related to me.

DEDICATION

*For everyone who took the time to review AJHC and mentioned
how excited you are for Oakley and Parker*

PARKER

NINE YEARS OLD

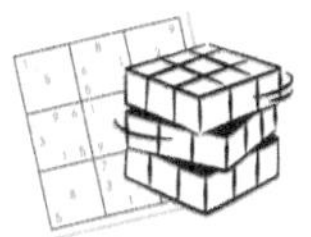

Today is my *fourth* first day at a new school, and I'm only in the third grade.

This one is a fancy private elementary school in downtown Chicago. The building looks super old, and the snow covering everything makes it feel magical. My dad said it's a really good school, but I'm pretty sure the things that make a school "good" to adults are different than what the kids there actually care about. *How's the food? Will I be the only kid with red hair again?*

There's a half-circle driveway in front of the building that's used for drop-off, and it looks like most of the kids are in fancy cars with drivers. My mom pulls into the line, but it isn't moving at all.

She turns around to give me a small smile. "It's okay to be nervous honey, just be yourself. Anyone would be lucky to be your friend," she promises me brightly.

I know that she means well and that she believes what she's saying, but I don't have the best track record when it comes to making friends.

"None of the kids at my last school seem to think so," I grumble, looking up at the fancy stone building that we're approaching. I wonder how old it is.

"That's what's so great about fresh starts," she agrees while nodding. "Smile, be kind. You don't have to be the most popular kid in school—one friend is really all anyone needs."

"Okay," I mumble, hoping to end this little pep talk.

I really like school. I love to read and learn about history, but math is my favorite. I love solving problems and doing puzzles. My dad and I do a lot of Sudoku, trying to see who can finish the same puzzle faster. Numbers have always made sense to me. My dad said that this school will be starting multiplication this semester, which is cool because he's been teaching it to me for years.

My last school talked about moving me into classes with older kids, but my parents were already so "concerned about me socially" after moving schools each year that they decided to leave me with the kids my age and teach me extra things themselves.

I've always struggled with making friends. My hair is a unique color, and I have more freckles than most kids, but I don't think the way I look would scare the other kids away. I just don't always have something to say. It seems like the other kids are constantly talking and joking around, but by the time I actually think about a joke and understand it enough to laugh, they've all finished and are onto the next thing.

I don't mind spending time alone, I just kind of wish that I had someone to talk to at school when I *do* have something to say.

My dad tells me that there's nothing wrong with taking my time and observing things. He says that I'm "analytical" and that it'll be a great thing when I'm older.

My parents are hopeful that this school will be different. Dad works for a restaurant that's been expanding to new cities over the last few years, and they move him to open the new locations and get them started. After about a year, when they've hired local staff and know it's in good hands, we move to the next location.

This time is supposed to be different, though. They promised my dad that the Chicago location is going to be more important than the other ones, bigger and hopefully more popular, and that they'll let him stay.

So the pressure for me to fit in here seems more important than ever to my parents. The school has a uniform, so I don't have to worry about having "cool" clothes, but my mom got me nice new shoes for Christmas that she said are popular right now, and she took me to get a haircut last week to make sure I look my best for the first day.

"You'll do great, I love you!" she says confidently as we finally pull up in front of the school and I get out.

"Love you too," I respond, turning toward the building.

My parents and I came a few days ago to tour the school and get all of the registration stuff done. It was still winter break for the kids, but the teachers were already back planning, so I was able to meet my homeroom teacher and see where my classroom is.

I make my way there and immediately notice a bunch of kids gathered around one boy's desk. I can't see much of him around the crowd, but I can tell that he's talking animatedly, gesturing with his arms, and making everyone laugh.

I wonder what it's like to be one of the popular kids... Do their parents ever have to tell them to smile, or give them pep talks about "being themselves"?

The teacher, Mrs. Ashley, notices my arrival and smiles warmly at me, gesturing to have me join her at the front of the room. "Good morning, Parker," she greets me when I'm next to her desk. "I'll just wait until everyone is here, and then I'll introduce you to the rest of the class."

I give a tight smile and nod, awkwardly standing next to her, looking out at the other kids that I'll be spending my time with.

A bell rings, and everyone moves to their seat.

"Good morning, and I'm happy that you're all back. I hope everyone had a lovely winter break," Mrs. Ashley addresses the class. "We have a new student joining us today: Parker Leighton just moved here from South Carolina. Despite the freezing temps outside, I expect you all to give him a warm welcome," she adds, and a few kids snicker at the attempted humor.

There's a general murmur of "hellos" from the class, and Mrs. Ashley directs me to sit in the only open desk in the room.

The desks are pushed together into tables of four, so that each desk has one directly next to it and is across from another two desks. I immediately realize that my desk neighbor is the popular boy everyone was crowded around earlier.

There goes any chance of a forced-neighbor friendship. I'm sure Mr. Popular isn't looking for any new friends.

He's got dark brown hair that's styled like the kids on TV and bright blue eyes. He smiles at me, and his teeth look very straight; he probably won't even need braces.

I reluctantly sit down and start to place my supplies into the desk as the teacher begins a summary of our plans for the day.

"I'm Oakley," the boy next to me says, and I quickly look up at him, surprised that he's talking to me at all.

"Like the tree?" I hear my mouth ask, even though my brain never gave it permission to.

See, this is why I don't have friends. I say things without thinking and offend people, or I take too long to think about what to say, and then they think I'm dumb or ignoring them.

This kid is going to think I'm teasing him, and he's going to tell all of his friends I'm mean, and I'll be all alone, yet again.

A laugh bursts out of his mouth. "Ha. Yeah, like an oak tree.

And you're Parker like a park," he says happily. "We're nature name buddies, it's like it was meant to be," he adds.

I am so confused. *Did he say buddies?*

"Um, what's meant to be?" I question, not following at all.

"Us, being desk buddies. It was meant to be," he declares casually.

Oh, he just means like neighbors. Not that he wants us to be friends. *That makes more sense.*

"Okay class, I know that I warned you all about this before Christmas, but it's officially time to move on to multiplication," Mrs. Ashley announces. There are a few groans, including one from Oakley.

"Don't worry, multiplication is easy," I whisper to him for some reason. I'm not usually a whisper to my neighbor kind of kid, but he was being so chatty, I guess it made me more comfortable.

He gives me a skeptical side-eyed look. "My older brother said multiplication is the hardest part of third grade," he challenges.

"Oh. My dad taught me about two years ago, and we work on it a lot, so if you need help I can show you the tricks he's shown me," I offer. *Why did I admit all of that?* He's probably about to call me a nerd or tease me for doing homework for fun.

"No way! Really? That's so cool," he whisper-shouts, earning us both a look from the teacher. We smile back apologetically as she tells the class what page to open our textbooks to.

"Sure," I say to him in a much softer voice.

"I think I'm going to like being your friend," he whispers back.

Did I hear that right? He definitely said friend that time, not buddy. Maybe he does want to be friends with the new kid.

Don't get ahead of yourself. Once he actually gets to know me, he'll realize that he's way too cool for me and leave me alone. It's happened before, people want to talk to the exciting new kid, but then they realize I'm me, and that there's literally nothing else that's cool about me. Suddenly being new is no longer that interesting.

We get through the lesson, listening to Mrs. Ashley explain what to do before having time to practice problems in our workbook. I finish quickly and glance at Oakley struggling with the second problem.

"Here, try this," I suggest, before writing out the way my dad showed me. I can do this stuff in my head, but I think the visual will help him.

"Ohhh, okay, that makes sense," he agrees, trying the next one. "Thanks, that's way easier!"

"No problem," I say with a smile before pulling out the Rubik's Cube my parents got me for Christmas. I've had a few in the past, but the colors were starting to wear off with how much I played with it, so they got me this new one. It's still a bit stiff, but the colors are bright.

I finish off the second side when Oakley notices it.

"There's no way you can actually finish that," he challenges.

"Sure I can," I say with a laugh. I do these all the time, my dad taught me how to last year after I found one in his desk. I picked it up quickly, and I like to carry one around with me to keep busy when I get bored.

Oakley stares at me, he must have finished his work by now too, and when I turn the last row into place a minute or two later, he grabs it out of my hand to inspect each side.

"Are you like a genius or something?" he asks, giving me a disbelieving look like he's actually impressed.

"No, it's just a pattern. I like patterns," I explain.

He gives me a huge smile. "Cool. Can you teach me? Maybe show me again during recess?" he suggests.

Is this really happening? Or am I having a strange dream?

Why would the popular kid want to hang out with me during recess?

"Yeah, sure," I finally agree, glad that I managed to sound so chill and didn't blurt out any other random thoughts.

He gives me that big smile again, and I wonder if this school might be different. Maybe my mom was right and one friend is all I'll need.

2

OAKLEY

ELEVEN YEARS OLD

"You okay, man?" I ask, worried for my best friend. "You barely reacted when that guy shot you."

School is finally done for summer break, and we're hanging out at Parker's house playing video games. He's usually a lot better at them than he seems to be today, though.

"Huh? Oh yeah, I guess I'm a little tired or something," he replies slowly. *He does look like he could use some sleep.*

"Want me to go so you can nap?" I offer reluctantly, not actually wanting to leave.

"Nah, just let me run to the bathroom again and grab another snack before the next round, I'm starving," he says.

"Didn't you just pee before we started that game?" I ask with a laugh, and he shrugs, heading toward the bathroom.

I go to the kitchen and grab a bag of his favorite chips and another sports drink for him to snack on. I'm full from what we ate earlier, but Parker has been growing a lot recently, and he looks way slimmer than he did a few months ago, despite how hungry he always seems to be.

I love hanging out at Parker's house.

It's so quiet. I have four brothers, and I can't remember the last time I heard actual silence at home.

I know Parker thinks that my place is cooler because it's fancy or whatever, but I like spending time here. He also wishes that he had siblings, but he has me, so he *obviously* doesn't need anyone else.

We've been pretty much inseparable since we met on his first day of school. I'm so lucky he moved here and that I get to have him as my best friend. Parker's really funny. I know a lot of people say *I'm* funny, but I don't think they realize how hard I'm *trying* to be funny, ya know? And when I am trying to get people to laugh at my jokes, I know they're actually funny if Parker laughs. I always make sure to look at him when I say the punchline to gauge his reactions.

Parker, on the other hand, is just effortlessly funny. He has the worst filter sometimes, and some of the stuff he blurts out will have me snort laughing.

He's also super smart, and for some reason, he doesn't mind helping me if I don't understand something in class. I've done way better in school since meeting him. I'm even getting higher grades than my older brother, Beckett, did in some classes, and he's the golden child who set the standard way too high for the rest of us to live up to.

Parker and I are both pretty competitive, and we try to outscore each other on tests and assignments. It's all for fun though, we don't actually care who wins. We're just as happy when the other succeeds in something as we are when we accomplish it ourselves.

Seriously, I must have won the best friend jackpot or something.

I bring the chips back to his living room where the video games are set up, and he thanks me, but doesn't eat them yet, saying his stomach is feeling off now.

We start another round, but Parker seems extra quiet today, slouched back on the couch like he's falling asleep, breathing kind of heavy. Maybe he's getting sick and I *should* let him nap.

Just as I have that thought, his character stops moving on the screen and out of the corner of my eye I see his controller fall to the floor.

"Parker?" I ask, turning toward him, where it looks like he fell asleep right next to me on the couch. *But if he was asleep, my talking would have woken him up, right?*

"Parker!" I say, a little more urgently. I shake his arm a bit, trying to make sure he's okay.

He doesn't respond.

"Parker! Come on man, this isn't funny." I think I'm shouting now, but my racing heart is beating way too loudly for me to hear anything else.

"Judy!" I scream his mom's name when he still isn't responding, and she rushes into the room, joining me in trying to wake him. She yells for his dad, telling him to call 911, and my vision blurs as his dad enters the room with their cordless home phone.

Am I crying?

I feel like I just finished a rough hockey practice with how I can't seem to catch my breath. I think his parents are talking, asking me what happened, but it all sounds far away, like we're under water or something.

I try to tell them that we were playing video games and then he fell asleep mid-game, but my throat is too tight to let out all of the words.

Two paramedics rush into the room and start touching him, holding his wrist and counting his breaths. One pokes his finger with a needle, and it starts to bleed before they stick a small machine right up to the blood. They seem to react to whatever is on the machine and draw up some medicine into a syringe before stabbing him to push it into his body. They tape another needle to his arm and connect a big bag of fluids to it.

Then Parker's moved onto a stretcher and rushed outside. I chase after them, determined to go with him, to stay by his side until he wakes up. I was there when he fell asleep or passed out or whatever is going on—I don't want him to think that I left him when he needed me.

I'm his best friend. I'm not going anywhere.

But his dad grabs my shoulder when we're outside, holding me in place and preventing me from climbing into the ambulance with Parker and his mom.

"Only one family member is allowed to ride with him," he says gently.

A part of me knows his mom *should* be that one person because I know my mom would want to be, and I'd want her there, too.

But another part of me is way louder and is very freaked out right now because my best friend just passed out next to me, and honestly, I feel like *I* should be that one person. I know I'm not technically his family, but I'm his best friend, so that definitely counts.

I think I might still be crying, but all I can feel is a bone-deep, paralyzing fear.

"I'll drop you off at home on my way to the hospital," his dad says, sounding far away again as he moves toward his car that's in the driveway separating me from my best friend, who obviously needs me right now.

I feel frozen in this spot. My breathing is still too fast, and my heart is trying to beat out of my chest.

What if he doesn't wake up? What if he isn't okay? What even happened? Is there anything that I should have done differently? Is this my fault for not noticing something was wrong sooner? Questions won't stop racing through my mind.

"Take a deep breath in for the count of five," Mr. Leighton says, gripping both of my shoulders and leaning down a little so that he can hold eye contact.

I try to do what he says, breathing in with him and out when he instructs.

"Oakley, they said that Parker will be okay," he assures me. "I don't think they'll allow extra visitors at the hospital right away, so I'll let your parents know as soon as you can come. I promise I won't let anything bad happen to him," he adds, looking into my eyes like he really wants me to understand.

Parker's dad is a super tall, muscular man who seems to fill a room when he enters it. When he makes a promise, it's really hard not to believe him.

"Okay," I manage to get out as my breathing starts to slow.

I've always liked his parents. They're really nice people, and I think it's cool how much time they try to spend with him on puzzles and extra school stuff that he likes to do.

They're so excited to have me over all the time, too. After we'd been friends for a while, Parker explained that he didn't really have friends before moving here because of how often he changed schools, and because he can be kind of shy.

So I guess they're happy that Parker has me now. *Well, so am I.* Parker is the best. They've all felt like my second family over the last two years, and I'm so happy that they got to stay in Chicago instead of moving around like they used to.

I'm relieved that Parker's parents were here. I don't know what I would have done if we were alone. I did not handle that whole event well.

I HAD to wait at home for *a whole freaking day*!

When I should have been in the hospital, waiting for Parker to wake up, I was stuck at home, alone.

Well, with my giant family. I'm not sure what's driving them crazier, my endless pacing or my nonstop questions about what happened to Parker—if he was awake yet, and when I could go see him.

Finally, my parents got a call from Parker's parents saying that I could come to the hospital, and I've never gotten into a car so quickly in my life.

The hospital is gigantic. I think it's the same one we came to visit my mom and Lincoln in when he was born, but that's the only other time I've ever been to a hospital. I don't remember it seeming so scary.

My mom and I have to check in at the front desk and tell them who we're here to see and get visitor passes. Security has to scan the badge and hit the correct floor in the elevator for it to work. Then we're walking down a long hallway, past all of these sick kids in big hospital beds peering out of the glass doors of their rooms.

Parker doesn't belong here. I can't believe that I let this happen, that I didn't know anything was wrong until he looked dead next to me on the couch.

We get to the room number they gave us downstairs and slide open the door. He looks so sick. Pale with huge bags under his eyes, and he's wearing one of those weird hospital gowns with snap buttons up the sleeves and a pattern that looks like it belongs on a movie theater's carpet.

We were just playing video games and joking around yesterday. Now he's in a freaking hospital bed, surrounded by monitors and wires. Bags are hanging on a pole next to him with tubes connected to his arm. Things are beeping and I want to know what they all mean. To understand what happened and know that he's okay.

His parents are both there, sitting on the couch that's on the other side of the room, and they smile as we come in.

"We'll go grab you some more water and give you guys a minute," his mom says, standing to leave with my mom.

His dad squeezes my shoulder as he walks past, whispering, "Kept my promise, he's all right," just for me to hear.

I let out the breath I didn't know I was holding and approach Parker, not sure what to do or say.

"I'm fine, Oak," he says, rolling his eyes.

"You don't look fine," I grumble, moving a chair as close to the bed as I can. "I thought you were dead," I admit even more softly, afraid to put that idea out into the universe.

I can't imagine my life without Parker in it. I don't even want to try.

"I'm so sorry you had to be there for that," he responds. As if *he* has anything to be sorry for.

"Are you kidding me?" I ask, grabbing his hand and looking at him, waiting for him to look at me too before I say anything. "Parker, don't you dare apologize for anything. I'm the one who should be saying sorry!" I tell him desperately. "I should have known something was wrong, I should have gotten help *before* you were passed out next to me. I should have called 911 sooner." I voice some of the regrets I've had in the last day, thinking of everything I did wrong.

"If I didn't even know something was wrong, how could you?" he questions.

"I'm your best friend, I should have known," I insist, and he laughs like I'm joking.

I'm not.

I don't care what I have to do, I'm never letting whatever happened yesterday happen again. "So, what did happen?" I finally ask.

"Apparently I have Type 1 diabetes; my blood sugar was

super high, and it made me pass out. They've given me a lot of fluids and medicine to bring it down, but I guess my pancreas doesn't work, and I'll have to give myself insulin shots now," he explains.

"What's a pancreas?" I ask and he laughs.

"I don't know, but the doctor said mine doesn't make insulin like it's supposed to, so I'll need to give it to myself with shots," he says with a shrug. "And I'll need to start paying more attention to what I eat and just be healthier so that it doesn't get high like that again."

"I'll help," I quickly add. "I can be healthier with you. Whatever you need. I promise you'll never end up back here," I say confidently, wrapping my pinky around his where I'm still holding his hand.

"What are we, five years old?" he says with a laugh.

"Dude, everyone knows how serious pinky promises are, don't laugh," I deadpan.

He twists his mouth to the side like he's trying not to smile. "Fine, I think they said the diabetes educator nurse will be coming by soon to teach me everything. You can stay and learn it too, in case I forget anything or need help."

"Sounds great!" I agree, relieved to finally have some direction. I drop his hand and open the backpack I brought with me to pull out the Rubik's cube I bought back when he was trying to teach me how to solve one, and hand it to him. I got it a few times, but I always needed his help remembering how to actually do it.

"Oh awesome, thanks, Oak," he says, his whole face lighting up as he immediately begins moving the sides around.

"Anything for you, Parker."

I hope he understands how much I mean that.

3

PARKER

TWELVE YEARS OLD

"Do you know June Smith?" Oakley asks, pulling my attention back to the lunch I'm supposed to be eating.

"Uh, the girl in our English class?" I guess.

"Yeah, with the long blonde hair, she always wears that choker necklace," he confirms.

"What about her?" I ask.

"Apparently, she told Doug Stewart that she likes me," he announces proudly. "She's like the hottest girl in seventh grade," he says with emphasis.

"Yeah, I guess she's pretty," I agree. I've never really thought about it before, but her hair is always shiny and she has a kind smile.

"*And,* he said her best friend, Grace, has a crush on you too!" he adds excitedly.

A girl has a crush on me? The idea totally catches me off guard.

The other kids our age *have* started dating, and Oakley is so popular that it surprises me he hasn't had a girlfriend yet.

But instead of worrying about dating, we've been pretty focused on being healthier and managing my diabetes.

Being diabetic isn't the worst thing in the world.

My parents, and even Oakley, have all been eating healthier with me, and we've learned how to count carbs so that I can give myself the right amount of insulin in the shots I need after I eat.

There was a lot of trial and error in the beginning—keeping track of my blood sugar levels throughout the day to see how much long-acting insulin I actually needed, as well as how the short-acting insulin affected me specifically. Everyone is different, and sometimes if I'm sick or more active, it affects my sugar levels, but now that it's been a year, I've gotten into a good routine with everything, and I've been able to avoid the hospital.

Our moms have both been teaching us how to cook so that we know exactly what we're eating, taking turns with whose house we're at. And we've been working out a lot more. I started playing hockey when Oakley suggested I join his team in fourth grade. Now, instead of just practice and games, on the days that we don't have hockey, my dad has been teaching us how to work out with him in the gym.

We've also all had to learn the signs and symptoms of low and high blood sugar so we can be aware of sudden changes. Oakley is always worried if I get sweaty or seem extra hungry or thirsty. I'm usually pretty good at picking up on the symptoms myself, but it's nice to know that someone cares so much about me to notice the signs too.

Middle school is way better than elementary school. We were able to pick some of our classes, so we picked all the same ones. Luckily, we were placed in the same accelerated classes, too. I also think they kept us together because he's my official buddy to walk with me to the nurse's office and back whenever it's time to check my blood sugar or give myself insulin shots. *Not sure why I need that lady to watch me do it when I can clearly do it myself.*

Hopefully in the next few months I'll get insurance approval for an insulin pump, a device that's smaller than a phone, that could hold the insulin in my pocket and be connected to my body by a flexible tube. The pump would continuously give me a small amount of insulin, and I could program right in the device with how many carbs I ate to calculate how much extra insulin to take instead of having to figure it out in my head and then draw up the correct dose to give myself as a shot each time. Then I won't need to leave class to take my medicine, but having Oak with me makes the whole experience more tolerable.

He's been super involved with everything from the beginning. My parents kept saying how cute it was that he wanted to learn everything with me, but I know how afraid he was after I passed out in front of him and ended up in the hospital.

Not going to lie, I was a little surprised by how upset he was when he first came to visit me there. I don't remember much about the day it actually happened, but my parents said he was with me and probably saved my life, or at least my brain from permanent damage, with how quickly he called my parents in to help.

I know he still feels guilty that he couldn't have done more, but I can't imagine what could've happened if I had been reading or working on puzzles or anything by myself that day. He's already the best friend I could have ever asked for, but now I literally owe him my life.

I've told him about the other schools I went to, my lack of friends, but I don't think he really understands how much he means to me, and I'm so bad at explaining things like that. So, I just keep trying to be the best possible friend to him, and hope that he somehow knows.

Now that I think about it, we've both grown a bit and added on some muscle. I guess I'd be considered attractive, even though I don't try very hard with my appearance. It seems like most of the guys our age have shaggy hair now, so other than the red color of it, I guess I fit in.

I think it will always be weird to me that I'm considered to be a popular kid here because of my friendship with Oakley. We're always surrounded by other people and I try to be nice to everyone, but I'm not naturally a social person, so I'd still consider him to be my only real friend.

I don't know why he chooses to spend so much time with me when so many other people want to hang out with him, but I'm not about to draw his attention to it by asking.

I've never given any thought to the whole dating thing. Oakley has commented on pretty girls in the past, but we usually don't bother to talk about girls or dating when it's just us hanging out. And his older brother, Beck, who lets us hang out with him sometimes, only likes boys, but I don't think he's dated any yet.

"So, do you like her back?" Oakley asks me expectantly, not waiting for me to respond before he continues. "Because I was thinking we could ask them to go on a double date. Doug said June's mom wouldn't let her go on a date alone," he explains. "We could all go to a movie together. I think that it's about time we start dating, don't you?" he asks, clearly very excited about the idea.

I'm not about to get in the way of him going on a date that he so obviously wants to go on. Plus, I kind of like that I would be included in such a big moment for him, even if I probably wouldn't have any interest in hanging out with Grace one-on-one.

"Sure, sounds great," I tell him.

"Awesome, we can ask them during English today! Let's get there early and do it before class starts. Are you free on Friday for the date?"

"Obviously. What would I be doing without you?" I ask with a laugh.

"Good answer," he teases.

We rush to finish our lunch and get to class early enough to ask them. Luckily, I do know who Grace is, we were assigned as partners for a project last year. She's very nice and way more outgoing than I am, and she seems really happy about the date when I ask her.

I got a cellphone last year, and I double-check that I still have her number saved from that project, which I do, so I tell her that I'll text her with details after I figure it out with Oakley.

WE'RE SEEING AN ANIMATED movie since we aren't thirteen and can't see anything rated higher than PG. It's about a family that all have superpowers, but society has decided superheroes are a liability and they have to hide their abilities. It's a great movie, so I'm not too focused on the whole date thing.

Oakley and I ended up sitting in the middle, with our dates on our other sides. I glance over and see that he and June are holding hands. *Crap, is that something I'm supposed to be doing too?*

I try to casually look at where Grace has her hand, and it's resting on the armrest between us, so I decide to go for it. I grab her hand gently with my own and interlock our fingers like I saw Oakley and June are doing.

Grace turns to smile at me, giving my hand a slight squeeze, so I think that made her happy. *Good.* I would hate to upset her because I didn't know that I should be doing something as easy as holding hands.

We watch the rest of the movie and I enjoy it way more than I was expecting to. We head out to the lobby afterward, and the girls giggle as they go into the bathroom while Oakley and I wait off to the side.

"I texted my dad that the movie just finished, so we should

have, like, fifteen minutes before the driver is here to pick us up," he tells me.

"Cool," I nod, looking at the coming soon posters hung up on the wall.

"That should be plenty of time to kiss them," he adds.

"Wait, what?" I question, shifting my attention to Oakley.

"Well, I didn't want us trying to kiss them in the car in front of the driver, he'll tell my dad and he'll turn it into a whole big thing," he explains. "And we're almost teenagers, we should have kissed someone by now," he laughs.

I guess that this is another one of those things I haven't thought about. I don't dislike the idea of kissing Grace. I just wouldn't have thought to do it on my own.

The girls come back and we all walk outside toward the benches in front of the theater. Oakley holds June's hand again and leads her to their own bench, so I do the same with Grace. I can hear Oakley talking to June, but with the city noises, I can't make out what he's saying.

"This has been really fun," Grace says brightly, pulling my attention back to her.

"Yeah," I agree, even though I'm feeling awkward.

How do you kiss someone? What if she doesn't want me to kiss her? But what if she does, and I'm too awkward to initiate it? She's a great girl and I don't want to hurt her feelings.

"Can I kiss you?" I blurt out.

She flashes a big smile at me, scooting closer on the bench. "I'd like that."

I lean in so that our lips touch, I have no idea what I'm doing, but luckily Grace seems to, and she moves her lips a bit so they rub against mine while I try to mimic her movements. We pull apart and she gives me another big smile. It must not have been too awful.

I was honestly so in my head about doing it wrong that I'm

not sure if I even liked it, but I smile back at her. I think this was a good date, I don't have any complaints and she seems happy.

Oakley's driver gets there and drops the girls off at their houses before taking us both back to mine. We have a hockey game in the morning, but his parents said it was okay for him to spend the night.

"I feel like we're more mature or something now," Oakley declares when we get to my room and out of my parents' earshot.

"Because we went on a date?" I ask with a laugh.

"Yeah," he agrees excitedly. "And finally had our first kisses," he adds.

"It was cool we got to do it together," I add, and he nods in agreement, a huge smile on his face.

4

OAKLEY

THIRTEEN YEARS OLD

’ve never known anyone who died before.

My grandparents are still alive, and my great-grandparents were gone before I was born. Luckily, no one in my family has been seriously sick. That day when I thought Parker might die was the closest I'd ever felt to death.

Until last night, when I heard Parker's mom sobbing.

We had been playing video games in the living room when she answered the door. We thought maybe she'd ordered food, so we ran to meet her, but we were still around the corner when we heard a man's voice start apologizing to her.

"I'm so sorry, Ma'am, there's been an accident. A drunk driver turned the wrong way down a one-way road without their lights on," he trailed off for a moment, taking a deep breath. "Your husband was crossing the street. Witnesses confirmed that he had the walk signal, but the driver didn't slow down at the intersection," he explained, pausing again. "He died on impact. I'm so sorry," he finally said.

His mom screamed and started bawling. I don't think I've ever heard an adult scream like that before. We both ran to her,

23

and there were two Chicago Police Department officers standing there with sad, apologetic expressions.

My stomach dropped through the floor as their words caught up to me. Parker's mom looked toward us from where she had sunk down on the floor, leaning against the wall, and I've never seen heartbreak written so clearly on someone's face.

"Is Dad really gone?" Parker choked out on a whisper.

His mom looked like she could barely move, let alone speak, but she managed a slight nod.

The rest of the night was a bit of a blur, unlike the night of Parker's hospitalization, where I can recall every detail, even now, years later. The officers left, and the three of us cried in their entryway, huddled around each other on the floor.

I know it might seem odd that I was a part of that moment, but for the last four years, Parker's dad was like my second dad, too.

Parker and I do everything together. So he was at every hockey game, he took us to half of the practices, and he helped us with homework. He showed us how to use the gym equipment and what workouts to do. I've spent nearly half of the last four years here in their house.

On the scariest night of my life, *he* was the one who calmed me down. He pulled me out of my panic and promised me that everything would be okay. Promised that he wouldn't let anything bad happen to Parker.

That was the moment that I realized how special his family really is, how lucky I am that I'm a part of it.

And now he's gone.

I know it isn't the same grief Parker is experiencing, and I'm glad that I can be here for him, but I'm not going to pretend like this is only his loss; that would dishonor his dad's memory and the impact he had on my life.

Parker lost his dad, and I lost someone who I truly considered to be my family.

I know it's my job to step up and be strong for Parker and his mom right now, but it won't be easy.

Parker ended up sleeping in his mom's room last night. I had already planned to spend the night, so I slept in his bed to give them privacy. I wish I could have been the one holding him though, giving him comfort, letting him know how loved he is.

I called my mom and told her what happened, and after she spent some time crying, she told me that I should stay here in case Parker needed me, and that she would be over first thing in the morning with breakfast.

Our parents have all gotten pretty close over the years with how often Parker and I are together, so I know his loss is hitting her hard too.

As soon as I tell her I'm awake, she shows up. Like the minute I text her. I think she'd been waiting outside. After giving me a very tight hug, she gets right to work preparing the food she brought.

Eventually Parker and his mom wake up, and my mom spends a long time hugging them both. My mom reassures Parker's mom that she's not alone, that she and my dad will do anything and everything that they can to help ease her burdens. Judy thanks her, still looking completely defeated.

I know they don't have any family in the area, so I'm not sure if she has anyone else to turn to.

After we eat, my mom tells me to take Parker to his room so that she can talk to Judy more about arrangements, *whatever that means*. I don't know what to say that could possibly help him as we both plop down onto his bed. Parker curls up, hugging his pillow and I'm not sure what to do at first, but I end up curling myself behind where he's lying so that I can hug him.

We've never cuddled like this before, and he's bigger than me, but I want him to know that he isn't alone, that he'll always have me, and my family. I'll never forget how loved his dad made me feel when he comforted me, even though his own son was literally on the way to the hospital.

"Parker, I never told you this," I start, trying not to cry. "On the night you got diagnosed, I was kind of a mess when the paramedics were there. I couldn't calm down enough to answer anyone's questions, and I tried to climb into the ambulance with you," I admit.

He's quiet, so I continue. "Your dad had to hold me back. He was so calm and supportive. He was able to talk me down from my panic, and he made me a promise that really helped me feel like the world wasn't ending." I have to stop again, taking a deep breath in before finishing. "He told me that you would be okay and promised me that he wouldn't let anything bad happen to you," I say as more tears run down my face. "That was the first time I ever felt like an adult, other than my parents, cared about me. I knew you were my best friend, and that you mattered to me more than anyone, but it was the first time I ever realized you can choose people to be your family. He had chosen to care about me like I was just as important as his own son," I explain.

"That sounds like him," Parker mumbles after a moment of silence, and I squeeze him tighter.

I grab his hand with mine and wrap my smallest finger around his. "I'm going to make another pinky promise," I explain, and he huffs out an almost laugh. "I promise that I am going to do everything I possibly can to help you and your mom. You guys are the best people I know, and no one deserves this. You have to know your dad didn't deserve this," I say with as much conviction as I can.

Then I take a deep breath, wanting my voice to be strong as I continue. "He promised me that he would protect you and make sure you were okay. Well, now it's my turn to make that promise in his honor. Parker, I promise I won't let anything bad happen to you or your mom," I say, and he pulls my arm around him tighter as his shoulders shake with his tears.

"Thanks, Oak," he eventually whispers, and I hope he believes me, that he knows how important he is to me, and that I never want him to feel alone.

"WILL Parker have to move or change schools?" I finally find the courage to ask my parents the question that's been eating away at me for the last few days.

We're leaving his dad's funeral. I wanted to go straight home with him, but my parents told me to give him some time with his mom and that they'd bring me over to his house later after we're all out of our suits.

"No honey, he'll still go to your school, he won't have to move," my mom answers, and I feel like a huge weight is lifted off my chest.

"His dad had life insurance," my dad adds. "So his family will get some money from that. But we also spoke to the school and your hockey coach. They've arranged scholarships for Parker to ensure that his mom doesn't need to worry about his tuition or fees. We were planning to keep that part anonymous, though, so maybe don't tell Parker. We don't want him or Judy to feel like a burden," he explains.

"Thank you, that was really cool of you to do." I'm so relieved I won't lose him. Not that anything could ever stop him from being my best friend, but I still want him at school and close to me.

"We've also spoken to Judy and let her know that if the time comes when she wants to work, we'll find her a job with one of our companies," Dad says.

"Has she ever worked before?" I ask. The whole time that I've known Parker, she's been a stay-at-home-mom.

Mom replies, "Yes, she has a degree in Hospitality Management and has worked in hotels. Maybe she'll want to help us at Caldwell House."

That's the fanciest hotel my family owns in Chicago. My dad took over after my grandpa retired from Caldwell Corporation. He runs a bunch of companies, multiple Caldwell Hotels, the Chicago Werewolves Ice Hockey Team, and more that aren't as fun.

"Yeah, that would be cool," I agree.

I'm so lucky to have the family I do. My parents really are amazing people. We have a lot of money, and even though we've had nannies and drivers and stuff, my parents have always been super involved with all of our lives. My dad's parents are also really close with us—we do dinners at their house once a week. My mom's parents are in Florida, but they're great as well.

Living with four brothers isn't always easy, but I would do anything for them. Beckett, my older brother, is probably my second-best friend after Parker. They're all Parker's family too.

I hope that he knows that.

5

PARKER

EIGHTEEN YEARS OLD

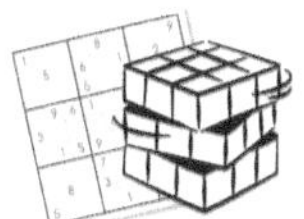

"Hurry up, we're going to be late for work," I warn.

I'm standing at my front door waiting for Oakley to put on his uniform. "Not everyone's parents own the hotel, ya know," I remind him.

"Yeah, your mom is just the General Manager, *totally* doesn't matter," he teases, finally passing me as he heads out the door.

My mom's been working at Caldwell House since I was fourteen. She became super involved in every part of my life after Dad died, like she was afraid for me to leave our house without her.

I think it helped that Oakley was always with me, though. We'd always spent a lot of time together, and we had sleepovers most weekends before my dad passed. But after he died, it was like we couldn't spend a full night away from each other if I wanted any sleep.

In the very beginning, on the few nights that Oakley's parents had him stay at home, I couldn't sleep without having horrible nightmares, and I would wake up screaming. My mom couldn't sleep either, so I think she was relieved when Oakley would stay over and she wasn't stuck lying awake in a bed next to me, or hearing my screams every night.

Luckily, Oakley has never been uncomfortable sharing a bed and was always willing to spend the night or invite me to his house. Something about knowing he's next to me calms me enough, even when I'm sleeping, that I don't have any nightmares if he's there.

After a few months of encouragement, Mom decided to start working for the Caldwells, and she slowly seemed to return to the mom I'd always known. In the months after my dad died, it was like she was a shell of her former self, going through the day to day but without any real emotions that weren't grief or fear. She seemed completely lost without him. But after settling into a new routine, she started smiling again, wearing makeup and doing her hair like she used to.

Caldwell House is a great fit for her. She'd worked in and managed hotels after college. She actually met my dad when his restaurant opened a location connected to the hotel she was managing at the time. She started at Caldwell House as a part-time front desk manager. The woman who'd previously held the position was expecting, and they spent her pregnancy training my mom to cover her maternity leave. When she returned to work, they split the hours, helping each other out when needed.

Mom loved it, and the flexible hours meant that she still had plenty of time to go to my hockey games and school stuff. If she did have to work, I would just go to Oakley's house. At first, I was worried I'd feel like a burden or like they were babysitting me, but I quickly realized that nothing had changed. His family has always welcomed me like one of their own, the only differ-ence now was that if it was a school night, I was allowed to sleep over.

The first time we visited my mom at work, Oakley and I were both fascinated by how much goes into the behind-the-scenes of running the hotel. We'd both stayed in hotels plenty with hockey tournaments and on vacations our families had taken, but when my mom took us on a tour and showed us all of the different jobs that were required to keep it all functioning, we were hooked.

That day, Oakley went home and told his dad that he planned to take over the Caldwell Hotel brand when he grew up. His dad took him seriously, and when we were both sixteen and were old enough to work, we started as bellboys, competing to see who could carry more or racing each other to see who could complete our tasks first. By then, we both knew hockey wasn't our future, so we decided to quit the team and focus on working. We still love working out though, and have always made fitness a priority to make time for around work and school.

Being best friends with the owner's kid had its perks, like being able to work the same schedule, which made it way more enjoyable. Mom had worked her way up to GM, and after a few months, we transferred into the housekeeping staff. After a few months of that, we spent some time working various positions in the food and beverage department. About a year ago, our parents decided that we were ready to work the front desk.

All of the different jobs have been interesting for different reasons, but I think we both appreciate everything that goes into running a hotel a lot more now. A few weeks ago, I got to spend time shadowing different people in the finance department and confirmed that that's where I see my future. I've always loved math, and it's cool to see how it's applied practically to the business I've spent years learning about.

We're both going to college soon, obviously the same one. Ivy League because of the *Caldwell* name, but only one actually has a hospitality management program, so we're going there. Oakley's older brother, Beck, goes there now though, and he said it's a lot of fun and is always going on about how great the parties are.

"Drew was telling me all about how he hooked up with

Angela again at some party last weekend," Oakley tells me as we walk the few blocks from my house to the hotel.

"And?" I ask. *Why does he think I'd care?*

"Well, it reminded me that we're eighteen-year-old virgins and that we're going to go to college as virgins if we don't do something about it soon," he says in a tone like his concern should be obvious. "I'm rich and popular, how am I still a virgin?" he jokingly adds.

"When would we have time to hook up with anyone?" I ask with a laugh. "We're always working or hanging out with each other," I point out.

"That's true," he agrees.

Honestly, I haven't given much thought to the whole virginity thing. My hand works just fine if I really feel the need to get off. Not that I even jerk off much, to be honest. Oakley and I are usually in the same bed, so I have to wait until I'm in the shower and he does the same. We've joked about it before because sleeping in the same bed means waking up in the same bed, morning wood and all. But Oakley and I talk about everything, so even that isn't awkward.

"Hey, what about next Friday, when our parents are all at that new hotel opening in California, we could invite Mia and Chloe over to your place, so my brothers don't bother us," he suggests.

Mia and Chloe are in some of our classes, and Mia and Oakley are constantly flirting, laughing, and casually touching each other. *I'm surprised that he hasn't tried to date her.* Chloe is Mia's best friend; they're both cheerleaders, and they definitely fit the stereotype of peppy popular girls, but they're nice enough.

Oakley's been on a few dates over the past few years, we both have, but neither of us has had a serious girlfriend. I've really only gone out with girls who've made the first move, and I've never cared to give much effort.

"Why would Chloe want to hook up with me?" I wonder aloud.

"Um, because you're already over six feet tall and are made of like solid muscle?" he answers. "Parker, you have to know you're hot," he adds, like it's an obvious fact. "Plus, you're like the coolest guy I know, I'm sure a bunch of girls want to sleep with you," he says matter-of-factly.

I can feel my cheeks heat a little at the compliment. People always tell me how much I look like my dad, which is great. That's really the only thing I've ever given much thought to as far as my appearance goes.

I'm also not as socially awkward as I used to be. After years of being friends with the most popular kid in our year, I've become more comfortable in social situations. Most of the time, at least. I would even consider some of the people we go to school with to be my friends, which is a big step up from where I was before moving here.

"We can have them over if you want," I concede, not wanting to hold Oak back if he wants to hook up. "Am I supposed to ask Chloe over, or can you handle it?"

"I'll text Mia and see if they're both free," he answers, already pulling out his phone.

I'm kind of hoping they aren't, but I guess Oakley has a point. We probably don't want to go to college with no sexual experience.

So when the girls are available, we all hang out at my house that Friday night. Oakley ends up in the guest room with Mia, and I ask Chloe if she wants to go to my room. When she eagerly agrees, practically dragging me there, I let her take control.

And once again, Oakley and I check off another first on the same night.

6

OAKLEY

NINETEEN YEARS OLD

College is awesome.

The classes are actually interesting and relevant for my future, and the independence of not having to constantly tell my parents where I am is amazing. We can go to parties and meet new girls, and I still get to spend all of my time with Parker.

I figured out pretty quickly that drinking heavily isn't for me, but I can still be my usual outgoing and happy self, and no one seems to notice if I'm not drunk.

The first week that we were here, Parker and I went to a frat party and got really wasted. We made it home okay, but Parker's continuous glucose monitor, the small wearable device that's attached to the back of his arm and is constantly communicating his blood sugar level to his phone, kept beeping that his blood sugar was too high to read. He was too out of it to program his insulin pump to give himself more insulin to bring his blood sugar level down. It was very scary and dangerous.

Luckily, I know how to work his pump and use his glucometer, the portable hand-help back-up machine that can read a higher range from a finger prick's worth of blood than his continuous monitor can, and I was able to program his insulin pump to give him the medication he needed to get it down safely.

Thank fuck the adrenaline and anxiety I had over not knowing if he was alright sobered me up, and I was able to do everything properly. But after that night, I decided that being so drunk I couldn't help him if he needed me, wasn't for me. Parker had a great night out, and I would never want to take that away from him, so if he wants to drink, then I don't care. But I'll make sure that I'm available both physically and mentally if he needs me.

That's also why I haven't been in a huge rush to hook up with any of the girls we've met while we're out. I'd rather know that Parker is home safe than have sex with some random one-night stand.

Obviously, we're roommates. We've spent almost every night together since we were thirteen, when I found out about Parker's nightmares and that my presence helped him not have any. I talked to my parents about getting rid of the "sleepovers are only for the weekends" rule, and they agreed.

I kind of miss us sharing a bed, though. Our dorm has two twin XLs, and I miss feeling Parker's body heat in the bed next to me. Sometimes, we would even end up wrapped around each other in the night, but it was never weird. It was nice to know that my favorite person was there.

Now we have the two beds, which is…fine. But it's created a new dilemma, since I'm a horny college kid after all.

Obviously, when we were sharing the same bed, I wouldn't jerk off with him there. No matter how fucking hard or desperate I was, I would excuse myself to the bathroom like the polite best friend that I am.

Now, Parker is all the way on the other side of the room. My dick is super fucking needy, but I don't feel like excusing myself to go shower. *Again.*

I swear my libido has no chill.

I don't want to make Parker feel uncomfortable if I just start tugging on my dick with no warning.

I should just ask him if he cares, right? He's my best friend, we can talk about anything. Maybe he feels the same way. I know I wouldn't mind if he needed to rub one out while I was in the room.

"Hey Parker?" I ask quietly. We're both lying in bed with the lights off, but I'm fairly certain he isn't asleep.

"Hmm?" he responds sleepily.

"I'm really horny," I start, not sure how to phrase my question in a way that doesn't pressure him.

"What do you want me to do about it?" he grumbles.

His question makes butterflies come to life in my stomach at the suggestion that he would do anything to help, and my cheeks heat with embarrassment at the implication. *Obviously not where I was going with that.*

"Ha-ha, nothing," I say with a laugh. "I was just wondering if you'd care if I took care of it in here?" I ask, wishing I sounded more casual. *This isn't a big deal. I don't know why I'm acting all nervous.* If he says no, then it's fine. I'll just go to the bathroom like I always do.

"Oakley, are you asking for my permission to jerk off?" he clarifies.

"I guess?" I say, like it's a question.

"I'm going to sleep, I don't care what you do in your bed," he finally answers.

My dick twitches and a flutter of excitement rushes through me at the thought of touching myself like that in front of another person.

"Oh, cool, I wouldn't care if you ever wanted to either," I quickly add. "Just in case you were wondering."

Parker grunts in acknowledgment and rolls to face the wall so that his back is to me. The room is dark, but the gap in the door lets in enough light that I can clearly see him turn over.

My dick is already thickening when I finally slip my hand beneath the band of my sleep shorts. I don't have any underwear on, so there's nothing in the way as I grip my hardening cock and give it a few lazy tugs. I love taking my time, appreciating every sensation and really enjoying the anticipation of my impending orgasm.

Since I'm usually only able to touch myself in the shower, I'm used to relying on shower products as lubricant, but I was optimistic when we moved in, and there are supplies in the nightstand next to my bed.

I try to be as quiet as possible opening the drawer and removing the lube, but I'm sure Parker can hear it. Not to mention the distinct skin-on-wet-skin sound of my hand coating my cock in the slick substance.

Fuck, this feels so good. It's been too long since I've been able to really enjoy jerking off. I slide my hand down to play with my balls and accidentally let out a soft moan.

I really am trying to be quiet, even if I don't think I'm doing a great job at it.

Every time I think about the fact I'm not alone, and that Parker not only knows exactly what I'm doing, but can obviously hear everything, it makes a tingle of pleasure shoot up my spine. I can't deny that I like knowing he's listening.

A soft whimper escapes my lips and my head falls to the side as I continue to work my aching cock. The muscles in my lower abdomen clench, and I know I won't last much longer. I realize that, completely unintentionally, I'm now looking at Parker's bed.

He isn't asleep. It's bright enough that I can clearly see the outline of Parker's body now lying on his back. I can also see the movement that's tenting his comforter.

Is he jerking off too?

Holy shit, the pleasure that's pooling deep in my gut seems to catch fire at the thought of what Parker's doing in the same room as me. I can't hold back my orgasm any longer, or the loud moan that I let out as cum coats my hand and soaks into my sleep shorts. Waves of pleasure crash into me and I ride out the euphoric feeling as I distantly recognize how fucking loud I must have been, but I honestly can't find it in myself to care.

I'm so consumed by my own gratification that I almost miss the soft grunt from Parker as his movements slow before stopping completely.

Holy shit. I just heard my best friend come. My dick twitches again. Probably just excited about being able to do this again without waiting for the shower, not because of Parker.

I strip out of my shorts, using them to clean up my hand and any remaining release the best that I can. I decide that sleeping naked under the covers is definitely less awkward than jerking off together, so I throw them toward my hamper and call it a night.

I'm assuming that Parker has done the same, but by the time I'm settled again, he's back to facing the wall, curled up in his blanket. I lay there for a few moments, still enjoying the post-orgasm high.

Should I say anything? I don't have any clue what the proper etiquette is in this situation.

"Thanks, Parker. Goodnight," I whisper after the silence becomes too uncomfortable.

After a few moments, I assume he's fallen asleep, or at least is pretending to be sleeping. But then I hear a soft laugh followed by, "Night, Oak," and a smile breaks out across my face.

I have the coolest best friend.

7

OAKLEY

THIRTY YEARS OLD

April

"Your insulin is ready for pickup at the pharmacy," I tell Parker as he adds pre-workout powder to his water bottle.

"Thanks, Dad," he replies sarcastically.

"That's Daddy to you," I say with a wink, slapping his ass as he walks past me to our front hall closet to grab his shoes.

He doesn't react, which makes me laugh. I ignore the way my dick twitches at the contact. It's been way too long since I hooked up with anyone. *I seriously need to find a girlfriend.*

"Oak, are you coming?" Parker calls out from our entryway.

I wish I was coming. Fuck, I need to get my mind out of the gutter. "Yup, one sec," I answer back, grabbing my own workout drink and meeting him to head downstairs to the gym.

We live in the penthouse of one of the newest high-rises in downtown Chicago, and one of the reasons we picked it was for the top-of-the-line fitness center that takes up the entire fifth floor of the building. It's also only a block away from my older brother,

Beckett's, building. We try to see him and his friends as much as we can, and even debated buying there, but it wasn't as modern as Parker and I prefer.

Some people think it's weird that Parker and I choose to share a condo when we're thirty, successful, and have plenty of money for our own places, but I can't imagine us *not* living together at this point.

It comforts me to know that he isn't alone in case anything happens with his blood sugar. Not that it ever really does, he's managed to stay out of the hospital since the scare when he received his diagnosis. But every time someone suggests we move into our own places, I picture him passed out again, with no one around to know he needs help, and I'm reminded of how much I love living together.

Plus, Parker is the best roommate ever. Why would I want to live by myself?

We make our way to the elevator and down to the gym, starting our routine on the treadmills like we usually do with a quick five-mile jog before we transition to the weight machines.

"Look, those girls are here again," I point out, nodding in the direction of the women I'm talking about. They seem to have a similar workout schedule to ours, and we've noticed them checking us out and glancing in our direction for a couple of weeks now. We've exchanged polite hellos and smiles, but nothing more.

Which seems stupid considering how hot they are, and how fucking horny I've been lately.

"Let's introduce ourselves after this rep," I suggest, nudging his shoulder with mine.

"Why?" he questions, like he honestly has no idea why I would want to talk to the beautiful girls who seem to be into us. I'm constantly amused by the way Parker's brain seems to differ from my own. He's always been more introverted than I am, and sometimes I wonder if he would still be a virgin if I didn't encourage him to talk to women as much as I have over the years.

"To see if they're single, and if they are, to ask them out," I spell out with an indulgent smile, endlessly entertained by how oblivious he can be.

"Oh," he says, sounding genuinely surprised. "Okay, which one do you want to ask out?"

This isn't the first time we've approached multiple girls together, and Parker always seems happy to let me take the lead and decide who I want to talk to first. He doesn't seem to have a type. At well over six feet tall, with broad shoulders and huge muscles, not to mention his unique red hair color and movie star chiseled face, with a jawline sharp enough to cut glass, he's yet to be turned down by any of the women he does approach.

I look back at the girls who are both smiling and chatting as they do their own routine. One is blonde and the other brunette, but they're both average height with fit curvy frames that look great in their workout clothes. "Honestly, they seem pretty similar. We can figure out if there's a good match when we talk to them."

We finish lifting weights and clean off the equipment before heading toward the girls. When they notice us, they stop what they're doing and stand up straighter, puffing out their chests, fluttering their lashes and smiling at our approach.

"Before I impress you with my cheesy pick-up line, are you ladies single?" I ask with a smirk. They both laugh and nod, so I continue. "Are you my next workout? Because my heart is racing, and you're making it harder for me to breathe," I say with an exaggerated wink. Parker snorts beside me, and the girls both let out short laughs. "I'm Oakley and this is my best friend Parker," I finally introduce us.

"Nice to meet you," the blonde girl says with a little flip of her ponytail. "I'm Sage and this is *my* best friend, Aspen," she waves to the brunette who's smiling and holding eye contact with Parker. *Looks like I'm asking out Sage.*

"Well, Sage, is there any chance that I could get your number so we could all go out some time?" I ask with my most charming smile.

"Like a double-date?" she clarifies, sounding excited.

It's been awhile since Parker and I have gotten to do the whole double-date thing, and it sounds like a lot of fun. "If you both would be up for that," I reply hopefully, glancing at Parker to see if he'd be interested. He gives me a slight nod before aiming his smile back toward Aspen.

"Okay," both girls say in unison before laughing. We all exchange numbers and I start a group chat so that we can plan something.

"Well, we'll let you get back to your workout," Parker says. "It was nice to formally meet you both."

"Bye, Sage," I say with another wink, earning a huge grin from her before we return to our own routine, showing off a bit in case they're watching.

"ARE you ready to present to the board?" Parker asks, knocking on my door as I'm scrolling through images of island resorts on my computer. We have a big meeting scheduled with the board of directors today about an idea I've been wanting to pitch for a while now.

My dad will be there as the majority shareholder of the Caldwell Hotel brand, along with some of the other executive VPs and board members. As President and CEO of the brand, I have a lot of independence in my day-to-day work, but this idea isn't going to be cheap, so I'll need the board's approval.

It's also the first major investment that's been proposed since Parker took over as CFO a few months ago, and I know some of the board members are concerned about our positions being filled by such "young" men.

I've been in my role for a few years now. After the various jobs I had in Caldwell House throughout high school, I shadowed Parker's mom, their GM, that first summer while Parker worked with their accountants. The summer after that, I filled in working as an assistant manager, and Parker shadowed their finance department's lead. For our final summer before senior year, we traveled to different hotels within the company. We saw more moderate options, as well as some of the deluxe resorts that are all over the world, learning about how each hotel operates.

We both did accelerated master's programs, and by the time we graduated, the previous President and CEO was getting ready to retire. I spent almost a full year studying under him and spending time with each of the executive VPs so that I was prepared to take over when he officially stepped down.

Parker might not have the Caldwell name, but given his vast experience within the company and his track record of excelling in the role below the former CFO, he was the obvious choice to take over when they retired. The majority of the board agreed with my recommendation, but a few didn't seem thrilled that we're such close friends outside of work, questioning if we would be able to focus or keep the best interests of the company in mind if we disagreed about something. There's still the occasional shared glance between some of the older members when he and I are both in a meeting, but our friendship has never negatively impacted our performance, so they don't have anything to legitimately complain about.

"Yeah, let's go win them over," I say with a false sense of confidence. I really want this to go well.

We're not the last to arrive, so I work on setting up my

presentation and exchange pleasantries with people as they enter. Once everyone is settled, I take a deep breath and put on my most charming smile.

"Good morning, it's lovely to see so many of my favorite people all in one room this early in the day. Oh, and Dad, you're here too," I say with a wink. A few people chuckle, and I relax just a bit. *I'm good at my job, no need to be nervous.*

"You're all aware that we're here today for me to propose a new investment opportunity for the Caldwell Hotel brand. I know that all you lot care about is money," I say in a teasing tone, earning a few more laughs. "So, I'll get right to the point. There's a resort in Bora Bora that's failed their health and safety inspections, and the family who owns it is looking to sell. They've been doing a lot of patchwork jobs over the years to pass the inspections and the repairs would be extensive," I admit. "But, it would still be cheaper than trying to find new land, given the remote location. It's a smaller resort, and they haven't offered as many amenities as their neighbors, so it's fallen out of popularity. There's a lot of room for improvement," I explain.

I'm already getting a few skeptical looks from the board, so I rush to get to the current plan. "I'm proposing we purchase the existing facilities and do a complete overhaul, turning it into *the* luxury destination-wedding resort for the rich and famous," I say with as much enthusiasm as I can while still sounding genuine.

"Obviously, we have other hotels with great wedding venues," I admit. "But, I think this could be an exciting investment opportunity to help keep our brand relevant. The wedding industry makes billions of dollars in revenue annually. Statistics from last year show that couples are choosing to invite fewer guests, focusing instead on the quality of their wedding, with extended destination events rising in popularity," I inform them.

My dad looks interested as I meet his gaze, so I focus my attention on him as I continue. "I think that this would be a great way to tap into that market in a way that stands out from our other venues." I pull up pictures of the resort as it currently stands, followed by some inspirational images that my team put together for me. There's some appreciative hums from the group, fueling my excitement. *They might actually go for it.*

Parker gives me an encouraging smile, probably thinking the same thing I am, and I hurry to wrap my part up so he can take over. "We can hire an in-house events specialist to coordinate the weddings or other large private events, and only offer the resort out to someone booking the entire venue. This will make it more exclusive and spin the smaller size as a benefit. It doesn't need to only be weddings, but that's where the majority of our marketing will focus. If a reality TV star wants to throw a birthday party at our private luxury resort, they can, but they need to book out the whole thing. We'll keep the costs lower if we're catering to the same large group rather than to couples, as most of these resorts do. Are there any initial questions before Parker goes through the financial projections?" I ask.

There are a few raised hands, and I answer some general questions about where Bora Bora is, *south of Hawaii*, how long of a flight it is, *eight hours from LA to Tahiti, and another fifty-minute flight to Bora Bora.* There are also questions about the island and the established resorts that are profitable there.

Parker takes over to give the rundown of the initial investment, as well as the projected profits after the first year. Most of the board members seem interested enough in the proposal, and after about an hour of everyone combing through the materials we've provided and asking more questions, the idea passes with a majority vote.

"Thank you all so much for your time today. I look forward to updating you all on our progress," I say brightly. "If you all would excuse us, Parker and I have another meeting to attend," I explain as we shake a few hands and wave goodbye before slipping back to my office.

"Fuck yes!" I whisper-shout, doing a happy dance as soon as I make sure we're out of sight. "We're going to Bora Bora!"

Parker laughs before joining in my silly dance, which I know he only does to amuse me. "It is a good idea, though," he assures me when we calm down. "Even if it'll be an expensive one," he adds a little more hesitantly.

"I know, I'm just really excited about this," I explain. "You know how much I love weddings, and islands are my favorite. This is going to be such a fun project!"

"Yeah, I think it will be," he admits with a big smile.

I love making him smile. Working this closely with my best friend and sharing these victories means the world to me.

8

PARKER

THIRTY YEARS OLD

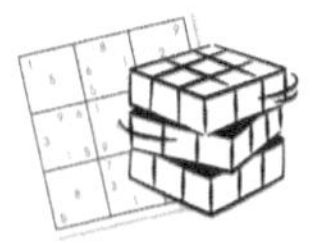

May

You would think that after twenty-one years as Oakley's best friend, I'd be used to the whole "super wealthy" thing. But there will always be that part of me that remembers how relieved Mom was to learn about the scholarships I qualified for at my school after Dad passed, or how stressed she was about paying bills while we were waiting for the money from Dad's life insurance.

I was so afraid that I would not only lose my dad, but the first real home I'd ever had, the first school where I'd fit in. My first real friend.

Moving around so much, and then losing Dad so unexpectedly, taught me to never take anything for granted. I know how quickly things can change or be taken away. I try not to take any of the luxuries that I've been afforded in life for granted.

Oakley on the other hand, sometimes needs reminding that not everyone is used to his lifestyle.

"Don't you think taking them on your yacht for a private

sunset cruise on Lake Michigan might be a little over-the-top for a first date?" I call out to him from where I'm finishing getting ready in my room. "Won't it seem like we're trying too hard, or maybe even be creepy that we're isolating them on the water like that?" I worry aloud.

"Um, noooo," Oak reassures me with a laugh, answering from his room next to mine. "We're not 'isolating them'. They'll have their best friend there, it *is* a double-date after all. Plus, there's a whole crew on the boat," he reminds me. "And they live in our building so I'm sure they're also used to a certain level of luxury. It's not too much Park, it's showing we cared enough to put in the effort to organize something nice," he says, and I can hear the smile in his tone.

It's early May, and the season to take out his boat has only just started. I'm fairly confident that's his main motivation for this date, not impressing them with his "efforts," but I don't bother to bring that up when I know how much he loves being on the water. It's always nice to see how happy he is when we're out there.

"Wow, someone cleans up well," Oak says with a whistle as he enters my room. I roll my eyes at his remark before noticing we're in similar clothes.

"Should I change so we don't look like we coordinated our outfits?" I ask. We both have on dark designer jeans, with the sleeves of our button-ups rolled up to expose our forearms, and a sweater tied around our shoulders for when the wind picks up on the lake. "We look like we're auditioning for a sailing commercial," I grumble.

"We look fantastic and the sweaters are practical," he assures me with a smirk, obviously less concerned with what people will think of us matching. "Are you ready to meet the girls?" he asks.

"I guess so," I agree, making sure that I have everything before we head down to the lobby. We're a few minutes earlier than the time we agreed to meet, but we thought it would be more polite to wait for them in the lobby than at their door in case they didn't want us to know the exact unit they're in yet.

Both girls are clearly excited as they exit the elevator and see us waiting, practically bouncing over to us. I like how cheerful they seem. I've noticed I prefer to surround myself with animated, peppy people, like Oakley, and they definitely seem to fit that description.

When it's obvious to me that the people around me are happy and are having a good time, I'm less anxious about my own behavior and wondering if I'm fitting in. I can just relax. But if I'm with other shy, introverted people, like myself, I tend to stay quiet because I'm so worried about what they're thinking or that I'll say the wrong thing and make things even more awkward.

"We all match!" Aspen says brightly, giving my forearm a light squeeze as she laughs. The girls have a similar boating look, with expensive looking button-up blouses and sweaters of their own, although they opted for skirts and will probably have cold legs if we're outside on the water. *I'll have to remember to offer her my sweater.*

"I'm not sure which look I like more, you hot and sweaty in the gym, or all cleaned up here for a date," Sage tells Oakley. He's one of those guys who never has to put in any effort and still ends up looking like a model.

"Well, I can think of a few other looks I'd like to show you in my apartment," he responds, with an overly flirty tone and a wink, earning more laughs from the girls.

I don't know how he always manages to pull off the cheesy flirty thing, not that I really have any desire to, but even if I did, I could never be that confident. I'm sure it only works because of how attractive he is, but women eat it up.

"You look beautiful," I say in a softer tone to Aspen as we all turn to exit the building, and her smile grows even bigger.

"Thanks! You always look really good, too" she adds with a

slight drawl I hadn't noticed during our brief first meeting. She must be from the South.

We make our way to Oakley's driver, who's waiting out front to take us to the pier. Oakley's family has a long list of people they can hire out to do odd jobs like staffing his yacht for a private date. I don't even want to think about how much tonight probably costs. I know logically that I make a lot of money now, especially as the new CFO, but I'll never have Caldwell money.

Once we arrive, the crew reminds us of the safety procedures before we're escorted to a romantic dinner they've set up on the deck. There's a table formally set for four with red rose petals contrasting against the stark white of the tablecloth, and after pulling out a chair for Aspen, I end up across from her and next to Oakley.

His presence at my side relaxes me like it always does, and the conversation between the four of us is easy. I'd forgotten how much I enjoyed going on double dates with Oak, how much more fun they are when he's there to remind me I'm not being socially awkward and I don't have to overthink everything.

The girls are obviously very close with each other as well. They constantly finish each other's stories, and the admiration in their gazes when they look at the other is sweet.

"We didn't meet until college, but we've been attached at the tit since we were roommates freshman year," Sage explains with her own faint Southern accent. Oak bursts out laughing before I can even register her unique phrase, but she goes on like nothing happened.

"We both knew we wanted to spread our wings a little after college, though, so we moved away from our families and up to Chicago," Aspen adds. "My father wasn't very excited about me moving so far away and ditching the life he had planned for me, but he makes sure that we video call a lot. Plus, he takes the jet up here when he really wants to see me, and Sage's parents do the same thing," she adds. I can tell her comment sets Oakley at ease, it's obvious they come from extreme wealth like he does.

Oak's always been very vocal about wanting his storybook happily ever after. The wife and kids with the big mansion in the suburbs. But, one of the *many* reasons that he's struggled to find this elusive "perfect" wife, is that so many women are only after his family's name and the lifestyle that they think is attached to it.

That's part of why I was surprised that he went so all-out planning this first date, but I guess that he was right about them having money of their own if they can afford to live in our building.

I'm aware that the *other* reasons he's still single have to do with me and our "codependent" friendship, so I try not to focus on them and the guilt that I feel about potentially holding him back. I know it's not my decision, and if he wants space from me to date more, I won't stand in his way. *No matter how much I dread the fact that he'll no longer be my roommate one day.* Maybe Aspen and Sage will be less likely than our exes to complain about us living together, how much time we spend together, or how often we bring the other up in conversation. They're the same way with each other.

I don't think there's anything wrong with our friendship because I know how lucky I am to have Oak in my life, and I'll never take it for granted. Oakley has also assured me, *and any of his exes who dared question our relationship*, that anyone he ends up with will understand how important I am to him. I'll never feel like I deserve that level of loyalty from him, even if I love it. Even after all of these years, there's that small part of me that's confused about what he sees in me, why he chose to be my friend when everyone else labeled me as awkward.

Sage and Aspen seem just as close as we are, though, so this could be the perfect set up. The whole "wife and kids" future has always seemed a little less certain to me than it has to Oak.

Maybe it's because of my grief over losing Dad like I did that I haven't been able to picture myself with a family of my own one day, or maybe I just haven't found my person.

I don't hate the idea. It's definitely easier to imagine that type of future for myself if Oakley and I had wives who were also best friends. We could live next door to each other and raise our kids together. That wouldn't be too different than having him in the room next to mine. And I know it would make him happy to have a big family like the one he grew up in and has always wanted.

Alright, slow down, this is a first date, not a marriage proposal. I don't need to put that kind of pressure on tonight.

We watch the sunset over the Chicago skyline and enjoy the fancy meal that Oakley's private chef manages to prepare on the moving boat, a feat which always impresses me. When the chill from the wind over the water becomes uncomfortable, we move inside to the couches that are in the boat's living room area. I did offer my sweater to Aspen outside, and she still has it wrapped around her legs where she's seated next to me on the couch. The crew are all upstairs, so it's just the four of us down here, and if it wasn't for the slight rocking of the boat, or the lit-up city in the distance, it would be easy to forget that we're not sitting in some-one's home.

We promised the girls, and the crew, we wouldn't be out too late. So, after another drink inside and a round of Scrabble that we are all probably a little too invested in, complete with special metal pieces that are heavy enough not to be disturbed by the motion of the lake, we head back. They've recently added docks for private boats on the north side of Navy Pier, and the girls suggest we do the Centennial Wheel.

The night has been full of laughter, and I've loved how easy it's been to get to know Aspen; turns out she's a popular wedding dress designer and Oak immediately starts listing ideas of how we can incorporate her dresses in promo for the new resort. With Oakley and Sage here, there hasn't been any awkward silences or wondering if I'm boring her. Looking at Oak's wide grin as he tells yet another joke, and remembering how often the girls exchanged smiles, it's clear that everyone's had a good time.

Aspen has her arm tucked into mine as we make our way over to the rides, her other arm through Sage's, who's in a similar position with Oakley so that the four of us are connected. It's easy to picture them spending time in our apartment with us, working out, eating dinner together, and watching our shows from the big sectional.

I feel like, for the first time in my life, I'm actually excited about the idea of starting a relationship. Maybe it *is* possible for us to settle down without sacrificing the friendship that's always been the most important thing in my life.

Hopefully I'm not the only one feeling this optimistic.

We get our tickets and skip the line because Oakley paid for that option. "Haven't you been on it before?" I ask when I notice that Aspen looks nervous.

"We've been here for years already, but I can't say we've actually been on it," she admits, and I note that both women tend to answer questions in a plural "we," as though they're a package deal. *Oakley and I probably do the same thing.*

"Don't worry, Ferris Wheels are statistically very safe, especially permanently constructed ones like this," I try to reassure her. "Plus, this one is enclosed, so there's little risk involved."

"I think I'll be safe with you," she adds, squeezing my arm and winking.

Oakley helps Sage step on first, and I follow suit, holding Aspen's hand as she leaps inside. There's bench seating on two sides of the private gondola, and she cuddles into me as we sit across from the others.

"I've always wanted to kiss someone at the top of one of

these," Sage announces while looking at Aspen, and they laugh at her not-so-subtle suggestion before she turns to face Oak.

"I think that can be arranged," he promises with a wink, putting his arm around her.

When we're at the top, he leans in for a kiss, and Aspen laughs at their cheesy display. I'm glad she isn't putting me on the spot like that, and her warm smile gives me hope that this could continue, that the four of us might just make something work.

"I don't want to overstep by suggesting this, but I had a fantastic time tonight and would love to do it again," Oak says when we're finally back in the lobby of our building.

"So would I," I quickly add, smiling at Aspen.

The girls exchange smirks and nod.

"Do you want tonight to be over already?" Sage asks Oakley coyly.

"Well, I didn't want to assume anything," he answers with his own grin.

"Come on, show us your place," Aspen says as she leads me into the waiting elevator.

When we're back in our apartment, we give the girls a quick tour, but it isn't long before Sage and Oakley excuse themselves to his room, already making out before his door is fully closed.

I hate this part of the night. The awkward navigating of expectations. *Does she want to hook up? Or does she want to get to know each other before anything physical happens?*

"Do you want anything to drink?" I offer.

"No, thank you. I was hoping that we could talk in your room?" Aspen suggests.

Hookup it is. At least she's taking the lead now. I'm always better at following clear instructions from the women I date so I know I'm doing what they want me to.

We get into my room and Aspen surprises me by climbing

onto my bed and sitting cross-legged with a pillow on her lap as she looks up at me. "Parker, I like you."

"Thanks, I like you too," I assure her.

"But I don't like you the way that you probably think I do. The way that Sage likes Oakley," she admits hesitantly, nodding in the direction of the wall I share with Oak.

He has music on in his room now, but it does little to drown out the occasional moan that makes it obvious that the two of them are hooking up.

Her response isn't what I was expecting.

If she doesn't like me like that, why would she ask to come into my room instead of going home? *Fuck, I don't think I pressured her in any way, did I?*

"I'm so sorry if I made you think you had to stay tonight..." I start, but Aspen cuts me off, her gentle smile still in place.

"No, don't worry. You didn't pressure me at all, or do anything wrong."

I let out a deep breath, relieved, though still very confused.

"Parker, can I trust you?"

I pause to think about how to answer her for a moment. A simple yes might be what she's looking for, but it also feels like a trick question. "You've only really known me for a day, so I'm not sure how much you should believe me. If you're asking as a polite way to protect sensitive information, though, I can assure you I'm trustworthy and I give you my word that I won't share your secrets," I promise.

Aspen laughs at my answer, her smile only growing. "You're going to be fun," she says, more to herself than me. "Can you sit down so we can talk?"

I opt for the chair that's at the desk in my room, spinning it around so that I can face Aspen where she's sitting on my bed.

"Alright, what would you like to tell me?" I prompt once I'm settled.

"I'd just like to start off by saying that I really did have a great time tonight."

"Me too," I agree easily.

She hesitates, biting her lip like she's afraid to go on, so I try to offer her a reassuring smile as she continues. "I really liked that we could all hang out together, and it's clear that you and Oakley are really close, like Sage and I."

"Yeah, it's nice to have someone who understands our friendship."

She looks at me expectantly, like I should be saying more, but I'm not sure what she's looking for from me.

Finally, she takes a deep breath in, exhaling heavily before a determined look takes over her features. "Fuck it, I won't know if I'm too afraid to say it, so I'm just going to ask. Parker, do you have feelings for Oakley?"

It's not the first time someone's asked me about Oakley in this way, assuming that we must be involved romantically because of how close we are as friends, so her question doesn't completely surprise me.

I let out an awkward short laugh before answering. "No, Aspen, it's not like that, and it never has been. I thought that you of all people, with how you and Sage are, would understand that just because two people are really close, it doesn't mean they're in love with each other."

I expect her to laugh with me, or to respond, say anything really, but she doesn't reply. Aspen just stares at me in anticipation, twisting the ring on her finger nervously.

After a few moments, it finally clicks and the thoughts start spilling out of my mouth before I can decide if they're polite. "*Oh.* You wouldn't understand, would you?" She shakes her head "no" a few times, still smiling at me. "Because you *are* in love with Sage?" I clarify, making sure I've understood the conversation up until this point.

She nods a few times, hesitantly, probably gauging my reaction. I'm immediately disappointed that all of the double dates and plans I hadn't been able to stop myself from imagining for the four of us will no longer happen, but I'm not upset. Aspen seems like a nice woman, and I want her to be happy.

Shit, what does that mean for Oak though? He clearly seemed happy with Sage, does she feel the same way about Aspen?

"Thank you for trusting me with that," I start. "Does she know?"

"God no, I can't tell her," Aspen answers quickly, tone full of regret.

"Are you worried that she won't feel the same way?"

"I know she won't, she isn't…" she trails off, looking around the room like what she's trying to say is hidden somewhere on my walls. "Even if she did think about other girls that way, which she doesn't, we're both from traditional southern families. They would never approve, and I'd never ask her to give up her family or their money for me."

"Your family would cut you off if they found out you were dating a woman?" I repeat back to make sure I've understood. I know that there are still a lot of horrible homophobic people out there. I've heard firsthand accounts from our friend, Adrian, about the bullying he faced growing up in the south, but the idea that her parents would shut her out so completely is hard to wrap my head around.

I was lucky enough to grow up with not only my own incredibly supportive parents, but also with the whole Caldwell family treating me like one of their own. As a straight man, I've never had to question if anyone would treat me differently because of who I was dating, but I know without question that the people in my life love me unconditionally, not because I fit some standard they've set for me.

Aspen scoffs. "Yup. My father is a politician in a very conservative state. There's also millions of dollars I'll lose access to if I don't marry a man soon," she confirms. "I've just never been attracted to men, I've tried to make something work with boyfriends in the past for my parent's sake, but I'm not built for that. My parents have been trying to get me to move back to Georgia for years to marry their friends' son."

"That's horrible," I blurt out, completely unsure how to react to all of that. It really is an awful situation to be in, and I feel sorry for her, but I'm also confused why she's sharing all of this with me. *Maybe she just needed to tell someone?*

"I know," she says sadly. "His dad is my father's campaign manager, and they've always wanted him to take over when my father retires. They've been trying to set me up with him since we were kids. It started as more subtle suggestions about how great he is, that we would be good together. He's a great guy, we're still friends, but now that I'm almost thirty it's like they think I'm an old spinster now and they're relentless. They've been threatening to cut off my access to my trust fund if I don't move home soon, saying the money is intended for my family and that I shouldn't be able to use it until I have a husband and children of my own."

"I'm so sorry you have to deal with that," I tell her honestly.

"Thanks, Parker. And the worst part is my father helped me start my company, so he's stuck in my life. I'd forget the family money in a second, but my business is my baby, I don't want to risk him sabotaging it." She hugs the pillow in her lap tighter to herself before letting out a defeated laugh. "I was actually hoping you'd be able to help me out, but I guess I was convincing myself that you had feelings for Oakley to try to justify what I wanted you to do." She shakes her head a few times before muttering, "It was a stupid idea anyway."

"What was?" I can't help myself from asking.

"Well, I thought that maybe, if you were in the same position as me, doomed to pine after your best friend while watching them fall for someone else, that you wouldn't mind dating me, or pretending to at least," she explains quickly.

My jaw drops and I can't help but gape at her. *That is not what I was expecting.* "Why would you want to pretend to date me?"

"Mostly to get my parents off my back," she huffs out. "They want me to move back there, and they keep going on about how 'it's clear I can't find a husband in Chicago.' But, if I were dating a successful, wealthy man like you, then they would have to shut up about it, and I could at least buy myself some more time here."

"Like a beard?" I don't know if that's even what it's called, *and that's so not the point, focus.* Whatever it's called, it does sound like it would help her out with her family. I wouldn't feel guilty about lying to them if they're such awful people. They're in another state, how would they know who she's dating anyway? We wouldn't actually have to be dating for them to think we are.

"It's also been referred to as a lavender relationship. I thought it would be perfect that we'd be able to keep going on double dates and spending time with our best friends instead of competing for their time with their new relationship," she adds with a shrug.

Now that really gets my attention.

That's exactly what I was going on about in my daydreams of a relationship with her earlier tonight. How great it would be to get to still spend so much time with Oakley, despite the fact that he was dating someone.

I didn't really care about the possibility of having a new girl-friend myself, I was more focused on how my friendship with Oakley would be affected. There's no denying the four of us all hanging out together was fun. Aspen and I definitely get along. We didn't even kiss, but more nights like tonight don't sound bad at all.

I only agreed to ask her out in the first place because Oak

suggested it, it's not like I was the one eagerly seeking a girl-friend. Even the thought of hooking up with her hadn't really been on my mind until I was worried about her expectations. Sure, I enjoy the release from sex when it happens, but I've never been as sex-focused as other guys seem to be.

The more that I think about it, the more the idea of agreeing to "fake date" Aspen sounds like a decent plan. At least while Oakley is seeing Sage. There would be a clear expectation of no physical intimacy between us, so I wouldn't have to waste any time wondering what she wanted from me. Dating always brings me back to feeling like the new kid, second guessing what people think of me, worrying if I'm letting them down by not behaving how they hoped I would. I usually wait for the woman I'm with to take the lead when we're alone so that I know I'm not making a fool of myself.

This could work. We could call it dating each other, and we'd get to keep going on double dates with the people we actually want to spend time with, without me having to stress about messing up the physical expectations that come with most rela-tionships I've never seemed to understand. It sounds way better than sitting at home by myself whenever Oakley wants to spend time with Sage.

Just because I'm not in love with Oak like Aspen was hoping, doesn't mean I wouldn't still benefit from her plan...

"I'll do it," I blurt out before I can overthink and talk myself out of it.

Aspen tilts her head, arching a brow, clearly confused. "Do what?"

"I'll be your pretend boyfriend. We can keep spending time with Oak and Sage, and you can get your parents to give you space to stay in Chicago and figure out a more long-term plan."

Her whole face lights up and she scrambles so that she's

kneeling on the bed now, bouncing slightly in her excitement. "Really? You'd do that?"

"I'm not going to agree to marry you or anything, but at least while Oak is dating Sage, I don't see why we can't all spend that time hanging out together," I offer.

Aspen is somehow off of the bed and jumping into my lap before I even know what's happening. She wraps her arms around me in a hug, squeezing tightly. Even in this position, with her practically straddling me, I'm not disappointed that our relationship won't be physical. Maybe there's something wrong with me, but I just can't find it in myself to care right now. I'm glad I can help her and, from the little I know, I do think we could be good friends.

And I don't have to give up any of my time with Oakley.

"So, do you want to go home, or spend the night here? We can watch TV or I have a lot of puzzle books if you do want to stay," I offer.

"You don't mind if I sleep here with you?"

"No. Oak and I used to share a bed all the time. I don't think it would be weird, if you're okay with it."

Aspen gives me a questioning look, like she wants to comment on that statement, but decides against it. "That would be great. I'm sure Sage will be staying," she says with another pointed look at our shared wall where things have finally quieted down.

"We can see what they say in the morning as far as seeing each other again."

"Want to watch that new blind dating reality show for a bit before we sleep?" she suggests.

"Where that guy thinks he's talking to a girl, but it's a man?" I check.

"Yeah, the commercials look so funny."

"Sure, let's get ready for bed first though." I head to my

ensuite, finding an extra toothbrush and some of my clothes that Aspen can sleep in before we settle into bed and pull up *Love Without Labels* on the TV. My king-sized bed is plenty big enough for us both to have our own space, and there's zero tension. It feels like I'm hanging out with Oakley's siblings.

I grab the constrained cube from my nightstand to keep my hands busy while we watch. It's one of the more difficult spin-offs of the Rubik's cube that Oakley's gotten for me over the years. After a few episodes, we're both drifting off, so we turn off the show and the lights, going to bed with simple, "goodnights." Maybe the situation should feel strange and I should be more worried about exactly what I've agreed to, but I feel a sense of calm about it in a way that I'm embracing.

In the morning over breakfast at our dining room table, Oakley asks Sage when she's free for their next date. I look to Aspen, who gives me an encouraging nod before I suggest we all plan something together again.

Oakley lights up even more at that, and I know he's thinking the same things I was last night. How nice it will be to go on like this, that we might have each finally found someone who could accept our friendship without having to constantly justify our bond. I should probably feel guilty about hiding this from my best friend, but what Aspen and I have agreed to doesn't feel like I'm lying to him. We *will* be going on dates, we just won't be having sex with each other. Despite us normally talking about everything, I don't bother to share the details of my hookups with Oakley. There's never really been much to tell.

Something about this feels right, like I'm on the path that I should be. So, I'm going to try not to get hung up on what I think I should be feeling, and just focus on the positives of the situation. I'm helping my new friend, and I won't lose my time with Oak to his new girlfriend.

9

OAKLEY

May

"I just got the email from our lawyers: the sale has been finalized and we're officially the owners of a run-down resort in Bora Bora!" I announce as I burst into Parker's room, too excited to wait for him to finish getting ready to tell him. He doesn't have a shirt on yet, and his abs are popping. "Damn, if I looked like that, I don't think I'd ever want to put on a shirt," I comment, forgetting why I came in here.

"What are you talking about? You're way hotter than me," Parker scoffs.

"My muscles don't look like these," I point out as I poke his rock-hard stomach, laughing as he tries to swat me away.

"Why did you come in here again?" he asks, but his tone sounds amused, not annoyed.

"Oh right! We got the resort! We officially have about eleven months to turn it into the best wedding destination ever before the tourist season starts," I announce as I bounce up and down, unable to contain my excitement.

"You do realize that we'll be hiring people to do most of the actual work for it, right? You still need to run a giant international company," Parker reminds me skeptically.

As if I could forget the job that has literally consumed my focus for half of my life now. "Yeah, yeah, but this will be my passion project! I want to be as involved as I possibly can with the decisions," I explain.

"I'm sure the designers will love that," he says sarcastically with a roll of his eyes. "But I'm happy too," he assures me. "Now, can you help me find my Werewolves jersey so that we aren't late?" he asks, reminding me that we *are* cutting it pretty close to the time we told the girls we'd meet them.

"Maybe it ended up in my closet again. I'll go check," I say. We send out our laundry, and the people who clean the apartment also put it away. At six-three, Parker's significantly taller than the five-foot eleven inches I claim on a good day. His giant muscles fill out a bigger size than me in most things, so it's usually easy to keep our clothes separated, but the jersey sizes can be confusing. Sure enough, the one I know he wants to wear is mixed in with my own collection, so I grab it for him.

"Your sweater, kind sir," I say in a weird formal British accent as I present it to him over my bent arm, bowing my head. He laughs like I hoped he would and throws it on over the Werewolves T-shirt he must have put on while I was gone. I like how silly I can be around him, like I'm allowed to still act like the goofy kid I was when we met, even though I need to have my shit together in front of everyone else to prove that I'm good at my job and have worked hard to excel in the position that I inherited. I love making him laugh or smile, even if it is just at something stupid that I do. He spends so much time in his own head, and he worries so much about fitting in around new people, so knowing that I can make him forget about all of that makes me feel great.

Tonight is game six in the second series of the Stanley Cup Finals. My family owns the team, so we're planning to take the girls to our box to watch the game. Neither of them were huge hockey fans going into the finals, but they've come to a few of the games with us now over the last few weeks and have had a good time. My family is amazing and they can welcome anyone, and the girls are so sweet, so there hasn't been any awkwardness over bringing our new girlfriends.

My older brother Beck, who's the team's CEO, is bringing his "friend" to the game too, and I can't wait to meet the guy who convinced my grumpy playboy brother to follow him to a self-help seminar in Florida, of all places. *They're definitely going to end up together.*

We swing by the girls' condo, and they look cute in the over-sized Werewolves jerseys we got for them at their first game. My driver takes us to the parking lot where all of the players and staff park, and we make our way through the Caldwell Center to the owner's suite.

All of my family is here, along with our closest friends, and I love being surrounded by so many people that I care about. There's a huge selection of food throughout the large space, a full bar with a bartender, a private bathroom, and through the door in the back is a balcony with two stadium-style rows of plush seating overlooking center ice.

The girls immediately get pulled into a conversation with my mother, and Parker says that he'll grab us some food, so I take the opportunity to say hello to Beckett before his new man arrives. Beck is the person I'm closest to after Parker, and I hope that he can find a way to work things out with this guy. He's never been in a serious relationship before, but it's obvious that he cares about him with how his face lights up every time his phone goes off with an alert from this Cody guy, or how often he brings him up in a conversation.

It wasn't easy growing up with a brother who was only two years older than me and seemed to be perfect at everything. He set a super high standard to live up to. But he's always cared about me, and even Parker, fiercely, and I know that I'm lucky to have him in my life.

Thank fuck we didn't have to compete over girls growing up though, because he's basically an older, cooler, taller version of me. I wouldn't have stood a chance.

"So, where's your boyfriend?" I ask when I finally find him talking with his best friend, Jordan, and our youngest brother, Lincoln. Beck is anxiously watching the door of the suite, ignoring whatever Lincoln is saying to Jordan, so I don't feel rude interrupting.

"*Cody* should be here any minute, but he isn't my boyfriend," Beck grumbles. "How's the girlfriend you're ignoring?" he asks, and I chuckle at his supposed dig.

"Sage is lovely, thank you for asking," I reply in a bright tone.

"How's that going?" Jordan asks. He, along with Beck's other best friend, Adrian, are also good friends with me and Parker, and we usually try to get together once a week or so.

"Great, it's easily the best relationship that I've been in," I answer honestly. "Parker and I get to hang out with them all of the time because they live in our building, and they're so chill it doesn't feel like I have to go out of my way to impress her or anything. The best part is that I haven't had to give up any of my time with Parker either, and the girls never complain about our friendship because they're just as close as we are," I explain excitedly.

"Do you all sleep in the same bed too?" Lincoln asks flatly.

"Ha-ha, it's not like that and you know it," I say, shoving his shoulder lightly.

"Do the girls sleep in the same bed at their place?" he follows up with a pointed look at where Sage is now sitting in Aspen's lap, sharing an armchair in the corner of the room, looking at something on Sage's phone.

"Women are just more comfortable showing affection than most men," I say with an eye roll. "That's just a sad fact of our society, and it doesn't mean anything romantic," I add with a laugh.

The implication that casual affection equals some sort of sexual relationship has always confused me. More than one person has thought Parker and I were romantically connected because of how comfortable we are around one another, and the assumption has never made sense to me.

"Do you ever spend time with *just* Sage?" Lincoln pushes.

I love my youngest brother, and I would do anything for him, but sometimes he likes to try to stir shit. I usually ignore his grumpy attitude and respond with as much enthusiasm as I can to piss him off. "Almost every night," I say with an obnoxious wink.

Even though that isn't *exactly* true. We've obviously slept together, and it's fine, kind of on the vanilla side if I'm being honest, but I'm of the opinion that all consensual sex is good sex. And we have a great time when we're hanging out together, so I know it's a good relationship.

Even though we all live in the same building, the girls like to spend any work nights in their own place to maintain their routine, which I totally respect. They usually only stay over on weekends. It's great because then we all get the sleep we need.

I also haven't taken Sage out on any one-on-one dates, because honestly, the thought has never occurred to me until just now. We've always gone out with Parker and Aspen. But, if we're all free, why wouldn't we?

Beck's not-boyfriend, Cody, shows up, and everyone is instantly won over by his bubbly charm. He's also hot, and I don't need to be into men to know that. He's tall with long blond hair, lots of muscles and a nice smile. Good for my brother.

"Here ya go," Parker says, handing me a plate with all of my favorite foods that he clearly picked out for me, then he joins me talking with Cody for a while.

Cody seems like a really cool guy, and he's obviously as into my brother as Beck is to him. His job sounds kind of weird though. He teaches self-improvement classes or something. I'm honestly surprised that my generally sarcastic and annoyed with the world brother signed up for that sort of thing, but I guess spending time with Cody was enough incentive.

The girls join us on the balcony for the game, and it's an exciting one with both teams scoring, but in the end, the Werewolves secure the win, advancing them to the semifinal round.

It's a weekend, so after the game, the girls join us in our condo, and when Sage comes into my room after brushing her teeth, I remember what Lincoln asked me earlier. "Does it bother you that we haven't gone on any solo dates, just the two of us?" I ask.

"Don't be silly," she responds with a smile as she hops onto my bed, pulling the covers over herself. "Why wouldn't we go out with Aspen and Parker if we're all free?" she asks.

"That's exactly what I was thinking. I just wanted to make sure that we were on the same page," I clarify as I crawl into bed beside her.

"I'm sure that eventually one of us will be busy while the other isn't, but we're both so used to our best-friend-schedule, I love that we didn't have to change that to start dating," she adds.

"Me too. I like dating you," I agree, with a kiss to her cheek.

It really has been my easiest relationship ever. She's the only girlfriend I've had who's never complained about my friendship with Parker. Which puts her right at the top. I've always known that the right girl for me would be able to accept how important he is. I'm glad that Sage might finally prove me right, because at the end of the day, I know Parker will always be my person, and I could never risk our friendship for anyone.

PARKER

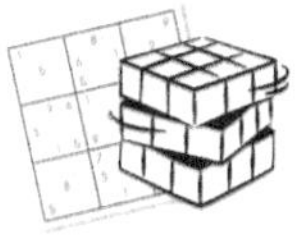

June

"Can I have another glass?" Aspen asks as we all move from the couch to the dining room table to snack on the low-carb charcuterie spread that's there. We don't completely avoid carbs, but snacks without them make it easier to keep my blood sugar levels stable, so they tend to be our default. I detour to the kitchen and grab a second bottle of wine from our built-in wine fridge. The Werewolves game was out of town tonight, so the girls are at our place and we all watched them lose from the comfort of our living room.

"We should play a drinking game!" Sage suggests, clapping at her own idea.

"What do you have in mind?" Oakley asks, sitting up straighter at the suggestion. *Competitive little shit.* I chuckle as I search for the wine opener. Oakley loves any type of game that he can win, but I don't think drinking games have a clear "winner" and he isn't usually a big drinker. I don't think he's had more than a glass all night.

"Truth or Dare!" Sage aims a conspiratorial grin at Aspen who nods eagerly at the idea.

I open the bottle of wine and bring it back into the room, refilling everyone's glasses before I sit down and ask, "Who goes first?"

"Me," Aspen volunteers, smiling sweetly up at me. "Parker, you can ask," she adds.

"Okay, Aspen, truth or dare?" I ask dramatically, playing along. I haven't had much to drink, maybe one glass throughout the whole hockey game, but it's easy for me to relax in our little group.

"Truth!" she answers quickly.

"Okay, um… What's the best date you've ever been on?"

"Hmm, that's a tough one," she says, chewing on her lip as she looks to Sage, like she'll know the answer. "I would have to say when Sage surprised me with a trip to Paris," she finally answers, grabbing her hand as she continues. "We got to go to shows during Fashion Week and then have dinner in the Eiffel Tower overlooking the city at night with all of the lights twinkling and the most delicious champagne," she adds with a dreamy tone.

I know she would have loved that experience, but I'm surprised that she's referring to it as a date in front of Sage.

"Wow, that sounds amazing. Best friend dates *are* the best," Oakley agrees.

Not what I was really going for when I asked. I guess I should have known that wasn't the best question for her, but I didn't think it through. With how she feels about Sage, anything they did would be more special than something she did with a boyfriend she didn't actually care about, so I nod, pretending it was what I meant all along. "That sounds like when Oakley surprised me with tickets to the premiere of one of the huge action, super-hero films that I love. We flew out and got to meet the whole cast and see the film before everyone else. It was unbelievable," I tell the girls.

Aspen gives me a big smile. "That sounds perfect for you. Okay, my turn to ask. Oakley, truth, or dare?"

"Definitely dare," he says, already sitting on the edge of his seat, ready to do whatever she requests.

Her smile grows. "Oakley, I dare you to kiss Parker in front of us," she says, looking pleased with herself.

I freeze, grateful that I wasn't taking a sip as she said that because I probably would have spit it back out. *Did I just hear what I think I heard?* Why would she want Oakley to kiss me? I told her that it's never been like that between us.

"Is that something you're into? Watching your boyfriend kiss someone else?" Oakley asks with a teasing tone.

"Maybe," she answers, sharing another conspiratorial look with Sage.

"It's not like you've never kissed before, we just want to watch," Sage adds.

Wait.

Did she just say that we've already kissed? Why does she think that?

"But, it *is* like we've never kissed before," I clarify.

"You two really expect us to believe that you've never fooled around?" Sage says with complete disbelief.

"Um, yes. Because it's the truth?" I answer, meaning to sound confident, but it comes out like a question.

"Come on, not you too," Oakley groans dramatically. "I thought you two, of all people, wouldn't buy into the whole 'best friends who are that close and live together must be fucking' thing that so many people give us shit about," he says sounding exasperated as he throws his head back, even though he's still smiling.

The girls exchange another look, almost like they feel guilty, probably about the assumption, before Sage turns to Oakley. "It's not a bad thing, honey," she assures him. "Aspen and I have kissed plenty of times," she adds casually.

"Really?" he asks, perking up at that. I look at Aspen who is definitely avoiding my gaze. Those kisses might not mean anything to Sage, but even if I didn't know how Aspen really feels, the blush on her cheeks and her guilty expression make it clear to me that Aspen does not feel the same way. *Probably why she's never mentioned that to me either.* We might be friends now and spend a lot of time together, but we haven't had any deep discussions. I'm not surprised that she hasn't been completely open with me about their history.

"Sure. It's not a big deal. Want us to show you?" Sage asks coyly.

"Okay," Oak quickly agrees. I don't think it's my place to intervene here, even knowing what I do. Maybe Aspen is wrong and Sage does want the excuse to kiss her? I'm a bit curious to see for myself how one-sided her feelings truly are. *And what would I say anyway?* Don't kiss your best friend after you just insisted it wouldn't mean anything because I know it would to her? *That would make me the worst fake boyfriend ever.*

Sage stands up from her chair and sits right on Aspen's lap. Then she tilts Aspen's chin up with her hand and brings their lips together. It's not a quick kiss, there's obviously tongue involved and both girls seem to be pretty consumed by the moment, bringing their bodies closer together.

I'm not sure how I'm supposed to feel about watching my "girlfriend" kiss her best friend. Should I pretend to be jealous, or should I make a comment that it's hot or something? I know some guys are into watching that, but it definitely isn't doing anything for me sexually. I don't want to fuck up appearances if I should be commenting, though.

"Wow, you really went for it," Oak says with a laugh, and it's like his comment startles the girls apart.

They join in laughing and Sage looks at Oakley expectantly, teasing, "Your turn."

I was so distracted by the girls kissing and the different layers of what that kiss meant to everyone in this room, that I completely forgot about the original dare. After their display, I don't know how I'm supposed to react. *Would protesting make it seem like I think kissing him would mean something?*

"Am I supposed to go sit in his lap too?" Oakley jokes but the girls both nod seriously, so he stands with a defeated huff and walks over to my chair. Instead of trying to sit sideways across my lap like Sage did, he pulls my chair out a little and fully straddles me. "Is this okay?" he asks softly.

I can't say that I've ever wished we would be in this position, but I also don't hate it. I decide to stop overthinking and follow his lead. Despite what the girls' kiss might have meant to Aspen, kissing Oakley really would be meaningless for us, and if he wants to joke around and put on a show, I might as well go along with it instead of turning it into a bigger deal than it needs to be. I rest my arms around him, gripping his hips so that he doesn't fall off of me and laugh. "Yeah, why not."

Then Oak mirrors Sage's earlier move, cupping my jaw with his hand to tilt my face up toward him. He looks into my eyes for a moment, before bringing his mouth to mine.

His lips are so much softer than I would have expected, and the feeling of the stubble on his face, rubbing against my own as our mouths move, is pleasantly intriguing. I let out a small gasp of surprise at the dual contrasting sensations and Oak takes the opportunity to slip his tongue into my mouth, exploring and tangling it with my own.

After a few moments, I realize that I'm kissing him back rather forcefully, meeting the movements of his mouth, battling for control. I also notice my grip has tightened on his hips, holding him firmly in place.

I don't do anything to stop though.

This is unlike any kiss that I've ever experienced. I've honestly never been a huge fan of kissing—it was just something to check off a list of things to do with a girl I was dating before we had sex.

This though? This is not *a line item.*

I could do this for hours. I feel like my entire body is buzzing with pleasure. Oakley moves his other hand into my hair and the feel of his fingers against my scalp is divine. The way his lips glide against mine feels sacred. He sucks my bottom lip between his own, following it with a slow little nip with his teeth. Then he licks the sore spot, and I let out a soft moan.

I'm unconsciously shifting my hips now, trying to grind my achingly hard cock up into his ass, and I realize all at once what's actually happening here—I'm grinding my very interested dick into my straight best friend while I basically fuck his mouth with my tongue. Kissing has never been like this before. I've never gone from zero to absolutely desperate from only a kiss. *What the actual fuck is happening right now?*

I pull away with a gasp, lifting Oakley off of my lap quickly as I shift my position, hoping to hide the very obvious erection that is now fighting against the zipper of my pants. *Seriously, what just happened? Why is my body reacting like this to a kiss?*

"See, that looked fun," Sage says, reminding me of her presence.

Her comment also reminds me how truly fucked up this whole situation is. Not only am I harder than I think I've ever been from the hottest kiss of my life, a kiss with my male best friend of all people, but that kiss was also in front of his girlfriend and my fake girlfriend after I insisted that I've never been attracted to Oakley.

Fuck.

"Really fun," Aspen agrees, smirking at me knowingly.

I look over at Oakley and find him staring at me with a sort of dazed expression. Maybe we drank more than I realized? But looking around the table, I confirm that our glasses are almost full, so I don't think he's had more than a glass or two of wine over the last several hours.

"Are you okay?" I ask quietly, internally panicking that he's re-evaluating our entire friendship after he felt my erection grinding into him.

Oakley blinks a few times, like he's trying to come back into focus and lets out a small laugh. "Why wouldn't I be okay? Like Sage said, no big deal. Right?"

My still very hard dick is protesting that statement, but if our kiss wasn't as earth-shattering for Oak as it was for me, I'm not risking our friendship over disagreeing. "Right. No big deal." The lie tastes bitter, and something in my chest sinks as I try to ignore the guilt I feel over lying to him.

Oakley suddenly turns to Sage and grabs her hand. "I'm ready for bed, honey, are you?" he asks, already starting to move toward his room.

"Sure," she says with a giggle, jumping out of her seat to keep up with him.

"You ready for bed too?" Aspen asks. "We can clean this all up in the morning," she offers.

My mind is racing with thoughts and questions over what the fuck just happened. But I'm still hard and I can't concentrate enough on anything other than how horny I am, so I agree and follow Aspen into my room, excusing myself to shower before we inevitably fall into our routine of watching reality shows while I do sudoku or puzzles on my phone until we fall asleep on opposite ends of the bed.

As soon as I've removed my insulin pump and I'm naked

under the warm spray, my hand is wrapped around my swollen cock, stroking, trying to focus on only the sensation and how good it feels like I normally would. I add some of the lube I keep in the shower to my hand, trying to fight the memory of that fucking kiss, and focus on anything else, but there's no use. That was by far the single hottest moment of my life.

Am I gay? Have I really been so ignorant of my own attraction to not know that about myself by now?

I try to picture another man, an actor, or athlete that I've heard people refer to as attractive, but despite how desperate I was feeling moments ago, picturing other men has my cock flagging in my grip. I try to think about my past hookups and relationships, about the women I've been attracted to before, but no one stands out.

Then the way Oakley's lips felt against my own comes rushing to the forefront of my mind, and all I can focus on is the way he was so aggressive, almost teasing as he nipped and licked at my mouth before exploring with his tongue. My cock is aching again, already leaking as the memories of that kiss consume me. His fingers in my hair. His firm ass on my lap as I ground my erection into him.

What would it feel like to have less clothes between us?

A part of me is shocked by the thought. Before our kiss I would have never cared what Oakley was wearing, let alone wished for him to be naked. But I've also never been as turned on as I am fantasizing about him. I'm enjoying it way too much to be overly concerned about the details of what it all means. I can stress about that more later.

Pleasure overwhelms me, spreading from where it had been building deep in my gut throughout my whole body until I feel like I'm on fire with how turned on I am, burning from the inside as my dick jerks and my hand is coated in cum. I'm panting under the warm water, one arm outstretched, leaning into the tiled wall for support as I struggle to stay standing.

Fuck.

I just jerked off to thoughts of my best friend. After sharing what was undoubtedly the hottest kiss of my life with him.

I have no idea what this means for us, or for me, but there is no denying now that I'm attracted to Oakley. Even as I'm filled with guilt over what I just did, my cock twitches again at the thought of our kiss. I've never been this horny in my life. Even in my teenage years when other guys seemed obsessed with the idea of having sex, I've always been sort of indifferent, content to take care of my urges myself.

I'm definitely not indifferent right now as I picture my best friend. *What the fuck is happening to me?* Is this what it's supposed to feel like when you're attracted to someone? How did I go this long without realizing that I'm into my best friend? Have I been ignoring feelings that were there before tonight because of how insistent we've always been that we're just friends when people make assumptions? Or did that kiss awaken something inside of me that I wouldn't have ever discovered if we'd never crossed that line?

Aspen must read the confusion in whatever expression I'm wearing as I leave the bathroom to get into bed. "Want to talk about it?" she offers.

"Nothing to talk about," I respond firmly. I don't know what any of this means and I'm definitely not ready to talk about my reaction to the kiss or the thoughts that it inspired with anyone. And even if I was, Oakley's girlfriend's best friend probably isn't the ideal person to talk about it with. Aspen might be able to relate to some of these emotions, but I don't want her projecting her situation onto me any more than she already has.

This might have been a fluke that will blow over and I'll forget all about it in a few weeks. No need to have her thinking

I'm in love with Oak because I enjoyed kissing him. Or what if she felt obligated to tell Sage about what I'm feeling? Oakley seems very happy dating her, and I would hate for something I said to Aspen to compromise his relationship.

Talking is definitely not a good idea. I'll just continue to question everything I thought I knew about myself internally.

That's way better.

OAKLEY

June

I've always been the oldest *straight* Caldwell brother. Beckett's been very vocal about being gay for as long as I can remember, so even from a young age, any girl trying to get in with our family name turned to *me*. Our younger brothers came to *me* with their questions about dating and what to do or say when trying to impress the opposite gender. I've never questioned that I'm *straight*.

But last night didn't feel very straight. My hard cock twitching when Parker's erection dug into my ass didn't feel very straight.

Then he was lifting me off him, ending our kiss and unleashing a storm of confusion in my mind. Questions about what the kiss meant, why it felt so good, and why we had never done it before still swirl violently around in my head, fighting for my focus while I attempt to stay afloat in my routine.

For the first time in over twenty years, I don't know how to act around my best friend. I don't know what he's thinking. And

I'm afraid to ask in case it shatters the calm facade of normalcy I'm desperately clinging to.

The girls left early this morning; they had brunch plans with some people from Sage's work and needed to get ready, leaving Parker and I alone.

We avoided eye contact for a few moments when we first ran into each other in the kitchen, but then, he asked if I was almost ready for our workout, slipping into our normal morning routine.

I eagerly agreed, happy that he wasn't ignoring me completely. Last night when he asked if I was okay after the kiss, I was completely unsure how to answer. I was entirely surprised by how much I enjoyed it and a part of me was pissed he ended it when he did. But I must have just been really horny, and I've always enjoyed kissing, plus our girlfriends were there. How was I supposed to respond? So, I tried to laugh it off like it was no big deal because I thought that was what everyone would expect me to do. And Parker immediately agreed, so I'm glad I didn't admit just how much I enjoyed it if he didn't feel the same way.

Parker is the most important person in my life, and if last night somehow fucked up our friendship, I would never forgive myself.

If he's going to continue with business as usual with no acknowledgement of what happened last night, then the kiss must not have been a big deal to him.

Which means I can't let on how big of a deal it was to me. I don't want him to worry that I want things to change between us. *Because I don't.* Questioning my sexual orientation doesn't mean I'm suddenly in love with my best friend.

Now we're in the fitness center, and I'm spotting for Parker as he bench presses a crazy high amount of weight. I've always been impressed by his physique, but I catch myself following a bead of sweat as it drips down the sharp edge of his jaw and wishing I could lick it off of him. *What the actual fuck? I'm not going to lick my best friend.*

Again.

There's no way that all of the people who asked us if we were more than friends over the years actually noticed something that I didn't.

Right?

It was only a kiss, and I love kissing. *Who doesn't love kissing?* Sure, my dick was really hard after a very short amount of time, but I had also just watched Sage and Aspen make out, so there was obviously a lot going on.

Just because kissing my best friend was hot, it doesn't have to mean anything more than that. My intense reaction was probably a result of the novelty of the situation; new things are exciting. He was hard too, but I'm sure that was just because someone was sitting on his lap kissing him, his dick would probably react like that to anyone.

And the girls were watching! I've always wondered if I had a bit of an exhibitionism kink. Jerking off in the same room as Parker in college was really hot. And after I heard Parker with a hookup in his room, I realized he could also hear mine. That realization has made sex, and even solo sessions, much hotter when I know he's home.

Parker also being involved in those situations doesn't mean anything. *Obviously.* He's just always around, and it's not like anyone else is near me enough for them to hear me having sex.

Of course, all of this thinking about sex has sent blood straight to my cock, so I attempt to subtly adjust my stance. Fuck. From the position I'm standing at, behind the bench, close enough to spot for Parker, my dick is basically right above his head. I really hope that he's focused on the weights and he won't look up at my bulging crotch.

There is no reason for me to be hard right now, dammit. I've watched Parker work out a million times, and it has never turned me on like this before.

I'm thirty years old. I shouldn't be randomly popping wood like I'm a teenager again. And it's obviously random, *not from staring at Parker and his muscles flexing as he shows off how strong he is.* I would know if I was into guys by now. I've known Parker for pretty much the entire span of my memory, so surely something would have clued me in during all that time if I was attracted to him, or any man, for that matter.

He finishes the set, and thankfully, brings up a topic that distracts me from these confusing thoughts. "So is dinner at your grandparents' house still tonight?"

"Yeah, I think Jordan and Adrian were going to come this week to drag Beckett away from work."

His flight back was this morning. The Werewolves' loss last night knocked them out of the playoffs. It must have been devastating for him. I'm glad he'll be surrounded by friends and family tonight for support.

"Are we all driving together?" he asks.

"Yeah, Adrian offered to take us all." I love that our smallest friend, I think I've heard him describe himself as a twink, drives the biggest car. He says that it's practical, but I've always thought it seemed a little more "soccer mom" than a single guy living in the city really needed. But, Adrian is a natural caretaker, and I think he likes being able to have the option to bring us all anywhere we need. He also likes to drive so that he can control the music selection. Apparently, my 90s and early 2000s punk-rock playlist really offended him the last time I tried to DJ.

I'm relieved we're all going together so I won't be alone in a car with Parker for the entire drive to the suburbs. Which is such a sad thought to acknowledge. Parker is my very favorite person, and there is no reason I shouldn't be able to spend a car ride alone with him, no matter how awkward I'm being about the kiss.

"Is he picking us up here, or are we all meeting at his place?" Parker asks. I'm sure he was in the group chat too, but sometimes he mutes it if they're sending too many texts while he's trying to focus on something, and then he forgets to turn it back on. Plus, he knows I'll keep him in the loop, so he doesn't really need to worry about it.

"We're meeting at Adrian's in an hour," I answer stiffly. I really hope Parker doesn't realize how strange I'm being. I don't want him to think I'm mad at him or anything. *Just super distracted by how soft your lips were last night.* Fuck. I need to get my act together before we're in front of our friends or they're definitely going to know something is going on.

ADRIAN HAS some upbeat pop playlist going as we head to my grandparents' house in the suburbs. "House" might not be the right label, but mansion sounds so pretentious. Jordan is riding up front with Adrian, and Beck is in the other bucket seat in the second row of the SUV, next to me. I'd offered it to Parker, but he told me to sit next to my brother and climbed into the third row, probably planning to do puzzles on his phone the whole ride anyway.

Jordan is a reporter, and he's telling us about some fluff piece his news station made him cover recently about local squirrels and the best at-home squirrel viewing tips. "They wanted me to hold one!" he says, and we all laugh.

"A wild squirrel?" Beck asks, and Jordan shakes his head.

"No, they were trying to get a wildlife specialist with a domesticated squirrel that I could hold during the taping, thankfully they couldn't find one in time and gave up on the idea."

"Thank fuck they did," Adrian adds. "Can you imagine if a

wild animal scratched up your pretty face? I'm shocked that they would risk damaging your moneymaker like that!"

"Ha-ha" Jordan responds with an eye roll. But it's a valid point, he's hot, and I'm sure his looks help with their ratings. *Have I always thought he's attractive? Is that something only someone who's attracted to other men would think?*

"I have to admit that I was expecting you guys to be in worse moods today, Beck and Adrian," I say, trying to stay focused on my friends and not thoughts of who's attractive.

Adrian is Beck's assistant at the Werewolves organization, but that title doesn't seem to accurately portray how important I know he is to the company. The loss must have been really hard on him too.

"I'm absolutely devastated! The only reason I even got out of bed was your grandmother's chef's baking. You know his fudge is literally to die for," Adrian answers. "Beck, on the other hand, has seemed perfectly fine about the loss. The traitor," he adds.

"I'm also very upset!" Beck argues with an eyeroll. "I just have other things to focus on right now that can distract me from hockey," he explains.

I gasp dramatically. "Nothing has ever been important enough to distract *you* from hockey," I tease.

"Fuck off," he says, giving me a playful shove, but he's also smiling. He's been doing that a lot more in the last few months since he met Cody.

"He's planning to abandon us all and move to some weird town in Montana to be with his one-true-love," Adrian adds theatrically.

"I am not moving to Montana," Beck says flatly. "I'm trying to plan a visit there for a few weeks during the off season, it isn't that big of a deal," he insists. Interesting that he ignored the whole "true love" thing, but I don't call him out on that.

"Your entire life has been focused on the Werewolves. You leaving for a month *is* a big deal," Jordan adds.

"So, Parker, you're awfully quiet back there," Beck says, obviously trying to shift the focus off of himself.

"Am I ever particularly *loud* in a group of people?" Parker deadpans, glancing up from what looks like a sudoku app on his phone.

"Good point," Beck admits. "But, what's new with you?" he asks, turning around as much as his seatbelt will allow to face Parker.

"Umm…" Parker mumbles and his cheeks pinken a little like they always do when the focus is on him. I hate when people try to put him on the spot in social situations, and usually I jump in, but I'm completely off my game today with how awkward things feel between us.

He doesn't ever struggle at work, he can talk business and numbers without hesitation, even in large presentations or important meetings, but when the focus is put on *him* and not the work, he doesn't love it. He doesn't seem to blurt out random thoughts as much as he used to growing up. I can tell the moment that Parker settles on what to say as he sits up a little straighter and the blush fades. "Your brother is trying to get me fired by demanding the most expensive resort renovations possible," he says with a slightly teasing tone.

Teasing is good. It's normal. W*e're totally normal*.

"That sounds about right," Beck agrees with a laugh, then launches into more questions about the resort.

"I'm invited to the opening, right?" Adrian asks in an over-the-top, sugary-sweet tone. He'd no doubt be batting his eyelashes at me if he wasn't driving.

"Yeah, we're hoping to do a friends and family soft-opening at the end of next March before the resort is officially open to the public for the peak tourist season. I know there will still be hockey, but I'm hoping that you'll all be there."

"Fuck yes, I'll be there. If the CEO can run off to the mountains for over a month, his assistant can go on a free island vacation to Bora Bora," Adrian eagerly assures me. "Beck, consider this my official time-off request."

"I have no doubt that you'll make it work," Beck agrees.

"I will also definitely be there. It sounds really cool," Jordan adds.

"We've already launched a marketing campaign in the bridal world and reached out to a few engaged celebrities to see if anyone would be interested in early bookings for next year. We've offered a discounted rate for their promotion," Parker adds. "April and May are already fully booked, so we need to make sure everything is ready before then."

"Sounds stressful," Jordan replies.

"It'll be fun!" I insist. Glad that we're focused on a topic that can distract me from last night. *Except there I go thinking about the kiss again.*

Dinner should be super fun and not awkward at all.

PARKER

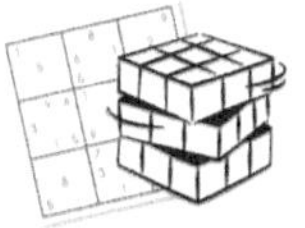

June

"You never think I'm awkward," I say as I pet Spot. Oakley's grandparents' five-year-old Dalmatian and I have always had a special bond.

Oakley's family has always included me in their dinners, even lovingly referring to me as his "better half." I love spending time with his brothers, parents, and grandparents, but it's also nice to take a break from all the noise and people, and soak up the affection from Spot while I can.

I've always loved animals, how uncomplicated their obvious loyalty and love are. Growing up, we moved around too much for us to ever have a dog of our own, and then, when it was just me and my mom, asking for another thing that she would have to be responsible for seemed selfish.

Oakley's offered for us to adopt a dog many times over the years. Our condo allows pets and even has some dog-friendly amenities, but I've never been able to picture one being happy in our indoor space with nowhere to really run.

If we're being honest, I've also been worried that if we did get a pet, it would become too attached to Oak, and I'd be forced to say goodbye when he inevitably found his wife and finally moved on from being my roommate. I know most people prefer Oakley's confident humor and easy-going nature over my sometimes awkward and quieter one. Odds are, any dog that we got would feel the same way.

Spot, though, has gravitated toward me since his grandparents adopted him. It gives me a confidence boost every time I see how excited he is at my arrival.

Today, more than ever before, I'm glad Spot has given me the excuse to hide out here and away from Oakley, our friends, and his family. I know I'm being awkward with Oakley, and I don't want anyone to call me out on it while I'm still so confused about what even happened. Spot looks so full of joy and love as I toss a ball as far as I can. It's a spacious yard, and he immediately bounds after it, tail wagging the entire time. *How could I be anything but happy around him?*

But I haven't been able to get out of my head. On the way here, I realized that Aspen and Sage have never come with us to one of these dinners, even though they happen every week. They've met the Caldwells in their box at the Werewolves games, but this house feels more sacred than the public arena. Bringing them here would feel like a very serious relationship move. I can't help but wonder what it means that Oak hasn't invited Sage, though.

Now that I'm alone, away from Oakley and pretending like everything is normal, there's nothing to distract me from obsessing over last night and what all of my confusing reactions might actually mean. Obviously, I'm not in a serious relationship, but no one else knows that. I'm feeling guilty about not being honest with Oakley about the arrangement between Aspen and I. But telling him now might make him think I'm only confessing because we kissed, and I don't need him reading into that.

When I agreed to go along with Aspen's idea of the whole fake relationship thing, I can't deny that my motivation was all about spending time with Oakley. But after last night, the situation seems a little less innocent. I was so confident I didn't feel anything more than friendship toward him, that hiding the fact that I'm not actually sleeping with Aspen didn't seem like a big deal. But now, it feels like I'm lying to my best friend for the first time in over twenty years.

Instead of innocently hanging out with Oak, something I'd be doing anyway, while also helping out my new friend, now I can't help but feel guilty. Like I'm manipulating someone I'm having very confusing feelings about to get them to spend more time with me. Which I guess is what I've been helping Aspen do with Sage this whole time, but she made that part seem like more of an afterthought, with the focus being on her shitty family and getting them to give her space. Hanging out with our best friends seemed like a convenient perk.

But I'm having trouble thinking about anything other than the kiss with Oak. It doesn't feel right to be so consumed by a kiss with someone and then claim I don't have any feelings for them. Oakley has always been my favorite person, and now that I'm apparently attracted to him too, it seems like the definition of having feelings.

Fuck.

Do I have a crush on my best friend? Is that what this is?

I don't think I've ever really had a crush on anyone before. I've had girlfriends I've been fond of, relationships I enjoyed being in, women I thought I had romantic feelings for, but I'm not sure I've had true feelings for any of them. To be honest, I was never that upset when things ended, and I only started dating them after they pursued me, or Oakley suggested I ask them out. I've never secretly pined after anyone. *Is that what I'm doing? Pining after Oak?*

I hate this. There's so much uncertainty. *Do I want to kiss him again?* Yes. There's no denying that. *But does that really mean I suddenly want to date my best friend?*

Fuck. I have no idea.

But I've never felt like time stopped when I kissed anyone else.

I seriously need to stop thinking about kissing Oakley. With our friends and family around who know how comfortable we are with each other, I'm worried it will be obvious just how strange things are between us.

I know it's my fault. I can tell that Oakley is trying really hard to act like things are normal between us. But it's been off. He was too careful with me all morning, formal and polite, compared to how we normally interact and give each other shit, how silly and competitive he can be. He's obviously uncomfortable with what happened last night. He felt my hard cock digging into his ass, and now he doesn't know how to act around me. *If it made him that uncomfortable, then this is obviously a one-sided situation. He isn't out there daydreaming about our kiss, wishing it could happen again.*

I can't believe I ground my erection into him like that, however briefly. He's probably wondering if the kiss was something that I'd secretly hoped for, if he'll have to let me down gently and put distance between us.

But, before last night, I'd never considered kissing him, or any man. I still don't understand why I had such a strong reaction. But I know that more than anything, I don't want our friendship to change. *I can't lose him.* I've gone this long without kissing him, I can do it again. I can try to forget how amazing his lips felt against mine, and go back to the way things have always been.

Oakley is obviously trying to pretend like nothing happened. He normally talks about *everything.* He tells me all of the mundane details of his day, every opinion he has, and his thoughts on any topic he's focusing on. He had no hesitation asking to jerk off in our room in college right in front of me all of those years ago, and he's told me all sorts of details about his hookups over the years for fuck's sake.

If he wanted to talk about the kiss, he would have brought it up by now.

So, if he's acting as though it meant nothing, that it wasn't some life-altering, make-you-question-everything kind of moment for him, *like I'm trying really hard to not admit it might have been for me,* then I need to follow his lead. I need to find some way to convince him that we're fine. We're still us, and nothing about our friendship needs to change. I can ignore whatever crush I seem to have developed, ignore the fluttering in my stomach that's happened every time I've looked at him since, and the heat that's flared deep in my gut when I've caught my gaze lingering on his lips.

I'm not exactly sure how to do that. But, for now, I guess I need to pretend like nothing happened, and eventually things will go back to the way they were before last night.

Right?

13

OAKLEY

June

*D*inner is…awkward.

There's no other word for it. I keep stealing glances at Parker, wondering if he's being his normal version of quiet, like he sometimes is in big groups, or if he's feeling uncomfortable about what happened between us. *Did I make things weird this morning at the gym? Did he see my erection and now he thinks I'm lusting after him?*

Despite my best efforts to follow Parker's lead today and act like nothing is going on, Beck won't stop giving me weird looks, raising his brow at me in that silent, inquisitive way of his that always gets me to bare my soul. *Not today big brother, this internal freakout does not need an audience.*

I'm sure that Beck would be supportive if I did decide to tell him about the kiss and how confused it's left me, but I'm not ready to talk about it with anyone. The gym this morning and my physical reaction to Parker during his workout left me with even more questions, and I need to deal with them without opening myself up to his teasing.

I've always been able to acknowledge if men are attractive, but I guess I chalked that up to growing up with an openly gay big brother who would comment on things like that. I didn't think it meant I was attracted to any of those men. The same way I can identify if a piece of cake looks good, but it doesn't mean I actually want to eat it.

But do I really not want to eat it? Or have I been so health conscious for so long that I don't even consider wanting the cake? And what does it mean that my mind immediately went to comparing being with a man to eating a universally loved dessert? *Have I been craving cake without realizing it?* What if I've been attracted to men this whole time, but I've just never considered being with one as a possibility, so I've dismissed those feelings? Did kissing Parker unlock that part of me I've kept shut away, even from myself?

I know I should probably talk to someone about what I'm thinking, but Parker is who I'd usually go to about everything, and I obviously can't go to him when we laughed it off last night and he's been avoiding the topic all day, acting like things are business as usual between us. And even though I know he'd be supportive, Beck would also give me so much shit after teasing me about being too close with Parker all of these years. I'm not ready to face his ribbing when I'm feeling so uncertain about everything.

The kiss last night was no big deal to Parker, which he immediately confirmed. Based on his caution around me today, I think he's only worried about how strange I've been acting. I need to evaluate my feelings by myself and figure out how to accept whatever's going on so we can get back to the way things normally are between us.

I refuse to let anything affect our friendship.

So maybe I'm bi. It's not like that's a bad thing. I've always been supportive of the entire LGBTQIA+ community. And really it shouldn't change anything. I already have a great girlfriend, so learning this about myself doesn't mean I suddenly need to break up with her so I can go experiment with men. I could live my whole life without another romantic or sexual encounter with a man and it wouldn't make that label less true.

I like Sage, she's kind, and we have a great time hanging out together. Parker and Aspen seem like they have a good thing going for them too. Before last night, I had no reason to even consider ending things with her, and just because I'm realizing that I'm probably attracted to men as well as women, doesn't make my feelings for her disappear.

But do I actually have feelings for her? Or did I just want to be in a relationship and one where I didn't have to sacrifice any time with Parker seemed like a perfect set-up?

I'm not sure.

So, do I want to end things between Sage and I?

That's the real question, isn't it? The one that's been bouncing around my head all day. *Did the kiss and how much I enjoyed it mean I should end things with her?* She kissed her best friend last night too, and I seem to be the only one who was so affected. Before last night, I'd been thinking of this as the best relationship I've ever been in.

Am I ready to ruin it over some confusion with my straight best friend?

I wish I was confident in that answer. I don't want to make any drastic changes I'll end up regretting. I guess all I can really do is try to continue to be honest with myself and with her. If at any point I realize that I don't want to be with her anymore, I'll end things.

But with Parker so unaffected by the kiss, it's clear that the internal struggle I've been having today needs to be more of a general "I'm into both girls and guys now" discovery. It can't be that I'm into Parker specifically. He's the most important person in my life, and I refuse to make things awkward between us by lusting after him.

Nothing has to change.

At least that's what I keep chanting in my head as I try my best to distract myself. It isn't working though, so I turn to my big brother, hoping he'll say something interesting to hold my focus. "So, when do you leave for Montana?"

"After the draft."

"And what exactly is there to do in Montana?"

"I have no idea, but Cody seems to really love it. He mentioned hiking, and he sends a lot of pictures of the mountains."

"Mountains are nice," I say, already losing interest in this conversation. I can't seem to stop my gaze from drifting back to Parker where he sits across from me. Has it always been so interesting to watch him eat? The way his mouth stretches around each bite of food and how his lips wrap around the fork suddenly feel like a tease. Like he's trying to remind me that I know exactly what those soft lips feel like moving against mine.

Fuck. I don't need an erection during family dinner.

"Oakley?" Beck asks in a harsh tone that makes me think it wasn't the first time he's tried to get my attention.

I shake my head slightly to try to clear the Parker-induced haze that seems to have consumed my brain. "Sorry, what's up?"

"I asked if you have any travel plans coming up," Beck says slowly, raising a brow at how oddly I'm acting.

"Oh yeah! Nothing is officially booked yet, but we're hoping to check out the resort in Bora Bora soon," I say, looking to Parker again, but at least I have a better excuse this time.

"Does the CFO really need to go?" My younger brother, Lincoln, asks from his spot further down the table. *Apparently, not far enough away to give us shit.*

"I actually do if I want to prevent Oak from demanding the

most expensive version of everything the contractors offer," Parker deadpans, making our friends laugh.

I don't think he was trying to be funny, which makes his comment even better in my opinion. I shrug, smiling at Parker, and when our eyes meet as he smiles back at me, something flips in my gut.

Nothing has to change. Nothing has to change.

I'm so fucked.

14

PARKER

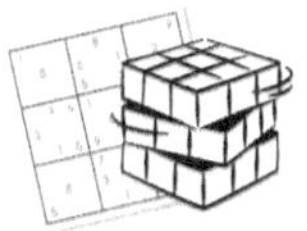

July

"For dessert, the chef has prepared lychee flavored mochi ice cream. Enjoy," the waiter says dramatically.

They've been the one narrating this sixteen-course Omakase dinner, and I've only understood the meaning of maybe half of the food we've eaten tonight. *Super fun for carb counting and insulin calculations.*

We're at this over-the-top, Michelin-star restaurant because Sage picked it for her birthday dinner. It's been a little over a month since *the kiss*, and I think things are finally back to normal between Oakley and I.

We never acknowledged that things *weren't* normal between us, but in the first week or so after the incident, there were a lot of stilted conversations and avoiding eye contact. Eventually though, things did seem to return to the way they've always been between us, just like I had hoped. It's hard not to fall into old habits with someone that you live with, work with, and basically do everything with.

Even if I still catch myself glancing at his lips when he isn't looking, or wondering what it would be like if I switched places with Sage when they're cuddling on the couch or holding hands as they're walking.

"Wow, everything has been amazing!" Aspen gushes, taking Sage's hand. "This was such a great idea, babe."

We're still dating the girls. Well, Oak is dating Sage, and Aspen and I are still going through the motions of a relationship when we're around other people so she can post pictures online and convince her family that we're dating. They've also never brought up the kiss. Either kiss, actually, between Oak and I, or between the two of them. I think Aspen is afraid to mess with our arrangement by asking me about it.

It's kind of wild to think that we've been fake dating for a couple of months now. It's definitely been the easiest relationship that I've ever been in, despite the fact that it isn't real. Even if we avoid any discussions of actual feelings, Aspen is one of my favorite people. Everything's fine between us. And fine is good. Plenty of people would be thrilled to be in an easy, fine relationship.

And I wouldn't even be questioning if I was one of those people if it hadn't been for that damn kiss with Oakley and everything that it's led me to question since then.

Looking at Aspen, it's clear to me that she's beautiful. She obviously puts in a lot of effort with her appearance. She's really good at doing her hair and makeup, she always wears nice clothes, she works out and eats well. I'd bet anyone attracted to women in this restaurant would agree that she's attractive.

But, even knowing that our relationship is fake, I still haven't been able to wrap my head around if I could actually be attracted to her if she wanted that from me. Oakley was the one that suggested we ask the girls out that day in our gym. He asked out Sage, so I went out with Aspen. If she had wanted to hook up that first night, I would have gone along with it. But am I attracted to her specifically? Have I ever been attracted to someone I was dating? Or anyone at all? Have I truly just picked my previous partners based on the idea of who I thought I should be dating?

I don't fucking know.

On paper, if this was a real relationship, she would be the ideal woman for me. We're similar ages, she wouldn't be after money or status, she's kind, a great friend, and most importantly, she doesn't care how close I am to Oak. But for the first time in my life, I can't help but wonder if there might be more out there for me than what I've always assumed seems perfect.

This past month has led to a lot of self-reflection on my part, even if I haven't been able to confidently answer any of the questions I have. I've realized I've simply gone along with what was easy when it came to dating. Even in middle school, my first date was a double so that Oakley could ask out the girl he liked. In high school, I had sex for the first time because Oakley didn't want us to go to college as virgins.

There were a few girls and dates over the years that he didn't introduce or help set up. But looking back, those girls always approached me first, I never pursued them. And they were typically during periods of time when Oakley also had a girlfriend. Would I have ever even dated if Oakley wasn't there to encourage me? *Would I have cared?*

I know I've never had a physical reaction to any of the women I've been with that could compare to the kiss with Oakley. I haven't had any problems performing, I think my libido is normal, even if I've been content to take care of things by myself. But would physical stimulation from anyone be enough? Especially when I wanted to have sex with them, and I didn't know it could feel like anything else, that it could be as explosive as the kiss Oakley and I shared. None of my previous experiences compare to the electricity of that moment.

So, one of the questions that's lingered in the back of my mind, one of the many that I'm not ready to confidently answer, but constantly tries to interrupt my thoughts and demand my attention—am *I even attracted to women?*

I would like to think that I'd have figured this out before I was thirty years old. Or that I would have at least questioned things *before* kissing my best friend.

But I feel blindsided by the situation, even now, weeks later.

Looking around the restaurant, I try to subtly note if I can find *anyone* who I'm sexually attracted to, man or woman, and fall short. *Is something wrong with me?* There are plenty of good-looking people here, but no one that I'm instantly drawn toward. Sex has just never been a huge priority for me. If I have it, cool. If not, no big deal.

So does it even really matter?

Looking back, though, there's an exception that I've never wanted to inspect too closely. It started that first night in college when Oakley asked if he could stay in his bed to jerk off. I'd laughed to myself about never understanding his libido that's always been much higher than mine. But I'd assumed it would be no big deal. We obviously knew we both jerked off, so did it really matter if I was in the room?

But then his soft moans and the sound of him touching himself had seemed to overwhelm my senses, and without making a real conscious choice, I'd joined in and gotten myself off too. I was worried back then that things would be weird between us, but they never were. I wrote off my reaction as no big deal, hearing him was basically a live-porn soundtrack, anyone would react that way hearing someone else get off. *Even though porn has never made me react like that.* I've even wondered if I might have a voyeurism kink.

Now, though, I'm debating if Oakley himself had something to do with that response, or if it was because he's a man, or maybe it was just the sounds and taboo nature of the situation. I can't confidently answer any of the questions I've been asking myself, but I also can't stop thinking about them.

But surely, if the answer was just that I was gay, I would be attracted to other men, *right*? Or at the very least, I would have known that I was attracted to my best friend before his tongue was in my mouth.

Maybe the connection that I'm remembering and obsessing over, wasn't even there. It's possible I've thought about it so much that I've exaggerated all of the details and imagined such intense chemistry, but it doesn't actually exist.

"Ready to go, sweetie?" Aspen asks, and I realize that I'm the only one still seated. I guess we're leaving.

"Yeah, just trying to decide if I gave myself enough insulin," I say as I get up to join them. I realize I really should have been thinking about that, and quickly program my pump. I've been counting carbs for so long that I'm fairly certain I put in the right amount, even if I couldn't tell you exactly what it is we ate. I'll just keep an eye on my monitor and adjust again if needed.

"You okay?" Oakley asks quietly enough that I don't think Aspen and Sage can hear from where they've started walking in front of us.

"Yeah, just a lot on my mind with work stuff," I mutter. I hate lying to Oakley, so I've tried to stick to half-truths the few times he has called me out on acting weird.

"If you're stressed about the numbers, try to focus on how much fun we'll have in Bora Bora! We get to start planning our first visit soon," he says excitedly.

I laugh at his enthusiasm. "You do realize that it's *my job* to stress about the numbers, so that you get to do things like plan visits to the island, right?"

"Yeah… And thank fuck you do, I would hate that responsibility," he teases.

"Eh, it's not so bad," I admit. I like to be the one who makes his vision work for the company from a financial perspective. I know that some board members don't love how young we are, or that we're best friends, but I think it only helps the company. Oakley has great creative ideas and passion, and I don't think anyone else would care as much as I do to find ways to actually afford them.

Because they're great ideas. *Totally has nothing to do with wanting to make my best friend happy.* And even if it did, everyone wants their best friend to be happy.

I don't need to admit if it means anything more.

OAKLEY

August

"I'm starving, I really hope the girls have already ordered dinner," I huff out.

I hit the elevator button more times than necessary, impatient to get upstairs. Parker laughs at my admittedly childish display, but I'm in a mood. The annoying summer humidity is in full swing. We were stuck at work late tonight, on a fucking Friday, with some of the other execs on an international call with the management team of our hotel in Tokyo. I was in other meetings all day and accidentally skipped lunch.

My hanger is real, and I need to eat something before I get really nasty to be around.

Finally, the elevator arrives, and we head straight to Sage and Aspen's place. They knew we'd be late, since we weren't sure how long the meeting would go, but we texted them when we left the office. I'm hoping their lack of response means they immediately ordered food, and that's why they didn't text back. I sent another one that we were in the lobby, though, and it doesn't look like it's been read either.

"Do you think they went to pick something up instead?" I ask Parker as we knock on the door after having no luck with their doorbell.

"I don't know. I think they would have texted us if they did," he says as he puts his ear up to the door to listen inside. "It sounds like the TV is on, maybe they fell asleep watching something?"

"Maybe…" I mutter as I give up knocking and try the handle. It's unlocked, so I hesitantly push inside. The lights are all on, but I don't hear anyone. I look back at Parker with a raised brow, unsure if we should just walk in, but also starting to get worried that something might have happened to the girls.

He shrugs and motions for me to go in, so we enter their condo together, looking around to make sure some masked murderer isn't about to pop out. Everything looks normal and I can hear the TV on, so I head in that direction.

As I round the corner into the living space, I start to hear… moaning? Is someone hurt? "Shit, Sage are you okay?" I ask as I rush into the space, only to stop on a dime when I see what's happening on the couch in front of me.

No one is hurt, that's for sure.

Sage is straddling Aspen, passionately making out with her

"What the fuck are you doing?" I hear myself demand. *Seriously what the fuck is going on?* I'm aware that Parker is standing mutely next to me, but I'm too confused by what we just interrupted to turn and see his full reaction.

The girls scramble apart so that they're sitting next to each other on the couch. "Oh, hi! Sorry, we must not have heard you come in," Aspen responds in her normal bubbly tone, although her wide eyes are darting between Parker and I, looking guilty.

"No shit. I mean why the fuck were you two hooking up?" I ask incredulously.

Sage is still sitting on the couch, a dazed expression on her face as she lifts her fingertips to her lips, the gesture so slow I'm not sure she's even aware she's doing it.

Aspen walks up to Parker and grabs his hand, finally pulling my attention to him. He doesn't seem upset, expression introspective as he stares blankly at the couch they'd just been on.

"I swear I didn't initiate that," she says in a low tone that's practically a whisper. "Can you give us a few minutes to talk? Maybe fill Oakley in and then we'll all sit down and figure out what's going on?"

Why the fuck does she need to talk to Sage first? To get their story straight?

Hell no.

"Or," I cut in loudly, "the four of us can stay right here and all talk together because we just caught you fucking cheating on us. You can have all of the time you want after we end things."

Aspen looks alarmed at the suggestion that we're about to break up with them, but what does she expect? *That we'd be totally fine with walking in on their hookup?*

"You've seen us kiss before," she reminds me weakly.

I roll my eyes. "Okay, telling us that you've kissed before, or even kissing in front of us, is very different than us walking in on you two hooking up, *alone*. Who knows how far you would have gone if we hadn't walked in?" I try to point out, but Aspen and even Parker look so calm, and Sage is still very quiet, not looking nearly as concerned as Aspen did at the idea of us breaking up, that I'm starting to question if this really is as big of a deal as I thought it was when I first saw them. "If you walked in on me with Parker's dick in my mouth, wouldn't you be upset?" I demand, trying to express my feelings in a way that they might understand.

Wait, what did I just say? And why would I volunteer to be the one putting a dick in my mouth?

I glance over at Parker and see him looking at me with more

shock than when we caught the girls. Aspen is smirking at Parker now, shaking her head no in response to my question.

Then the doorbell rings, interrupting this awkward moment. "That must be the concierge with our food," Sage says, still seeming like she's lost in her own head as she gets up to answer it.

Food. I desperately need food.

Apparently, the doorbell works just fine. They were just too busy making out with each other to notice.

Fuck. I am way too hungry to be dealing with any of this right now. I look over at Parker again to try to gauge his reaction to any of this. My first thought when I saw them tangled up together was that we had caught our girlfriends cheating on us and our relationships were done.

But no one else seems to be upset.

Am I overreacting? Am I missing something? What the fuck is going on?

Sage comes back into the open concept kitchen and living space, and Aspen helps her unload the takeout bags from one of our favorite local Mexican restaurants. They look nervous, both girls' gazes pinging from each other to us and back, but they're still going through the motions like we're all about to sit down for a normal meal.

I grab Parker's arm to stop him from following them to the table. "Come on, isn't this really weird? Why am I the only one freaking out?" I frantically whisper to him.

"We should let them talk," he mutters. "I have to admit something, and I don't know how you're going to take it…" he trails off, confusing me even more.

This is all way too much for my level of hunger, so I grunt an agreement and decide that eating is the most important move I can make right now.

I reluctantly sit next to Parker at their table where Sage and

Aspen have already put a few of our favorite tacos on plates for us. Parker nods at Aspen, and she looks to Sage, acting far more hesitant than she had when she was whispering with Parker.

"Sage, would you mind coming into my room for a few minutes? There are some things you should really know before we all sit down," she slowly asks as she stands.

Sage finally makes eye contact with me, brow furrowed, what I think is an apology shining in her eyes before she follows Aspen into her room.

I let out a very confused huff before taking a bite of a taco. No use letting the food go to waste when I definitely need it. I finish the whole thing before turning to face a very worried-looking Parker. I'd hoped that he would start his explanation while I was eating, but it looks like he needs more encouragement. "Okay, spill. What the fuck is going on? What is it that you haven't told me?"

He stares at me for another moment, eyes wide and mouth open like he wants to speak, but nothing is coming out.

I'm starting to panic that it's something awful with how hesitant he's being. "Come on, Parker, spit it out!"

"Aspen and I have never really been together," he *finally* blurts. The words are said quickly, but I'm able to understand them. Even if their meaning completely blindsides me.

"What the fuck are you talking about? You've been dating for months. I've been there the entire time." Obviously, I'm missing something. I need to shut up and listen, but that was the last thing I expected him to say. Parker's my best friend, we're always together, we talk about everything. Surely I would know if he wasn't actually dating his girlfriend.

Right?

Although, we never talked about our kiss, so we don't *technically* talk about everything.

Fuck.

"That first night, when you and Sage went into your room, Aspen admitted to me that she's in love with Sage. She told me all about her horrible judgmental family who would disown her, sabotage her business and cut off access to her money if she was ever with a woman, and she asked me to pretend to date her to get them off of her back about moving home to marry some family friend that they have picked out for her." He's talking so quickly that I can barely hear the individual words he's saying, let alone process what they mean.

It's been fake the whole time? "Why didn't you tell me?" I interrupt, honestly more surprised that Parker and I apparently have so many secrets than by what he's saying. *He's got a huge heart, of course he'd want to help her.*

"Honestly, I didn't think it was a big deal at first," he says with a shake of his head. "She seemed convinced that Sage didn't feel the same way. I figured that we had a great time that first night, the four of us could keep hanging out, and you and I wouldn't have to split the time we usually spend together with your new relationship. I know previous girlfriends have complained about how close we are, and I thought maybe you and Sage would have a better chance, because she would understand with how close she is to her own best friend. Plus, Aspen would get the freedom she was after, and we'd all get to keep spending time with each other. The fact that her and I weren't having sex seemed unimportant."

"You didn't care that you've been in a relationship for months without any of the physical benefits of being in a relationship?" I can't stop myself from asking.

He's avoiding eye contact now as he twists the bottom button on his shirt. "I guess I don't think sex is the most important aspect of a relationship," he says softly with a shrug. "I've enjoyed all of the time the four of us have spent together, but I'm really sorry that I didn't tell you the entire truth. I've thought about it so many times, but I didn't want to mess with what you and Sage have."

He finally turns to look at me for that last part, and I let out a soft sigh, my tense muscles physically relaxing in response to his concerned expression. I can't be mad at him. It sounds like he had good intentions of helping Aspen out with her family. And obviously I would have been really bummed to miss out on all of the time I've gotten to spend with him over the last few months.

I know Parker better than anyone else, and I'm confident that he didn't keep this from me to hurt me. I take a deep breath in, counting to five as I do, and again as I let it out, trying to gather my thoughts before I respond.

The last two months since our kiss have been so confusing. *This is just another thing to add to the list.* I've completely refused to acknowledge how often I've thought of that moment we shared, or how many times I've caught myself checking Parker out since then. I've also found myself looking at other guys in the gym or when we're out at restaurants too.

I've come to a sort of hazy acceptance that I'm bi. That I've probably been ignoring the signs for years in favor of what I've always thought to be true. But I haven't told anyone else about the new label I'm claiming.

Has Sage been dealing with a similar realization?

I don't think I would have understood before kissing Parker, but now, I can appreciate that Aspen, and most likely Sage, are dealing with their own confusing feelings. I don't know their own situations well enough to completely judge them and what happened here tonight, if it was a spur of the moment thing or if it's been building and something finally snapped. But I feel like I've gotten to know Aspen well enough to believe she didn't mean to hurt anyone with her fake relationship with Parker.

Apparently, she's been in love with my girlfriend this whole time, but I've had some not-so-innocent thoughts about my own best friend recently, and Parker said she didn't think Sage felt the same way, so I don't think she ever thought we'd be in this situation. I don't believe she's been scheming to steal my girlfriend or anything malicious like that.

"Are you mad at me?" Parker finally whispers and that snaps me out of my introspection.

"No, I could never be mad at you, Park," I assure him. "Just trying to wrap my head around all of the new info."

"I should have told you the full truth," he insists, but I cut him off.

"Parker, you're right. You've never really talked about your past hookups, so that isn't new. Still, I should have known something was up when I never heard you guys through our thin walls, but I think I just assumed we were all on the same schedule or something," I say with a nervous chuckle, not willing to admit how much I'm enjoying the way his cheeks darken at the implication that I *have* heard him in the past. "I've had a great time dating Sage the last few months, but I'll be honest, I have no idea what our relationship would look like outside of the four of us spending time together. Maybe that means it wasn't actually that great of a relationship…" I trail off, voicing my thoughts as I have them.

To be honest, I'm not all that upset about the idea of ending things with Sage. I was more upset about being cheated on, that feeling of embarrassment and betrayal that instantly flared when I saw them kissing. It wasn't so much about Sage specifically but about the situation in general.

I hurry to eat another taco as I contemplate how uninvested I actually am in my girlfriend. She's smart, kind, and funny, but the best things about her all point back to Parker. That she didn't care how close we are, that she had her own best friend to understand how important our friendship is to me, that her best friend was dating Parker, so we got to spend so much time all together. I've fantasized about the four of us advancing through different stages of life together, getting married at similar times, finding houses next to each other, raising kids all together.

I'm upset about the loss of that daydream, but maybe not for the reasons I should be.

It would have been perfect.

Except for the fact that Aspen is in love with Sage. Sage kissed Aspen tonight, so clearly there's more going on there. Aspen and Parker were never really dating. And I can't stop thinking about the one kiss Parker and I shared months ago. There hasn't been a day since then that I haven't thought about how amazing it felt to be on top of him, exploring each other's mouths and bodies in a way that we never had before.

But even now, in this night of shocking confessions, he hasn't mentioned our kiss once. I'm the only one still stuck on it, and I seriously need to move on.

So, yeah, not so perfect after all.

But what the fuck does that mean for us all going forward?

The door to Aspen's room swings open down the hall. "Is it okay if we join you?" Sage asks, and I nod before the girls hesitantly sit with us at the table. They're both fighting grins, and I have a feeling their talk was a little more dramatic than the one Parker and I had.

"I'm so sorry, Oakley," Sage starts, and I can't even be mad at her either. I don't have it in me, not with the way they both look so excited and happy. Sage has never looked at me like that. I'm not an angry person and I usually let things slide pretty easily so I can focus on the positives, despite knowing that, I feel like I should probably be mad at someone tonight, and I'm just…not.

"Are you guys together now?" I guess.

"I swear I wasn't lying to you, or trying to hurt you," Sage rushes to explain. "I've had a great time dating you. But I think I've been lying to myself for a long time. I've always been so drawn to Aspen, and I told myself that it was just because of our friendship, but I think maybe it's always been more than that. I had no idea she felt the same way." By the time she finishes talking, the girls are staring at each other with such adoration and love that I can't believe I never suspected anything between them before tonight.

I've probably been so used to dismissing everyone who's questioned me and Parker, that I didn't stop to consider that it could actually be true for them.

Even though I've been thinking a lot about my own best friend and our relationship recently, he's given me no indication that our situation could be like theirs, so I won't entertain the idea.

I need to focus on what's happening and stop fantasizing about my straight best friend dammit.

"I'm not mad," I finally admit. "I was upset about how this all came out, but it sounds like it wasn't some conspiracy to hurt me. If you guys will be happier together then I wish you the best. I don't want to be dating someone who would be happier with someone else."

"So what does this mean for our arrangement?" Parker asks Aspen.

"Fuck… I don't know." Her eyebrows are scrunched together, and she's picking at her nail polish, looking far more worried now that she's been reminded about that. "My father still owns a huge part of my company, I'm worried that he'll try to sabotage it if he finds out I'm with a woman. I'd love to have some time to try to convince him to let me buy him out before it actually happens."

Sage reaches across the table, squeezing Aspen's hand that's resting on it. "We'll figure it out. We won't let him ruin everything you've built."

"We can keep up the pretend dating thing for them if that would help," Parker offers.

"Really? Even after all of this, you wouldn't mind?"

Parker glances to me, maybe looking for approval. I'm not sure why he wants my opinion, but I nod. Her family sounds awful, and she should definitely try to secure some of their money if they're going to do bad things with it.

"Sure. I do really care about you, Aspen. You're one of my best friends, and I don't want to speak for Oak if he'll want to keep hanging out, but you and I can at least get together to take pictures for you to post or send to them or whatever you've been doing."

"That would be amazing," she sighs in relief, every single inch of her visibly relaxing. "Thank you so much."

Parker gives her a small smile before turning back to me. "Do you want to leave?"

I take a second to really think about it. I've experienced so many emotions tonight, but ultimately, what Parker told Aspen is true for me as well, they've become some of our best friends. I might need a minute to adjust to the romantic aspect of my relationship with Sage being over. I do like her as a person though, and I think we could continue to be friends. I don't actually want to cut her out of my life.

"Nah, we can stay and finish dinner," I say, looking pointedly at the uneaten tacos on Parker's plate. We don't need his sugar crashing on top of everything else that's happened tonight.

"So, how was the meeting with Tokyo?" Aspen asks, obviously trying to move onto something more casual for us all to talk about.

"It was fine, there was a lot of using translators, which isn't always easy, but they needed our approval on a new budget," Parker says. He also sounds calm, like we're back to our usual nightly plans with them and nothing's changed. *But I guess for the two of them, nothing really has.* "They've had an upgrade planned for over a year now, but ran into some trouble with their contractors. They'd resolved it and just needed our approval, which we gave quickly," he adds. "We would have been there much later if there had been an actual problem."

And then we might not have walked in on the girls. *Would Sage and I still have ended things tonight if we hadn't caught them?* I guess it doesn't really matter. Now that I'm single again, I'll just have even more room for questions to obsess over about myself and my sexuality.

Great.

The rest of the evening is pretty normal. It's clear to me that I'm the only one still thinking about who in this group should be kissing who. *Plus, I have the fun addition of my stupid blowjob comment earlier to obsess over too.*

Seriously, why did I say that? I've never thought about being on the other end of a blowjob, even as I've been questioning things, looking at other men, my thoughts haven't really solidified beyond wondering what it might be like to kiss them. Yet without hesitation, I volunteered my mouth for the pretend scenario with my straight best friend.

If I'm being really honest, though, I think the reason I can't stop thinking about it is that it sounds kind of hot.

And I don't hate the idea.

PARKER

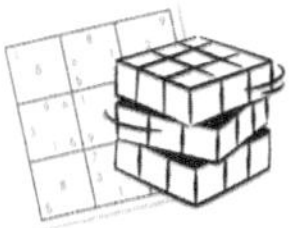

September

Gregory Caldwell is the type of businessman who will move any meeting he possibly can to a golf course.

The Chicago weather hasn't gotten the memo that it can start to cool down, so we're out here sweating in the heat of the cloudless day on a fancy golf course at one of the country clubs Oakley's dad belongs to.

He asked us to join him so that he could "have some quality bonding time with his sons," and get some updates on Bora Bora. I appreciate that he includes me in the family bonding time, and that he's remained such a positive part of my life after all of these years.

I know he isn't trying to replace my own father. I started golfing with Oakley's dad and brothers in elementary school, and Greg is probably one of my favorite people. I really admire how he manages to balance prioritizing his family and his work. He makes supporting his sons' careers and happiness look effortless, all while maintaining his own. It can't be easy.

"Alright, boys, let's hear some resort updates," he encourages as we wait for the group ahead of us to struggle out of the sand trap. "I know you're excited, Oakley, so hopefully you won't mind talking about it here, instead of waiting for the next board meeting," he teases, knowing full well that Oakley would talk about this resort all day every day if given the audience.

"I thought you would never ask," Oak deadpans back before excitedly launching into the plan. "Turns out we had to tear everything down and start fresh.""

"The good news is most of it was made of local organic materials," I cut in before Oakley gets too into his speech. "Which meant that most of it could be recycled in other ways, and the new projects won't have a negative environmental impact. We're also planning to use solar panels on all of the new roofing structures to remain as self-sufficient and environmentally friendly as possible," I add.

"Good to hear," Greg responds. The group ahead of us has finally moved on, so we take our initial shots. Greg is almost as competitive as Oakley, and the three of us take our game very seriously finishing the hole quickly.

"We get to create everything from scratch." Oakley jumps back into his spiel. "It's perfect because we'll have so many options for the events we want to host there."

"That sounds nice. Good to have options," Greg says, nodding.

"We're going to have a few beachside villas to cater to different types of visitors, too," Oakley continues with the same level of excitement.

"It'll still remain exclusive, though," I add.

"I can't wait to see it all in person," Greg says, now matching Oakley's level of excitement.

"They've already started construction on the new structures. Plus, we've lined up a ton of different activities to offer!"

"I'm excited for it to be over so that Oak can stop coming up with new expensive ideas," I add in a teasing tone. Greg will understand better than anyone just how ambitious Oakley's suggestions can be.

"He's lucky to have you at his side to rein him in," Greg adds with a laugh, giving me a solid pat on the back.

"Seriously, though, Parker has been amazing at helping me figure out how to justify the cost of everything, or even finding more affordable ways to bring my vision to life, I don't know what I would do without him," Oakley agrees, smiling at me, and the comment makes my stomach squirm. *He's just complimenting your work, stop twisting everything into more.*

"My biggest concern is making sure that we're ready before the season next year. We have a pretty tight timeline, and I don't want to give up our friends and family trip," Oakley teases.

"Glad that you've got your priorities in order," his dad jokes back.

The group in front of us finally offers to hang back and let us pass them, and the rest of the day flies by as we all try to outdo each other and end up with the lowest score. We all do pretty well, but Oakley ends up on top. Watching how happy he is about it makes me glad I missed a few easy shots. *Definitely missed them on accident. I would never lose on purpose just to see Oakley happy.*

"THE GIRLS SAID we don't have to be ready until five thirty, right?" Oakley asks me as we enter our condo after having a drink with Greg at the club.

"Yeah, we'll meet them at their place then, and our dinner reservation is at six," I confirm. Sage and Aspen got us all tickets to one of the Broadway in Chicago shows tonight. The four of us have still been hanging out once or twice a week, and Aspen posts the pictures of us so that her family will continue to believe we're dating.

The first few times the four of us were together after the night Oakley and I walked in on the girls kissing, I was concerned he might have a hard time hanging out with Sage after the way they ended things. The last thing I wanted was to put him in a situation that would make him upset or uncomfortable, but it was immediately evident that he was completely fine. It was almost as if they had always just been friends because there was no awkward tension or silences like I was expecting.

We really do always have a great time with them, and Aspen and I's reality show nights have turned into the four of us watching in our living room, Sage and Aspen cuddling, while Oakley and I are usually close enough that I spend half of the time too distracted by fantasies of *us* being the ones casually tangled together to actually watch. I think we all can agree that the four of us were always meant to be friends, even if we did have an unconventional beginning.

I'm looking forward to the show tonight, but we have a few hours before we have to get ready.

"I might take a nap after I shower," Oakley says, more to himself than me.

"Have fun," I respond anyway, heading into my own room to shower off the day in the sun. I've always had to worry about burning, even more than Oak does. We probably put on sunscreen three times today, and I'll still end up pink later. *The joys of being a redhead covered in freckles.*

After I shower, I decide to figure out what I'm wearing tonight, so I wrap the towel around my waist and head into my large walk-in closet. Aspen informed me that she would be in a lilac sundress and that she'd like me to wear my purple button-up. She doesn't want to give her family any reason to dislike me, so she usually requests something specific that she knows they'd approve of for me to wear. I don't mind because I like not having to worry about something so trivial myself, but I can't remember when the last time I saw that shirt was.

Sure enough, a thorough search of my closet reveals that it isn't here. The cleaning staff probably put it in Oakley's closet again. I don't want to wait and find out it needs to be ironed, or worse, isn't actually in there, so I might as well grab it now. Even if Oak is napping, I'm pretty confident I can be quiet enough that he won't know I was there. Plus, he wouldn't care that I'm in his room without knowing, we've always shared everything, so it won't be the first or last time one of us is in the other's space without asking first.

I slowly open his door, hoping that it won't creak as I do, and slide through the gap as soon as I can fit. My back is to his bed as I try to quietly step toward the closet, but I stop in my tracks when I hear a moan, accompanied by the distinct sound of a lubed hand working a hard cock, what can only be Oakley jerking off.

My own dick thickens, instantly interested in the situation we've found ourselves in, and the towel that's still wrapped around my waist isn't doing anything to hide it.

I clutch the towel to make sure it at least stays in place, and slowly turn, unable to stop myself from looking. Oakley is laying back, propped up on a few pillows, with absolutely nothing covering him. His abs are flexing, showing off each curved ridge of his muscles, and a thin dusting of hair framed by the V of his hips seems designed to draw my attention right to where he's roughly tugging on his very hard cock. The angry-looking purple head is swollen, and he looks completely consumed by how good it must feel, his eyes squeezed closed and his face twisting in pleasure.

It's the hottest fucking thing that I've ever seen.

If I thought lying across the room and hearing Oakley pleasure himself under his duvet in college was arousing, it has absolutely nothing on watching it happen in a bright room with him fully exposed to me.

My own cock is fighting to free itself from the towel, and I quickly adjust myself. I attempt to tuck it up under the waistband I've created, pressing my hand where I'm still holding the towel closed against as much of it as I can, trying to give myself any sense of relief. I don't know that I've ever felt this desperate. I feel both consumed by my desire, and completely frozen in place as I watch my best friend's private moment.

I know I should leave, try to slip out as quietly as I came in, and hope that he never learns I was here. But I can't seem to translate those thoughts into actions.

What if I never get to see this again?

Then Oakley shifts his other hand to play with his balls, letting out another deep moan, and the sound is so erotic that a soft whimper escapes my mouth.

Fuck.

Oakley's eyes fly open and immediately lock on mine. He doesn't stop his movements, though. His eyes drop to my towel and the poorly concealed erection there, and a myriad of emotions flash across his gaze in an instant. Surprise, confusion, pleasure, amusement, and finally something a little darker, almost wicked, maybe teasing.

"Well, are you going to just stand there with that giant thing waving at me?" he asks, nodding his chin at my visibly rock-hard dick. "Or are you going to address the monster-cock in the room and get off too? It's not like we've never jerked off at the same time before," he taunts, all while maintaining his slow twisting rhythm up and down his shaft.

I don't remember making the conscious decision to join him. The towel is suddenly on the floor, and I'm automatically reacting, catching the small bottle of lube that he tosses at me where

I'm standing near the foot of his bed. I quickly coat my dick and am consumed by how good it feels. I don't think I've ever been this close to release so quickly. *Is it always supposed to be like this when you have a crush on someone?*

Oak lets out another moan and my focus is once again drawn to him. He's looking at me, only now, his eyes are clearly locked on my hand where it's moving, working my erection. He still has that wicked glint in his eyes, but they're hooded. He looks so fucking sexy. If *this* is sexual attraction then I've definitely never felt anything like it before. I don't want this feeling to end, but I know I won't last much longer.

Oakley must have been approaching his own climax when I walked in, because he looks desperate now, his movements are faster and less coordinated. The muscles in his lower abdomen clench, and he crunches forward as his expression reveals his obvious pleasure. He lets out another deep moan as thick ropes of cum shoot out across his abs and chest, coating his hand.

How is that so fucking hot?

I wish it was my cum covering him, dripping down the ridges of his muscles... The intense pleasure that had been building at the base of my spine crashes over the edge, spreading throughout my entire body as my own climax washes over me. I can't hold my eyes open any longer to see where my release lands as the most intense orgasm of my life consumes me.

When I finally come down enough from the high of my gratification, my eyes lock with Oakley's, and I catch what almost seems like a look of awe on his face. He quickly blinks it away and replaces it with a smirk.

"Well, I wasn't expecting that to happen," he says in a light, teasing tone.

"Sorry—" I start to say, but he cuts me off.

"Don't apologize, that was hot. Just...unexpected. Plus, like I said, it wasn't like we've never jerked off in the same room before," he reminds me casually.

I guess he isn't going to make a big deal about the fact that we just masturbated with a whole lot of eye contact while staring at each other's dicks. *Totally normal.*

And my intense reaction to watching him was also *totally normal, and I'm handling this crush so well, super casual.*

When he finishes cleaning himself with some tissues, he tosses me the box and I see that most of my cum landed on his sheets. I quickly clean myself up, but sheepishly point to the wet spot, ignoring how something deep in my gut heats at the idea of his bed smelling like me. "Sorry."

He just laughs. "I was going to need to change them anyway. So, was that your plan when you came in here or…?" he trails off, and I wonder what he's expecting me to say.

"What? No," I sputter. "I think my shirt ended up in your closet again, I thought you were sleeping, and that I would just sneak in and grab it without bothering you," I explain, hoping he blames my sunburn on how hot my cheeks feel right now.

"Which shirt?" he asks as he confidently struts completely naked across the room to his closet.

I know I've probably seen Oakley naked hundreds of times over the years, but I don't think I was ever *looking* before now. In the confusing months since the kiss and my newfound attraction to him, I've avoided changing near Oakley.

No going back now. *He's really hot.* I can finally admit that his dark hair and blue eyes, which seem to pop against his sun-kissed skin, are really captivating in a way that makes my blood heat. His toned muscles that bunch and flex as he moves, drawing my attention to his ass, are already making me want to go for a round two, my dick twitching in agreement.

Fuck, he has a really nice bubble-butt. Seriously, how did I not realize how attracted to him I am?

I have no idea what to do with this information right now, though.

I can't risk things between Oakley and I. The kiss was months ago, he's been single for weeks, and if his feelings toward me had changed at all, he would have brought it up by now. There would have been signs, some hint that he was having any of the same struggles I've been having. I might have accepted that I wish things could be different between us, that I would love to explore my newfound attraction and see what it really means, but I know those fantasies need to remain in my head. I can't risk him finding out how I'm really feeling.

There are so many ways it could go wrong. Oak could apologize that he doesn't feel the same way, and in his confusion on how to handle the situation, end up putting distance between us. Or worse, what if he attempts to force himself to reciprocate my feelings when he doesn't actually share them in some well-intentioned attempt to make me happy?

I can't risk that. I can't lose Oakley. Which means he can't know how spectacular that mutual jerk off really was for me. That was a gift. A shared orgasm I will probably never get again, and I should be grateful that strange circumstances led to it happening at all.

I need to calm down and stop focusing on the possibility of losing him. My breathing is too fast right now... I really need to get out of this room.

"So, which shirt was it?" he calls out from his closet.

"Um, the light purple one," I manage to get out, sounding surprisingly calm, despite the internal freak out I'm definitely having.

"Yeah, it's in here," he responds, bringing it out to me on a hanger. "Guess I'll have to thank the cleaning crew who put it in there for an exciting afternoon," he says with a wink.

He's fucking *winking* at me and joking like this was all just a fun little surprise in his day, completely normal best friend behavior.

I manage a short chuckle in response, muttering "thanks" as I grab the shirt and spin to leave the room.

"Parker?" Oak asks before I can leave.

"Yeah?"

"Are we cool?" he asks, finally sounding a little less confident.

I turn back to him so that he can see the sincerity in my expression as I respond. "Of course, Oak. We're always good," I promise, and I can see his shoulders relax a bit in relief. Then I rush back to my own room for another shower, determined to take as much time getting ready for tonight as I can. If Oakley and I try to hang out alone before dinner, I have no idea how I'll behave around him.

I'm probably going to be super awkward. But, there's also a part of me that worries I'll try to recreate the kiss we had months ago.

Now that I've confirmed just how good things with Oakley can make me feel, will I be able to resist the temptation?

17

OAKLEY

September

All throughout dinner and the show last night, I could not get Parker's O face out of my mind.

Or his giant cock. He's been my best friend for long enough that I knew he was packing, but I've never seen him hard before, and that thing is massive. I'm surprised that his exes weren't constantly walking funny. Do people really even like dicks that are that big?

My own cock twitches as I picture it, *so I guess I seem to like how big it is.* The whole situation was pretty hot too. Especially when I was thinking about *why* he was so hard. Was it just from watching me? Is he a voyeur or something? We've never talked about kinks, mostly because I assumed we didn't really have any to talk about, but maybe he likes to watch other people get off.

I would definitely volunteer again.

Ugh. I shouldn't be thinking that. Things are complicated enough between us right now. I don't need to be adding more mutual orgasms to the mix.

Parker is my person, and the last few months of us being so stiff and careful around each other have left me feeling completely untethered. I need to get my act together so that things can go back to normal between us.

Not that coming my brains out while watching him get himself off was ever our norm, but things were never awkward after hearing each other do that same thing in college. Maybe we can use this as a tipping point, a fun moment that pushes us back to the way things have always been.

We kissed and I made things weird when I was surprised by how much I enjoyed it. Yesterday, I confirmed that Parker is sexy as fuck, and now that I know that, I can move on.

Maybe I just need to get some of my confusing thoughts out, and then when I actually talk about it, everything will make sense again. I've always been the type of learner who needed to explain things out loud to someone else to fully grasp them myself. In school, Parker used to let me pretend to teach him concepts that he definitely already knew, so that I would remember them. As an adult, I always have my best ideas for the company when I'm talking them through with Parker or other members of my team.

Why didn't I think of this before? Maybe the reason I've been so weird with Parker is because I've been trying to suppress my feelings. I'm so used to sharing literally every mundane detail of my life, so maybe bottling them up has turned me into this awkward version of myself.

Obviously, Parker is not the ideal person for me to talk this through with. If I end up confirming that the kiss, and now the shared orgasms, meant more to me than they did to him, I don't want to make things even weirder between us.

But Parker isn't my only friend. Actually, I have someone who might know exactly what I'm going through. Cody and my brother are back in the city, officially together now. Cody didn't realize that he was bi until he was almost thirty. Even knowing he went through that didn't clue me in, though. Apparently, my own bi-awakening took me literally kissing my best friend, and then watching him come, for me to acknowledge a desire I've been ignoring for most of my life.

I pull my phone out and find Cody's number, immediately hitting the call button. I don't want to wait around for him to respond to a text.

He answers on the second ring. "Hey, Oakley! Everything okay? I don't think you've ever called me before. Not that I'm not always happy to hear from you," he says before I can respond to any of it. He's kind of a rambler, always excited and peppy. It's cute how he and my brother balance each other out with how different they are.

"I'm fine," I assure him. "Just wanted to check if you guys were home. I was wondering if I could stop by for a bit?"

"Oh, yeah, we're home for the next few hours at least, you guys can come by whenever!" He sounds thrilled by the suggestion, and I smile, but realize that he said "you guys," so he must assume Parker is coming too.

"Just me today," I say, not sure what excuse I'll give, but I know I want to talk to Cody without Parker there.

"Oh, no wonder you're bored if Parker is busy," Cody says with a laugh. "See you soon!"

Parker should still be showering; we finished up our workout for this morning not too long ago, so maybe I can leave before he's done. I don't want to give Parker the chance to assume I'm inviting him with me. I don't think I'd be able to turn him down, which would defeat the whole purpose of my visit. So, I sneak into the living space, and when I don't see him around, I quietly slip out of the condo.

I send him a quick text saying I needed to grab something at the store and didn't want to wait for him to be done, but I'd be back soon and to let me know if he needs anything. *I hate lying to him.* I don't think I've ever had a reason to lie to him before, but I need to do this.

WHEN I GET to their condo, my brother is the one who's waiting to answer the door.

"Why would you call Cody and not me?" Beck asks, already sounding suspicious.

"Because I knew he would be more excited to see me than you, obviously," I tease with an eye roll. I push my way past him into the large space and find Cody waiting at their table with snacks and an assortment of beverage options laid out.

"I wasn't sure if there was actually a reason that you wanted to come over, like if you needed to talk about something with me, since you called me and not Beck, so I wanted to be prepared," he explains, gesturing to everything that he's set out. "If we're just bored, then there's low-carb, high-protein snack options and sports drinks. But, if we're upset about something, there's also chips, desserts, and beer or hard liquor. I know you like wine, but we don't usually drink it, so I couldn't decide what type to put out. I think there's some on display somewhere in this fancy place if you want it, though," he offers with a shy smile.

Cody is always super high-energy and tends to ramble, so I'm not surprised by his over-explanation or by how prepared he was for my arrival.

I love how much he clearly cares about me already. My brother really did find a good one. "Um…" I hesitate, not sure if I want to get right into it, or what *it* even is that I want to get into exactly. "Maybe the beer," I finally answer.

I've never been a huge drinker because I don't like to put myself in a situation where I couldn't help my friends or family if they needed me. *Fuck, even leaving Parker alone like I did now feels so wrong.* But I know talking with Cody and Beck will help, so I try to ignore the unwelcome thoughts about bad things happening if I drink, or am away from Parker, and casually pull up the app on my phone that has his continuous glucose monitor reading. He's at 115, which is great, so I actually do calm down a bit.

I open up the offered drink, and Cody and Beck each do the same, looking at me expectantly. I'm not sure how to begin, so I just go for it. "So, Cody, you realized that you were bi later in life than some people do, what was that like?" I ask, hoping that my question isn't offensive.

"You finally fucked Parker," Beck accuses with a huge smirk on his face.

"I did no such thing!" I assure him. *I really hope that my cheeks aren't as red as they feel.*

"Did he fuck you then?" Beck deadpans, and I involuntarily shudder at the thought of his giant cock somehow fitting inside of me. "That's a no," he continues, sounding disappointed for some reason.

"No need to look horrified. Bottoming is awesome," Cody assures me.

This is so not how I thought we'd start this conversation. "I'm not horrified at the idea of bottoming," I hurry to say, really worried that I've put my foot in my mouth and forced this conversation to end before it could even begin. "He just has a huge dick and there's just no way…" I trail off my attempt to explain when I see how smug Beck is back to looking. Cody starts laughing at our exchange, and I left out a frustrated huff. "I was *trying* to talk to Cody, thank you very much," I say, rolling my eyes at Beck and dramatically turning my chair away from him so that I'm directly facing Cody's direction.

"So, *Cody*, you were going to tell me about your bi-awakening," I prompt with a sugar-sweet smile, ignoring Beck's laughter on my other side.

"Yes, what a normal topic of conversation for this random get-together *without Parker*. I'm sure it has nothing to do with you or why you two have been so weird lately," Beck adds, unhelpfully.

I ignore him.

"There isn't really much to say," Cody apologizes. "I think that I grew up without a lot of LGBTQIA+ influences and assumed that I would end up married to a woman. But, when your brother tried to kiss me, I realized I really wanted him to, so I must not be as straight as I had assumed," he says with a shrug.

"Wait, you didn't realize it until *after* Beck tried to kiss you?" I ask. I don't think I've ever heard the details about how their relationship began, I just knew my brother was obsessed with him.

"Yeah, looking back, it's obvious I cared more about him than I did other random people I'd met traveling. I was really excited to hang out with him, to talk to him. I was constantly finding excuses to message him or even talk about him before I realized what it all meant," Cody says.

Well, that's not helpful. I've cared about Parker more than everyone else for the last twenty-one years of my life, nothing has changed there.

"But then the kiss?" I prompt. That's the part that sounds familiar.

"Yeah, he tried to kiss me and I knew my reaction meant I must not be straight," he explains with a shrug.

"Wasn't that confusing?" I ask. I've been a mess for months over my own kiss.

"Not really. I try to follow what makes me happy, and I really wanted to keep kissing him," he says enthusiastically making Beck laugh.

"Cody is not a good example if you're looking for someone who went through an identity-crisis," Beck apologizes. "And neither am I, but if you do have anything else you want to tell us about, I promise to stop giving you shit and actually be a supportive big brother," he says with an encouraging smile.

I know he means it, but I don't want to tell them everything. At least not yet.

When Beck accused Parker and I of fucking, I realized that I don't want to betray his trust and share anything that Parker might not want them to know. Even though Beck is my brother, he and Cody are also some of Parker's closest friends.

"Thanks, Beck, but there's nothing else to share," I say, attempting a relaxed smile. I'm not sure I pull it off, but he nods in understanding.

"Well, if anything changes, you know we're both always here for you. Or for Parker, for that matter," he adds. I really am lucky to have him as a big brother.

We move on to discussing the Werewolves because preseason is about to begin, and Beck is really excited with how training camp has been going. It's their captain's final year before retirement, and he's convinced that they'll win the cup. I hope so, but it's also not the first time I've heard him say that.

After about an hour, I decide that I've been out long enough and head back home, stopping at a pharmacy to grab some allergy meds in case Parker asks what I needed. When I get home, he's on the couch with his laptop open, SportsCenter on in the background, focused on whatever work he's doing. It's a scene that I've seen hundreds of times before, but I've never stopped to appreciate its domesticity. I like coming home to him relaxed in our space.

I'm not going to think too deeply about what that means. I've decided to try to take a page out of Cody's book and just go with the flow, try to act on what makes me happy. I'll acknowledge these thoughts about Parker and then move on. If he wants to continue on the way we always have, the way that we've both always been happy with, then there's no reason for me to stress about it.

If anything changes, I'll deal with it then.

18

PARKER

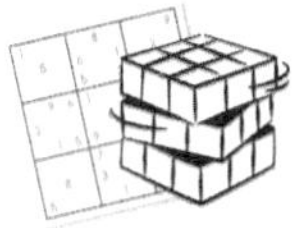

October

Almost eighteen hours later, we've landed in Bora Bora for the first time. We had a four-and-a-half-hour flight from O'Hare to LAX, spent a couple of hours there before an eight-hour flight to Tahiti, then a few more hours waiting around for our hour-long flight to Bora Bora. But, we weren't done there, because that single runway airport required a boat transfer to actually get to the island.

I'm exhausted.

Apparently, the amount of effort it takes to get here is a *good* thing, and makes it a more "exclusive" experience, or whatever rich celebrities and influencers care about. All I know is that I would have really enjoyed a direct flight. All of the getting on and off planes, and worrying about making all of the connections, meant that I didn't sleep at all.

Not that I'm ever really able to sleep on a plane. Our longest flight was overnight, and did have the little business-class sleeping pods that lay down, so Oakley was out for most of it, but I'm never able to relax enough to actually sleep. I worked for a bit, but when I was too tired for actual work I switched to a sudoku book. Our flight was so long that I finished the entire thing.

I'm dragging my suitcase behind me, feeling like a complete zombie, but Oak is practically skipping toward the resort entrance when we finally arrive. It's a complete construction zone, and we definitely don't *need* to be here, but for the past few months, Oakley has been complaining about not being able to visualize things because he needs to see it in person to be able to make decisions.

After the confusing mutual jerk-off session last month, I was looking for a way to distract him, to give him something other than our shared orgasms to focus on around me, so I asked his assistant to rearrange his schedule and book our tickets. This was the soonest that we could both come and they could accommodate us being here, but he's been so excited planning everything that I do feel like things are back to normal between us.

What will eventually become a luxury resort is currently a whole lot of empty beach. They've finished taking down all of the old structures, and started the framing on the new over-water villas. New construction began with the main building and the few beach villas, so those parts actually look like a hotel, at least.

When we told the main contractor that we wanted to visit, they explained that none of the rooms would be ready yet, but Oakley refused to stay at a competitor's resort. They rushed to finish one of the beachside villas enough that we could stay there. Oakley probably would have slept on the sand if it meant he got to visit, though, and I'm a sucker who wanted to make him happy, so here we are.

There's a man in a hard hat waiting to greet us at the entrance to the main building. "La Orana, hello and welcome, I'm Arii. We've spoken over the phone," he says with a warm smile. I attempt my own smile and mumble back the traditional greeting as best I can manage with the level of exhaustion I'm working with. Oak is much more enthusiastic with his own response.

"I'll show you to the only functioning room. As I explained over the phone, it's not fully set-up yet. We'll bring in the decorators after the construction is finished, so for now, you'll have a very minimalist layout. I apologize that we couldn't accommodate more in the time given," he says, leading us down a wooden pathway that trails beyond the main building toward the beach.

"I'm sure it will be better than staying at any of our competitor's resorts," Oak replies with a huge smile. I'm less certain of that, though.

The villa is situated in a small alcove surrounded by tropical trees on the edge of the beach, giving the illusion of being in our own private oasis, rather than staying in a hotel. It's not small, but most of the space is obviously designed to maximize the ocean views with large windows revealing a very open-concept layout.

From what I can see, I don't think there's more than one bedroom. *Did Oak realize that when he agreed for us to stay here?* It's not like we've never shared a bed before, but since we moved in together in college, there hasn't really been a need, so it's been over ten years.

Arii lets us into the villa, leaving the key on the dining table before pointing out some of the features that will eventually be in the space. As I assumed outside, it's all one large room. The only door leads to a luxurious bathroom with waterfall showers and a soaking tub big enough for two set in front of a large floor-to-ceiling window. Arii assures us that the water does work, *thank fuck,* and then excuses himself to go back to work on another part of the property.

"This place is amazing!" Oak declares as he hurries around the room, taking it all in.

"I'm sure I'll enjoy it more once I've slept," I mumble. I put my suitcase on the floor next to the dresser and hurry to move my clothes into it. I unpack my insulin, placing the small glass vial into the fridge, grateful that it's already working, before I grab sleep shorts, and turn to the bathroom. "I need to shower all of the plane off me and then probably sleep for a day."

"Well, I slept great on the second plane, so I think I'm going to go check out the rest of the property," he responds, already headed for the door.

"Oak?" I call out before he can actually leave.

"Yeah?"

"Don't forget this is a construction zone. You can't just wander around by yourself," I warn.

"Ugh," he groans, throwing his head back. "Fine. I'll go to the beach if I can't find a worker to show me around," he agrees with an eye roll in my direction, but he's smiling the whole time.

"You probably shouldn't swim in the ocean by yourself either," I remind him.

"Aww, are you worried about me, Daddy?" he asks in an over-the-top teasing tone, batting his eyelashes up at me in the bratty way that he likes to taunt me with.

Usually, I laugh it off and tease him back, but right now I'm trying very hard to ignore the lust pooling in my gut, not at the Daddy comment, but just everything he does seems to do it for me now, even his taunting. The instinct to play into his comment, to be a little firmer than I have in the past, maybe put him in his place and show him just how much I care about him is surprisingly strong. I'm unsuccessfully trying to ignore the fantasies my mind is not-so-helpfully supplying, of crowding him into the door he's yet to open, backing him against it, using my size as an advantage to surround him so that he can't leave. In my fantasy, he would keep taunting me, egging me on until I'm forced to kiss him to shut him up so that I don't give into my desire to be more physical in other ways.

But picturing all of that is not helpful right now. I'm

supposed to be ignoring sexual thoughts of my straight best friend so that we can continue on as normal. "I'm not your fucking Daddy, you brat. Obviously, I care about you," I finally respond.

His smile falters for a moment, but I can't read the meaning before it returns as big as ever. "Go shower and sleep. I'll be okay," he promises with a laugh. "How's your blood sugar?"

"Normal, just like it was ten minutes ago," I assure him.

"Goodniiiiight Parker," he sings out, blowing me a kiss before walking out of the villa, leaving me alone to daydream about the man I'm about to be sharing a bed with.

THE SOUND of waves crashing into the beach rouses me from my sleep. I'm not ready to actually wake up, it's so peaceful and I'm so comfortable and warm despite passing out on top of the covers. There's a solid weight wrapped around my bare waist, holding me in place and making me feel safe and secure in a way I don't remember feeling in years.

Is there an arm wrapped around me?

It takes me another few seconds to blink myself fully awake and remember where I am.

Bora Bora. In the villa. With Oakley.

My whole body tenses as I slowly turn my head to confirm that Oakley is in fact, wrapped around me. He's sleeping peacefully, looking completely at ease. *Not going to focus on how great having him surrounding me in bed feels.* Maybe I can slowly ease my way out of his hold and pretend like I'm not loving every second of this.

Just another moment and I'll move.

Except when I do finally shift, Oak tightens his hold on me, pulling me in even closer to him. Then he grinds his hard dick into my ass and lets out a soft groan.

Holy shit.

My cock is immediately interested, thickening and tenting the thin sleep shorts that I'm wearing. He's slowly rocking his cock into me, and completely without my permission, I realize that my hips are shifting back into him, meeting the motion.

I freeze. *Fuck, what do I do?*

If I make any sudden moves and wake him up, he'll know that he's humping me in his sleep, and he'll see the very obvious evidence of what that's doing to me. For all I know, he's actively dreaming about a woman. But I'm awake and I have no excuse to offer for my own arousal. I guess I can pretend to be asleep, but I'm such a bad actor. Oakley would know I was lying and that would only make things more awkward.

Before I can decide to do anything, Oakley stops rutting into me and lets out a soft chuckle. "Sorry, Park. I must have been having a good dream," he says in a soft tone that's full of gravel.

"You're fine," I mumble, still frozen, hoping that my breathing is somewhat normal so he won't notice I'm freaking out. He hasn't actually moved away from me at all yet, his strong arm still wrapped tightly around me.

"Just like high school, huh? I wonder how many times you woke up with my morning wood digging into your ass," he says in that same raspy tone that has no right to be so sexy. His hand loosens his grip slightly, only now it's resting lightly on my lower abs, which is definitely not helping my cock get the memo that it needs to fucking calm down. *Is this a dream? Some sort of twisted fantasy where the man I'm obsessed with teases me but doesn't actually touch me?* I'm pretty sure that this is real though, even my nightmares don't have this level of detailed torture. I don't think I'm creative enough for my mind to come up with a scenario so bittersweet.

"I miss sleeping together. I always got the best rest when we used to share a bed back then," he goes on, still spooning me, his hard dick still pressed against me.

My own aching erection that was already straining toward my abdomen twitches at the mention of us sleeping together. I panic that Oak would have somehow noticed and try to shift away from him slightly, but when I move, my shorts must catch on the sheets and don't quite go with me.

To my absolute horror, the movement allows my cock to free itself so that it's now sticking right out of the loose waistband. Oak's fingers are mere centimeters from the tip.

I have no shirt on, there's no blanket covering us.

I have no idea how I'm going to get out of this without Oakley finding out about my attraction to him.

19

OAKLEY

October

I know that I should move. Put distance between my aching cock and Parker's ass. But what I *should* do, and what I *want to do* are very different things right now.

What did Cody say about chasing what makes you happy?

I fidget, tracing my fingers over the defined muscles in his abs as I admit how much I miss being able to sleep with him every night.

I hadn't intended to go to sleep as early as I did, but I came in from my brief tour of the property, and Parker's brows were furrowed as he squirmed in the bed. I couldn't tell if he was actually having a nightmare, or was just struggling to sleep, but I didn't hesitate. I just stripped down to my underwear and climbed onto the bed.

He relaxed slightly when I scooted in right next to him, but he continued to toss and turn. I eventually stopped resisting my own desires and pulled him into my arms like I had wanted to from the moment I walked in. He finally settled, and knowing that I'm still able to help him sleep after all of these years offers me my own deep sense of peace.

I decide to finally stop being inappropriate and go to slide my hand away from Parker's abs, but he shifts at that same moment, and I graze something that's both silky and hard. It takes my still sleep-hazy mind a moment to catch up and realize the only thing it could be.

I just touched Parker's hard dick.

I'm fully awake now.

"Oak, I'm so…"

"Horny? Join the club," I offer with a laugh, cutting off what I'm sure was about to be Parker's apology as I move my hips into him to remind him of my own current erection.

I don't want an apology. I want an excuse to do it again.

Does it mean something that we're both so aroused right now? Is there any chance that he'd actually want me to touch him again? To do more?

I haven't been able to stop thinking about Parker.

It doesn't seem to matter that I can now casually acknowledge when I think other men are hot. I try to tell myself that the reason Parker seems to be the focus of my newfound most-likely-bi label is convenience, due to proximity and all of the time we spend together.

But it feels like an excuse. I can't deny how much I want *him* specifically.

Kissing Parker was amazing. Jerking off in front of each other was one of the hottest moments of my life. There's no pretending, even to myself, that I don't want to do more. I want to touch him. I want to be the one drawing moans from his lips, making his face twist with pleasure.

I told myself to focus on what makes me happy, that I'd enjoy my friendship with Parker like I always have, and that I'd deal with any changes as they came. Well, Parker's erection is *right there* as my own is digging into his ass.

I think it's safe to say that things are changing. I would be lying if I said I hadn't wondered what it would feel like to touch it, to do way more, honestly.

I decide to completely throw caution to the wind and go after what I want. "I could help you, ya know?" I finally say, sounding far more confident than I feel.

"Help?" he whispers in a pitch much higher than his normal voice.

"Yeah, I could help you with this," I offer, moving my hand closer to his hard cock.

He inhales sharply, but doesn't move at all, doesn't push me away. This whole situation feels charged. I woke up hard, I don't remember much of my dream, just feeling safe and happy. Now, though, teasing Parker like this, me wrapped around him in *our* bed, I feel out of control, desperate, completely at the mercy of my own desires.

My head is trying to tell me this is a risk, that this isn't how Parker and I interact, that I could fuck up over twenty years of friendship, but I'm so turned on right now. *I want Parker.* I'm not even sure what that means, but maybe we can help each other out in this moment. I take another deep breath and try to convince myself that I'm brave. I'm the CEO of an international billion-dollar company dammit, I shouldn't be nervous to go after what I want.

He hasn't said anything, but gives the slightest nod of his head, and I go for it. Moving my hand to his swollen dick, I trace my fingers over the tip before working my way down his erection with the same feather-light touch, still surprised and impressed by the size of him. I repeat the motion, and the lack of pressure must not be what he's looking for because he lifts his hips as a groan escapes his lips. It makes me giddy. As much as I want him, want this, I also want him to admit that he wants it too. I've always gotten a kick out of joking around with him, and this is just a whole new level of teasing.

"Stop fucking around. Are you going to help me or not?" he grits out, thrusting his hips toward my hand more obviously.

"Should I? That wasn't a very nice way to ask..." I joke, trailing off when a deep, growly sound rumbles from his throat, sending a bolt of lust straight to my core. "What the fuck was that noise?" I manage to ask with a laugh, still trailing my fingers up and down his shaft without applying any real pressure.

"*That* was a very frustrated sound because you're being a brat," he huffs. "Oak, will you please touch my dick?"

"Much better," I answer, my smile evident in my cheery tone as I finally tighten my hold, his hips jerk into my touch, and he lets out a groan. It's easily one of the hottest sounds that I've ever heard. *I want more.* I feel like an addict who's been given a taste, a tease of my drug of choice, and I know it won't be enough. *I don't just want. I need more.*

But his stupid pants are in the way. I don't want there to be anything between us, so I momentarily let go, gripping his waistband as he lifts his hips so that I can lower his shorts and completely free his erection. I'm careful not to pull his insulin pump, removing it from the pocket and setting it on the bed next to us before slowly closing my fingers around his hard dick again.

We're both completely still, frozen like that as we take in the moment.

I just removed my supposedly straight best friend's shorts so that I could have better access to his cock.

But then he relaxes back into me. "Well, what are you waiting for?" he taunts, spurring me into motion. I don't know what this means for us, but Parker is letting me touch him and I can't think about anything else.

Obviously, I've had my hand wrapped around my own dick,

but the feel of him in my hand as I slide my grip up and down his long shaft is unlike anything else I've experienced. Holding him like this seems so different than when I get myself off, but I love thinking about how each movement or motion must be for him, how I can almost sense the ghost of it on my own aching cock.

Parker lets out a low moan and shifts his hips forward into my hold. I feel high off of the power I have right now, knowing that I'm the one forcing sounds of pleasure from his lips.

I try to focus more on what I like, what feels good for me, and quickly pull off to add some spit before returning my hand to his cock. I shift so that I can watch over his shoulder. "Fuck, that's so hot," I mutter, unable to stop myself from commenting as I watch what my hand is doing to his dick. "You're huge. I can barely wrap my fingers all the way around."

He lets out another soft moan as I pick up the pace of my motions, up and down, twisting and adjusting how tight my grip is. "I wish that I had both hands to work with so that I could explore a little more, maybe play with your balls, or even use my mouth," I admit softly right by his ear.

Apparently, I've lost all filters in my lust-filled brain. I've had plenty of time to imagine that scenario after my blowjob comment a few weeks back, so I don't even care.

I can't seem to help myself as I continue. "But my cock is grinding into your ass again and there's no way I'm giving that up if you don't want me to." He slowly shakes his head no as he shifts his hips back to meet my movements. Even as a teenager, I don't think I've ever been this close to finishing just from rutting into someone, but that's definitely where this is headed. I have absolutely no intention of stopping my building orgasm, and I don't think I could try even if I wanted to.

I rub my thumb over his angry-looking purple tip, smearing the precum that's leaking, and he lets out more of those intoxicating moans as he relaxes his head back further, drawing my attention to the sharp line of his stubble-covered jaw. Without really thinking, I leave a sloppy wet kiss there, licking and nipping up the exposed slope of his neck. He seems to have given up on trying to hold back his sounds of pleasure, and he's picking up speed as he rocks his hips forward into my tight grip and back into my hard cock

"Fuck, Oak, why does this feel so good?" he asks desperately.

"I am pretty great, right?" I joke, earning another huffed "brat" from Parker. "I don't know why," I reply honestly this time, exhaling against his neck. "But I'm close, are you?"

He nods again in response, panting, like words would be too difficult right now. He gives a couple more thrusts before I feel his dick twitch in my grip and I hurry to watch over his shoulder as thick ropes of his cum cover his chest. The sight of his release sends me barreling over the edge as well, the buzz of pleasure that had been building at the base of my spine quickly spreading throughout my whole body as I grind my cock into him. I continue to work him through his orgasm, spreading his release over his shaft as it coats my hand. I wish that I had taken the time to strip as well, so that I could have painted his ass with my cum instead of ruining my underwear.

Okay slow down. That might be a little intense for whatever the fuck this taunting hookup was.

Because that's what this was. A hookup.

I just hooked up with my best friend.

When we're both supposedly straight. I'm definitely *not* straight, but I don't think Parker knew that.

Nope. *That's way too much for my brain to process right now after I just came that hard.* I'm going to enjoy the aftereffects of my orgasm.

Eventually, when I've come down a little bit from the high, I remove my hand from his cock. It's covered in his release, but we've already gone this far, so I internally shrug and subtly lick it clean. I don't think Park even notices. I'm not sure what I was expecting it to taste like, but the salty flavor isn't bad, and knowing that it's Parker's cum sends another jolt of arousal through me.

I'm not ready to let go of him, so I wrap my arm back around his waist and pull him in close. I don't care that we're both covered in cum. I just want to hold him and fall back asleep.

This moment feels perfect. Just the two of us, relaxed and sated in each other's arms.

I have no idea what Parker's thinking about right now, and I'm definitely afraid to ask, but I really hope he isn't freaking out. I know I should probably admit how much I enjoyed that, how much I enjoyed kissing him, and jerking off together when those things happened over the last few months, too.

Parker is my favorite person in the world, and I am far too attracted to him to keep pretending like it doesn't mean anything. I don't know *what* it will mean for us going forward, but this did mean something to me, and it definitely made me happy.

So I'll try to ignore all of the questions that are vying for my focus, and enjoy this moment for what it is as I give into my fatigue and drift back asleep, wrapped around the person who matters to me more than anyone else ever could.

PARKER

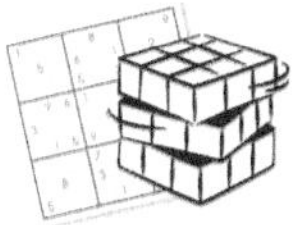

October

I'm still kind of in shock over what just happened.

I can't believe that Oakley and I...*hooked up?* I don't know how else to label it. He almost immediately fell asleep, still wrapped around me while my mind spins with questions of if that was real and what it meant.

He was the one who offered to get me off while he humped my ass like a horny teenager until we were both covered in cum. He seemed so fucking confident, taunting me with all of his bratty dirty talk. He barely even hesitated to touch me, like it was no big deal that my best friend who I've always thought was straight was suddenly giving me the best handjob of my life.

I'd accepted that I'm attracted to him, that I have feelings for my best friend, but that nothing could ever come of that. Now, though, I feel like everything I had previously known to be true, no longer is.

Was it really just a friendly offering while we were both horny? It felt like more, but I don't know if I'm reading into things and letting my own hope distort my perception. Still, if he was so quick to hook up, could there be a chance that he's attracted to me too? Is he bi? Maybe the kiss, and our other encounters, have him questioning his sexuality, and I'm a safe person to experiment with.

That would be fine with me.

Until he decides to move on.

Fuck. I don't know what is going on between us, but I know that I care way too much about Oakley for anything we do to feel casual.

Still, if this is my only opportunity to experience this kind of attraction, I don't want to pass it up in some attempt to protect my feelings. I'll take whatever Oakley offers if he ever does again and deal with the consequences later.

But I won't let anything ruin our friendship.

I've always expected him to end up married and to no longer live with me eventually, and this doesn't change that. It just might make the time that I have left as his roommate a little more interesting if he wants to do it again.

I'm not sure how long I lay there bouncing between disbelief and gratitude over what happened, stressing over what comes next. Eventually, my pump starts to alert me that I'll need to add more insulin soon. I don't want it to wake Oak up, so I slowly ease out of his hold and grab what I need before taking a quick shower, trying not to focus too much on why there's cum all over my abs and chest so that I don't get hard all over again. Then I get dressed and carefully use the needle to draw up insulin from the glass vial it comes from the pharmacy in, into the syringe to transfer it to my pump. When I can no longer procrastinate, I take a deep breath, gathering the courage to face Oakley in the main room again where I heard him moving around.

He's sitting on the edge of the bed, so he must have recently woken up. His head snaps to me as I exit the bathroom, a soft smile on his face as the island sun washes over him in a warm golden glow through our window. *He's perfect.* His sun-kissed skin is a beautiful canvas for his striking features, and his thick brown hair and bright blue eyes are such a lovely contrast. He looks like he belongs on a screen or in a magazine, but I'm lucky enough to be standing here, the solo viewer of the art-worthy display that is Oakley lounging in the bed we just shared.

I can't take another moment of not knowing how he expects me to act around him. All of the awkwardness between us over the last few months has been horrible, slowly driving me insane as I've overthought every single interaction, every word either of us has said, every movement we've made in the other's presence.

I've been fooling myself that things could ever be the exact same as they were before the kiss. How could I ever think that I could continue on the way we'd always been after knowing what Oakley's full lips felt like moving against my own? That I could ever look at him with anything other than awe after seeing the expression he makes while he comes?

I need to know what he's thinking, even if I don't like his response. I feel like the not knowing might somehow be even worse. I've never been very good at difficult conversations, but I know it's well past time we had one. As much as I like to pretend I'm no longer the socially awkward kid who doesn't laugh at jokes at the right time, moments like this always bring me back to that period of my life. I feel just as lost, just as confused about how I should act or phrase things. I know that there's no good way to do this, though, so I give up trying to find the perfect words and just go for it. "What happens now?"

I think that he knows I mean with us, but in true Oakley fashion, he takes the easy way out with a joke. "I should get cleaned up," he says with a shrug and a cocky smile. But then to my immense relief, he answers again rather than brushing off my question. "And we should probably talk about what we did and if either of us regrets it… Or if we might want to do it again." Then he quickly adds, "I don't regret it."

My heart is racing so quickly I can barely hear his words over the pounding in my ears. I'm quiet for a moment, staring at the beach outside our window with my brows furrowed, biting my lip as I try to figure out what to say. There's no way I could look into his ocean blue eyes right now, so much more captivating than the water out there, and form any coherent thought beyond "want," or "mine." I try to gather the courage to tell him the truth, and force myself to speak. "I don't regret it either," I admit, but I know he deserves more than that.

Fuck it. It's now or never. I might not ever be attracted to anyone like I am to Oak again, and I can't miss out on the chance to explore that because I'm worried about him not feeling the same way.

I take a deep breath and say, "I'd like to do it again."

He lets out a huge exhale, like he'd been holding his breath. "I was hoping you would," he responds, and my gaze snaps to his, my wide eyes probably giving away how little I was expecting that answer. There's a huge grin taking over his face as we stare at each other for a moment, my mouth twitching as I attempt to hold back my own.

I want to make sure he's being serious before I get my hopes up, but there's no teasing in his expression for once, just a large, genuine smile, and I know that look, he's being sincere.

I let out a short laugh. "Okay, good," I agree with a nod, unable to get anything more than that out as I realize what we've both just admitted. *Oakley wants to hook up with me again.*

"I mean, obviously. Why wouldn't you? I'm amazing" he teases.

"And so humble," I deadpan before finally mirroring his grin. "Are you bi?" I hear myself asking before I think it through as I wonder what exactly changed for him and when.

"I think so. How about you?" he asks, sounding even more excited now. Even though the label doesn't feel like the perfect fit when Oakley seems to be the only one I'm attracted to, I'm definitely not ready to have *that* discussion, so I opt for a nod, and he smiles even bigger. "This is perfect! We can explore our newfound attraction to men with each other. We've always done everything else together, it feels sort of fitting that we'd do this together too, don't you think?" he adds with a laugh, sounding eager as he looks up at me hopefully.

My chest feels tight as I process what he's suggesting, even if my logical brain agrees that it makes sense. Oakley has figured out he's attracted to men, and he's suggesting we explore that together, probably go through some sort of checklist of new experiences so that he can build up confidence for when he decides he's ready to move on and potentially date another man for real. We're already so comfortable with each other, it makes sense that he'd want to ease into the unknown with me before attempting something potentially so vulnerable with a stranger.

I know I should be happy that he's offering me anything at all, but there's a growing knot of tension in my gut at the thought of that arrangement ending, of him wanting to move on.

"So, we go through all of the 'first times with another man' together?" I clarify, wanting to make sure I'm understanding his suggestion.

"Yeah, we can keep hooking up. It'll be great, and so easy, we're already together all the time."

And no one else has to know, is what he seems to be implying. I don't think either of us would mind other people knowing that we're attracted to men, but it would be a bit more complicated than that with living together, and work, and all of our friends and family. They would jump right to wanting us to be together forever, and we definitely don't need that kind of pressure for what will likely be a short-term thing.

And who knows what sort of implications there would be if anyone at work found out that we'd hooked up. Oakley is technically my boss, and I can't imagine people would be as trusting of me and my position with the company finances if they thought I only got the job because I was sleeping with the CEO. Or worse, if they thought I was being untrustworthy with the money after finding out I'd hidden something from them. Even if we got back and disclosed a physical relationship with HR, people might assume that we'd been doing this for years.

Plus, there are all of the posts I'm tagged in from Aspen that would make it seem like we're dating. I'm sure people would have opinions or questions on why I was seeing her and sleeping with Oakley if they ever did find out about him and I being together. Better to keep such a temporary situation between the two of us.

It will also be easier when Oak inevitably ends things. I can save myself any embarrassment of having to explain to anyone that Oakley just wanted it to be fun from the beginning.

"Alright, go shower. That can't be comfortable," I tell him, happy that we're finally on the same page.

"If you insist," he teases with an eye roll, jumping out of the bed. I know that there's still a lot more we need to talk about and don't know what I even want to happen with Oakley. I just know that was the best wake-up of my life.

I'm hoping there will be more mornings like that in our future.

OAKLEY

October

My life is amazing.

I'm in Bora Bora, at a resort I'm helping design so people can throw the best parties, because what's a wedding if not the ultimate party? I'm here with my best friend that I'm super attracted to, and he just agreed to keep hooking up with me. Does it get any better than this?

There's only so much to see of the construction zone that is our resort, and we only actually have one more full day here before we're needed back in Chicago, so today we're spending time exploring the island and participating in some of the experiences we're hoping to eventually offer to our guests. We're doing a helicopter tour around the island first, and I can't wait to see how this new luxury Caldwell venue fits into the island as a whole from above.

We've hired an interpreter-slash-guide, Teva, for our trip even though many locals speak English as well as Tahitian and French, and he'll be joining us on the tour. He also drove us to the beach with the helipad that we'll be taking off from, and as we approach the four-seater helicopter, he greets our pilot as though they're old friends.

"La Orana, I'm Amand, and I'll be your pilot and guide today as we fly around one of the most beautiful islands in the world. My English is okay," he says with an obvious French accent. He tilts his hand side to side as he offers us a self-deprecating smile before continuing. "As I focus on flying, though, I may slip into French. Teva can take over if that is the case, or of course, add even more to the tour if I forget anything."

"La Orana," we echo before introducing ourselves. Parker and I have both been in helicopters before, but we pay attention to the safety briefing before climbing into the second row of seats. Teva offers to have one of us sit up front for a better view, but there's no way I'm giving up sitting next to Parker, so we politely decline.

Once we're all situated with our own headsets so that we can communicate with each other over the roaring of the aircraft, we take off. The island is beautiful from the shore, the white sand beaches with light blue water, crystal clear and inviting in a way that's so different from the dark shores we're used to with Lake Michigan. From the air, it's even more stunning as it seems to glimmer in a million different shades of blue.

"On your left at the center of the Lagoon, you'll see Mount Otemanu standing at seven hundred and twenty-seven meters, or over twenty-three hundred feet for you Americans," Amand points out. The green peaks appear to be grazing the few white clouds in the clear sky and the entire scene seems more fit for an oil painting than my business trip.

Again, my life is amazing.

I may have grown up in a wealthy family, but my parents never let us forget how lucky we all are. My mother had us volunteering in soup kitchens and shelters throughout the city from a young age so that we could see firsthand how important it is to give back and actually help people. It's not enough to write a check for the tax break or PR opportunity like some people do. How can you know what people really need if you don't talk to them yourself, if you don't see exactly what kind of struggles they're really dealing with for yourself?

Driving throughout the island earlier, and even glimpsing the scattered homes from above now, it's obvious that not everyone here is living in luxury. I know our team has been working with locals here to learn about the best way to create jobs and fulfill needs within their community. I've done the research on local living conditions and know that French Polynesia has high unemployment rates and many people live below the poverty line.

The clientele we'll be attracting are the wealthiest in the world, but I don't want them to ignore what life is really like in paradise. Hopefully, when they visit the island and see for themselves how amazing it is here, they'll be inspired to help as well. I make a note in my phone to make sure our staff has information to pass on to any of the guests who ask about donation opportunities to local charities.

I make another note to call my mom and see when and where I can be the most helpful back home since it's been too long since I joined her volunteering.

"That's the birthplace of the Polynesian islands in local mythology," Teva adds, pulling my focus back to the moment. I know I'm not going to help anyone from up here, so I focus back on my present, trying to soak in the beauty of my surroundings.

Focusing is hard though, because Parker is very close to me, and as gorgeous as the island is below us, I keep thinking about the fact that we agreed to have sex.

I'm going to fuck my best friend. Or will he want to fuck me? Do I have a preference? Cody was very enthusiastic in his advocating to bottom, but I've seen Parker's dick, wrapped my hand around it, and I'm not sure how that thing could possibly fit inside of me. But I'm also not completely opposed to trying.

Maybe we should ease into it though, like Parker suggested, share some other first times before we jump right into anal. Will he want to start tonight? I definitely do. Or we could just repeat what we did this morning. Maybe he'll want to touch me this time too… *Okay nope. Don't need to be hard right now. Focus. Pretty island, try to ignore the hot man next to you that happens to also be your favorite person.*

Parker glances over at me with a warm smile and bright eyes, and I realize it's been awhile since I've seen him look so at ease. The last few months we've both been a little more hesitant around each other, but hopefully now that we've finally realized we're on the same page, I'll be seeing that look a lot more.

"This really is amazing," Parker comments, turning to face me as he speaks even though we can only hear each other through our headsets. "Even though we're only here for such a short period of time, I'm glad that we were able to come."

And I'm glad that we were able to make each other come.

Nope. Need to stop thinking about naked fun with Parker when we can't immediately do more. "Me too," I agree, but I can't help but wiggle my eyebrows at him, knowing he'll understand my implication.

He bursts out with a laugh, causing Teva to turn to us with an arched brow. We wave him off, and Parker glares at me, only making me want to work him up more, but there will be time for that. So, I give him my most innocent wide-eyed expression and shrug before grinning and turning back to look at the view.

Teva and Amand continue to point out different parts of the lagoon, telling us about local customs and culture as they do. We circle above a smaller island, its beaches stretching and connecting so that they form a heart around more dazzling blue waters, and start to descend.

"This is Tupai, the famous heart-shaped island. The resort will offer this tour to guests, and we anticipate it being popular among the wedding crowds," Amand informs us. "I've brought along the same spread we're planning to offer them so that you can have the full experience. Give me a moment to set it up after we touch down."

We land smoothly, and he quickly disappears down the beach while I ask Teva if he knows of any local charities that he'd recommend trying to partner with. I get the names of a couple that he's seen do actual good for the community, and then Amand is back, leading us across the pristine white sand to where a table is set up with two chairs featuring an elaborate picnic spread atop it. It's rather formal for the setting, with a white tablecloth, fresh flower centerpiece, and even a bottle of champagne chilling in a bucket of ice. There's cut fruits and sliced meats and cheeses, and Amand helps us sit down before popping the champagne and filling our flutes. Once he confirms we're settled he heads back to the helipad with Teva.

I pick up my glass and hold it out to Parker for a toast. "To old friends and new adventures."

"We're not old," he points out, clinking his glass with mine.

I laugh at the literal interpretation. "I just meant we've been best friends for a long time," I clarify with a warm smile. "This will be perfect for the couples getting married: heart-shaped beach, fancy private date with champagne. Not that this is a date," I quickly say in response to his confused expression before looking back out at the water.

But is that true? Could this be a real date?

Parker and I agreed to keep hooking up, and I was so thrilled about the fact that he wanted to keep doing it that I didn't really think to clarify what that would change between us if anything.

Do I want this to be a real date?

I look back over at my best friend, his unruly copper hair, the freckles covering his already sunburned skin despite the sunscreen he's used hourly since our arrival. I want to map out each spot, memorize the ones I don't already know, and spend hours learning every single inch of him.

Warmth is spreading throughout my body as I take in the curves of his muscles. But that feeling isn't just lust. The attraction is there, but so is all of the love and affection I've always felt for him as my best friend.

I think I want this to be a real date.

But as I acknowledge that thought, another realization washes over me. Parker's question from this morning sends a chill down my spine as I try to think about what *exactly* we agreed to. He asked if "we'd go through all of the first times with another man together," and I was too excited agreeing to more sex to stop and think about the specifics of what he meant.

Parker is very literal with his word choices, if he offered to check off some sort of first-times list, then that's probably exactly what he intends to do, nothing more. He isn't wanting to turn our friendship into something more. He found out we were both bi and figured it would make sense to get our first experiences with other people's dicks out of the way with someone that we're comfortable with.

Which I guess it does…except for the fact that I don't want to stop after that.

Okay, this is fine though, no need to panic. Parker loves lists, I just need to find the longest list of gay sex acts and make sure that he's using that one for our plans. Maybe suggest we really master each act before actually crossing it off. This doesn't need to be over quickly. I'll be the best damn friends-with-benefits ever, make sure that Parker knows how happy I could make him, and then maybe over time Parker will realize how great we could be together. He'll understand that we already live together and work together and spend all of our time together, so that by adding sex to the mix we'll basically already be married, and then maybe he'll agree to us being together for real.

Great plan. Totally not setting myself up for heartbreak.

Parker asks me about the other experiences I'd want to try out that we'll offer the guests and we talk about kayaking and snorkeling as we finish our food, mostly ignoring the champagne. When we're done we make our way back to the helipad, I successfully resist the temptation to reach out for Parker's hand as we walk along the beach.

Maybe one day.

AFTER THE HELICOPTER brings us back to the main island, we spend some time driving around with Teva, exploring local shops before having dinner with the crew working on the hotel. By the time we get back to our villa, I'm buzzing. I haven't been able to stop thinking about if Parker will want to hook up again tonight. *I really fucking hope so.* I don't want to wait until we're back home. What if something's different once we're no longer on the island? I don't want to give him time to overthink anything and change his mind.

I don't go far once we step inside, pausing where I've just closed the door behind us, hyperaware of the tension that's been building on the walk back here. Should I wait until we're ready for bed? Bring it up now?

"You okay?" Parker asks, turning back to look at me with a raised brow as he realizes I didn't follow him inside.

"Are we going to start tonight?" I ask, unable to wait any longer with how excited I am. *Both figuratively and literally.*

Parker's expression shifts to worry. "Oak, we don't have to do anything, if you're having second thoughts—"

"No second thoughts," I interrupt. "I'd like to. I just wasn't sure what you were thinking…" I trail off as Parker slowly approaches me with a lopsided, cocky grin that I'm not sure I've ever seen on him before. *Holy fuck it's hot, though.* Even more of my blood rushes south as he gets closer, surrounding me with his wide shoulders and towering height. But he doesn't say anything and I can't seem to shut up as I whisper, "What do you want to do?"

For a moment, he just stands there, eyes darting around my face like he's searching for something in my expression. Then his gaze lingers on my mouth, and he's stepping in even closer, crowding me back against the door. "This," he says on an exhale before reaching down to cup the back of my neck in his hand, guiding my face up toward him as he looks down at me.

Our lips meet, and I immediately confirm that our first kiss was not a fluke. His mouth on mine sets my body alight in a way that I'm beginning to associate only with him. I'm buzzing with the pleasure he awakens in me, and I'm desperate for more. He grips my hips as I push my tongue into his mouth, deepening the kiss as I bring my hand up around his neck to grab his hair, holding him firmly in place against me. Our tongues tangle, exploring each other, fighting for dominance, and it still isn't enough. He slides his hands around my hips to grip my ass before moving them lower to lift me up and closer to him. Without hesitation, I jump up and wrap my legs around his waist so that he's holding me as he grinds his hard cock into mine.

I groan at the sensation, and he moves to kiss and suck down my neck as I continue to rock my hips into him. I love being in his arms like this, surrounded by him. I feel completely lost in the euphoric feelings Parker inspires in me.

Us hooking up was the best idea ever.

"Oak, *fuuuck*," Parker says before letting out another moan followed by a soft chuckle.

He stops kissing me, and I finally open my eyes, which I'd apparently closed, and shift back in his hold to look down at him. He's staring up at me with a look of wonder.

"Why'd we wait so long to do that?" I tease.

"No idea," he replies with a grin and a shake of his head. Despite all of these new concerns that he's inspired in me about what this will mean for us long-term and if he could ever want more, I love that he's still Parker, still my best friend who I can joke around with, who makes me feel comfortable in any situation. We're grinning at each other like complete idiots, and I'm loving every second of it. The electricity between us builds as we enjoy the moment.

"Now, where were we?" I ask, leaning in to kiss him again.

Kissing Parker is amazing. I can't believe it took us over twenty years to do this. The feel of his stubble against my own is hot as hell as we battle for control. He's so much more dominant than any woman I've ever been with, and I love that I don't have to hold back either, don't have to worry if I'm being too rough.

Then Parker shifts his grip so he's fully supporting me, backing away from the door and turning toward the small kitchen area of the villa. He's walking, holding me in his arms like I don't weigh almost two hundred pounds, and the casual display of his strength is making the desire pooling in my gut even harder to ignore. Eventually he places me on the counter, still holding me flush against him.

My cock is rock hard as I grind it into him, the counter is the perfect height, and the way he's squeezing and kneading my ass is putting all sorts of ideas into my head. *Is he thinking about fucking me? Do I want him to already?* My cock twitches at the idea, and I think I'd be up for anything at this point with how fucking desperate I feel.

Then I remember that *this is Parker.* I don't need to wonder what he's thinking, I can just ask him.

Hooking up with your best friend is awesome.

I finally force myself to pull back from the kiss, and he immediately moves his mouth to my neck, kissing and sucking like he did earlier. It feels so fucking good. I hope it leaves a bruise too. I want him to cover me in his marks, to have the proof of this moment even if no one else will know they're from him. "So, what should we do first?" I ask breathlessly.

A small moan escapes from my lips as he sucks on the pulse in my neck but eventually he pulls back. "What do you mean?"

"Well, there's so many new things for us to try," I point out eagerly. "Blowjobs, frotting, rimming, anal; we've been hearing Beck and his friends talk about this stuff for years. Now that I know how much I like kissing you, and how hot it is to watch you come, I want to try it all."

He lets out a soft laugh. "So even though you've never been with a man, just like that, you want to jump right into rimming and anal?" he asks with the same teasing tone he'd use to taunt me if we were playing video games or competing against each other in the gym. I love that we can still be *us* while we're casually grinding our hard cocks together.

"Maybe not right to rimming. I feel like that might require some more prep work than I have the patience for right now," I deadpan, making him laugh even louder this time. His laugh always makes my chest feel lighter and I can't stop a huge smile from taking over my face. This is already one of the best hookups I've ever had with how easy everything is between us. I'm definitely going to need a longer list of things for us to do, try out kinks too, just to be sure we haven't missed anything else we might like. Honestly, I'd try anything, and I'm looking for any excuse so that we can keep this up indefinitely. "Okay, we'll save rimming for another day. What about blowjobs?" I offer. "I bet I'll be really great at blowjobs."

"Have you been practicing? You seem a little too confident

about that," he teases, biting his lip like he's trying to hold back his smile.

"No, but I really like getting blowjobs. I'm sure it's transferable knowledge," I say confidently, trying to get him to laugh again.

"I'm happy to have you test out your skills. But, you gave me a handjob this morning, so I'm kind of feeling like I owe you the first blowjob," he offers, moving to unbutton my pants. I help him, lifting my hips so that he can pull them off with my underwear. My swollen cock slaps against my abs when it's finally freed, but he takes his time removing the rest of my clothes. I'm left completely naked on our kitchen counter while he stands between my legs, still fully clothed.

A shiver runs up my spine as I realize how exposed it makes me feel. It's vulnerable to be the only one without that layer of privacy, but *it's Parker*, so I'm still completely at ease. When I notice him checking me out, I shift my hands behind me to lean back on my arms, flexing my abs to really put on a show.

"Fuck, Oak, you're really attractive," he mutters, more to himself than me.

"And you should have already known that," I tease.

But then he pulls his gaze away from my muscles and back to my face. "Something changed when we kissed," he says softly, like he isn't sure if he should admit it out loud. But the words settle something in my chest at the confirmation that our first kiss might have meant more to him than I'd previously allowed myself to hope.

"Yeah, it did," I agree softly, and his entire face lights up. Then he's pulling me in for another kiss before I can say anything more. I hear a scraping noise, and realize he's used his foot to drag one of the barstools over as he sits on it, right in front of me.

He reaches out, wrapping his hand around my dick, and I immediately let out another moan. I've been aching for him all day, and his large hand feels amazing. Then he lowers his head, taking just the tip into his mouth, and my hands fly up to grip his hair on instinct, burying into the unruly copper strands, grateful that there's enough for me to properly hold. I'm trying really hard not to give into the desire to pull him further onto my cock, and it's really fucking difficult. But I don't want to scare him away. I already know one blowjob won't be enough.

He takes more of me into his mouth, bobbing his head a little to go deeper and the sight of him trying to swallow me down is hotter than any porn I've ever seen. He gags when he goes too deep and shifts his hand to work what he can't fit in his mouth. It's nothing fancy as far as blowjobs go, but…*it's Parker. With my cock in his mouth.* I feel like I'm already close.

"Fuck, babe, that feels so good. You look so fucking hot choking on my dick like that," I tell him, wanting him to know how amazing this is for me. "Your mouth is perfect. Are you going to swallow my load?" I ask, not sure what's coming out of my mouth right now. I've never talked much during sex before, but I feel consumed by the pleasure he's giving me, and I want him to understand how much I'm enjoying it. He must like it too because my words seem to inspire him. He takes me deeper and his rhythm is faster as he hums around my cock, nodding slightly in response to my question that he plans to swallow.

The vibration feels too good, and I'm glad he doesn't want me to pull out because it's too late. My cock is pulsing, and I can feel him swallowing around me as I finish in his mouth. I don't want to miss a moment of this visual, but the orgasm is too intense. I can't help but close my eyes as I ride each wave of pleasure. He doesn't pull off of me until my overly sensitive cock is completely spent, and even then, he licks it completely clean.

"So, how was that?" he teases as I slump back on the counter. My arms feel shaky as I try to support my weight and remain seated.

"It was alright," I joke after a few deep breaths.

"Think you can do better?" he taunts with a huge grin.

"Give me a minute for my limbs to cooperate, and I bet I can make you come even faster than I did," I promise.

"I'm sure you will, that dirty talk had me ready to finish while your cock was still in my mouth," he says, his expression shifting to alarm like he's surprised he actually admitted that aloud.

It motivates me even more, and I don't want him to have to wait. I take a few more deep breaths and hop off of the counter so I'm standing next to him before I grab his hands and pull him up too. I work quickly to remove his clothes as he disconnects his insulin pump so that he's standing completely naked in front of me.

His giant cock is sticking straight up at me and I don't give myself any time to hesitate. I drop to my knees and wrap my hand around the base, bringing the swollen purple head to my mouth where I leave a wet kiss. I know there's no way in hell I'm fitting this entire thing in my mouth yet, *something else to work up to,* so I lick up his long shaft, exploring with my tongue and coating him in spit so I can use my hands more easily. His hips jerk as I stretch my lips around the tip and suck, forcing more than I had intended to take into my mouth and hitting the back of my throat. I immediately gag.

"Fuck, sorry," he apologizes, pulling back.

"Do you actually want me to stop?" I tease, looking up at him as I continue to slowly work him with my hand. "I knew you were big, but this thing is practically a weapon."

"If you need to stop…" he answers, and his concern is sweet, but I'm just fucking with him. I'm loving every second of this.

"Not happening," I assure him. *I'm determined to be good at this.* I recover quickly and double down, trying to take as much of him as I can into my mouth.

"Oh thank god," he mutters as I use one hand to stroke the rest of his cock, and he lets out a deep moan when my other hand moves to play with his balls. To my surprise, the sound causes my spent dick to twitch. I didn't think there was any way I would be able to get hard again so soon, but this entire experience is way hotter than I expected.

I'm on my knees, with Parker's cock in my mouth, and I'm in no hurry for this to end. The way his thick erection stretches my lips, the weight of it on my tongue, the way he keeps shallowly shifting his hips forward like he can't control himself. It's addictive. The feel of his smooth shaft sliding through my fist, and *the fucking sounds he's making*. I could stay like this for hours. Knowing I'm the one making him feel this good has me feeling invincible.

Making Parker happy has always made me happier than anything else. Now that I can do this for him too, I never want to stop. Unfortunately, I don't think I have that option. The way he's gripping my hair with both hands now and the desperate noises leaving his mouth makes me suspect he's close.

Each moan that he lets out has me thrusting my hips forward, my dick is somehow hard again and seeking friction that isn't there. I finally give in and move one hand to jerk myself off. I look up at Parker through my lashes and meet his blissed-out expression. His eyes are hooded and he's staring at me like he can't believe that I'm real. I've never felt closer to another person than I do right now.

"Fuck, Oak, I'm..." his words turn into another moan. His grip in my hair tightens as his cock twitches in my mouth and hot thick ropes of his cum shoot down my throat. I try desperately to swallow it all, the salty taste of him is heady, even better straight from the source, and I don't know if I'll ever get enough. The slight jolt of pain as he pulls my hair only intensifies my pleasure in this moment, sending me over the edge once again as I enjoy the high of a shorter second orgasm.

"Holy shit, did you just come again?"

I nod and blink up at him after he slowly pulls his cock out of my mouth. I don't want it to be over yet. I want him to stay there and to feel that connection to him until he's also ready for another round. *Another time.*

He drops down, joining me on his knees, and pulls me in for a desperate kiss, holding my face in his large hands. I melt into it, loving my taste on his tongue as I grab him just as fiercely. After we make out like that for a while, just enjoying the feel of each other in this new way, he finally pulls back, still cupping my jaw with both hands as his gaze meets mine. "It's never been like this for me," he says quietly.

"Me either," I admit. There's something about hooking up with Parker that makes everything better. I don't know if it's just how comfortable we are together, or that I can read his reactions so well, or hell maybe it's that he's a man, but being with him is like a whole new level of enjoying sex for me.

He relaxes a little with my answer, smirking. "I think I'm the winner of best blowjob if you came twice," he taunts, and I let out a surprised laugh at his topic change.

"I think that makes me the real winner."

"True," he agrees, joining me laughing.

We both stand and hesitate for a moment. I'm not sure what we're supposed to do next. "Want to shower?" I finally offer. I don't know what the etiquette is after you exchange blowjobs with your best friend, but the thought of leaving him right now, even if it is just to wash up separately, causes a knot of tension to form in my gut.

I'm so glad there's only one bed.

"Yeah, that sounds good," he agrees easily and follows me into the bathroom.

"Do you need help getting clean?" I offer in an over-the-top suggestive tone once we're in the shower. I hold out the soap and raise my eyebrows a few times to really sell it.

Parker bursts out laughing before playing along in an equally dramatic tone. "Yeah, I think I do."

We take turns cleaning each other, laughing and teasing as we're clearly more focused on groping and massaging than on only getting clean. I can't stop thinking about how easy and fun this is, being with him in this new way.

I have no idea how long he expects our new arrangement to last, or what his long-term relationship goals even are. Sure, I've always wanted a big family like the one I grew up in, and I had always assumed that meant a wife and kids, but that was before I knew how amazing being with Parker physically could be. I don't see any reason why we couldn't have that together, other than the fact that Parker's never really expressed the same interest in having a family. I'm not sure if losing his dad so young affects his own vision of his future, but I'm determined to show him how great it could be if he spent it with me.

For now, I'm happy to focus on the fact that Parker and I are sharing a bed, and on how amazing it feels to have him wrapped around me as I drift off to sleep.

PARKER

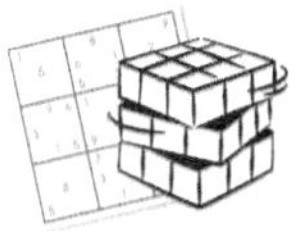

October

"So, our families will expect us to come home for either Thanksgiving or Christmas," Aspen says.

We're having brunch in their apartment a few days after we returned from Bora Bora. "No way Parker is missing Thanksgiving with my family," Oakley immediately responds. "My grandparents do a huge party, and we have a very competitive Turkey Bowl football game that would fall apart without both of us present."

Aspen's family has been asking me to come visit and I had agreed weeks ago to plan something. That was before Oakley and I decided to become friends-with-benefits *or whatever we are*, but I don't think our temporary new situation should affect the promises I made to her.

"That's fine," Aspen says. "Would you be able to get the time off for Christmas then? As much as I'm not looking forward to seeing them, going when there's other parties and distractions might be for the best."

"Yeah, we typically take the week off anyway," I respond.

"My family's been asking for me to come visit for months too, so I'll let them know I'll be there for Christmas," Sage adds.

"So, how will that work? We start in Georgia for your family, Aspen, and then split our time in South Carolina for yours?" Oakley asks Sage.

The girls exchange a concerned look. "Well, no honey," she says hesitantly. "You would stay here with your family, I'll go to South Carolina, and Parker would go to Georgia with Aspen."

"We can't do Christmas all together?" he asks, sounding genuinely surprised.

"It would be kind of weird to blow off our parents for our roommate," Aspen says apologetically.

Oak looks to me, eyes wide and brows scrunched together, clearly concerned about the idea. But the girls are right. As much as I hate thinking about giving up any holidays with him, it's not like we're dating. Aspen assured me that during this visit she should be able to talk her dad into selling his shares of her company and that meeting me in person would hold her family over until she's ready to cut them out of her life for good.

So, I try to play it off like it's not a big deal that we'll be missing our first holiday together in twenty-one years, shrugging before I move my hand to squeeze his thigh under the table, wanting to touch him in some way, to show him that we're in this together. "We'll still have Thanksgiving," I remind him, and he relaxes slightly.

"Yeah, that's fine, I guess," Oakley finally agrees.

"Fantastic, I'll let them know we'll be there for Christmas then!"

I'M AT WORK, going over yet another email from our Bora Bora interior designer requesting a budget increase to accommodate Oakley's new plans. They seem to have trouble saying no to him, and I've had to help them compromise on more cost-effective alternatives. I know that Oak can get set in his ways when he gets excited about a new idea, and that he listens to me more than other people, so I don't mind. But I still need to coordinate with the designers to find out what cheaper options exist to suggest to him.

"Knock, knooooock," Adrian sings as he walks right into my office. "Did you forget I was coming for lunch today?" he asks, holding his hand over his heart and scrunching up his face, pretending to be offended.

"No, sorry, I just lost track of time," I apologize.

"Well, I'm here and I brought your favorite sandwich, so your workaholic-ass doesn't even need to leave the office!" he says, holding up a takeout bag like he's showing off a prize on a gameshow, clearly back to his normal peppy self.

"You work just as much as I do," I say with a laugh.

"Don't call me out on my bullshit like that, it isn't polite," he teases.

Adrian and I have always been friendly, with our best friends being brothers we've spent a lot of time together over the years, but we've only recently started hanging out outside of the group. Adrian and I helped Cody out a few months ago by making a fake company for him to "invest" in to trick his old boss into approving money transfers. The money was all Cody's so there wasn't anything illegal about it, but his boss had access to his accounts and he needed an excuse to move it into a bank that his boss wasn't an authorized user on.

Adrian and I posed as the fake company's founders and made a whole pretend online presence to back up the story. We had a lot of fun putting it all together, and since then, he's decided we're "besties" and has shown up at least once a week to drag me to lunch. *Not that I don't appreciate the effort.* I really do enjoy spending time with him, and I know if Adrian didn't force his friendship on me I probably wouldn't think to initiate anything myself, so I'm thankful he does.

"So, what's new with you?" he asks, pulling out my wrapped sandwich and putting it on my desk in front of me. I know there is absolutely no way for him to actually know anything has changed between me and Oakley, but of course that's where my mind immediately goes, and I can feel my cheeks heating.

Last night Oakley bet that he could make me come first from a blowjob, and we ended up laying next to each other in his bed with our heads on opposite ends in a sixty-nine position so that we could blow each other at the same time to find out. He was right, and I finished first, but having his cock in my mouth turns me on way more than I would have ever guessed. I love knowing I'm the reason he's so hard, that he's moaning and clearly feeling so much pleasure *because of me*. All of that combined with his mouth on my dick, and I was a goner.

No wonder people think about sex so much if it feels that good when you're actually into the other person.

"Well, what the fuck are you looking all embarrassed about?" Adrian asks excitedly, folding himself into the seat across from me, abandoning his food and propping his face in his hands to bat his eyelashes as he leans in.

"Nothing," I insist, trying to focus on slow, even breaths in an attempt to appear normal. "How's living with your favorite hockey player?" I ask, clearly trying to change the subject. He recently had the Werewolves' captain move in with him after Hudson's wife very publicly served him divorce papers. Hudson was worried about paparazzi following him if he tried to stay in a hotel, and Adrian was there when it happened, so he offered his place.

"Nope, we're talking about you. You do not blush like a schoolgirl over nothing! Spill."

Fuck. I know I'm going to have to tell him something, but I have no idea what to say without exposing Oakley, and I definitely don't want to do that. I trust Adrian not to say anything to Beckett if I ask him not to, but I still don't want to feel like I'm betraying Oak in any way. I take a few more deep breaths, as I attempt to gather my thoughts, and realize that Adrian might actually be the perfect person to talk through some of my more confusing emotions with. "Have you always known you're gay?" I ask quietly.

I think my question throws him because he doesn't immediately respond. Instead, he sits back in his chair and furrows his brow, looking confused, but eventually his expression softens into a reassuring smile. "I've always been pretty fabulous. People assumed I was gay before I even knew what being gay meant, and a lot of them weren't happy about it," he finally says with a shrug. I nod because I know some of the details about what Adrian had to deal with growing up as the only out gay kid at his school. There's a reason he hasn't been back to Arkansas since.

"I'm sorry people are assholes. You deserved better," I tell him. I know it's my turn to say something, but I'm not sure how to even begin to explain what I've been questioning.

"Did something happen?" he prompts when I don't say anything else. "We don't have to use any details or names, but I'm here if you need to talk to someone."

I nod, liking that plan. I'm sure he'll guess who I'm talking about, but I feel better not actually saying it. "I've always assumed that I'm straight..." I trail off, shifting in my seat, hesitant to admit the next part aloud. I can't look at him, so I focus on the view out my window as I force myself to go on. "But dating and sex in general have never been a huge priority to me. Something happened recently that has me questioning if I've ever actually been attracted to anyone before now, though."

"Oh, Parker," he says, pushing up and out of his chair to round my desk. He wraps his arms around me from the side in a hug, squeezing me tightly, despite the somewhat awkward angle.

"Why are you hugging me?" I finally ask when it seems to go on for far longer than the average embrace.

"Because, you've clearly been dealing with these feelings by yourself, and I don't want you to forget that you aren't alone, duh."

"Um, thanks?" I mutter, unsure of what I can say to get him to stop hugging me.

Eventually he lets go and returns to his seat across from me, still giving me that supportive smile. "Okay, I don't want to over-step or ask specifics because I promised I wouldn't, but I just want to make sure I understand what you're saying so that I can support you properly." I nod, giving him permission to continue. "So, something happened recently where you *did* feel sexual attraction? And that was a new experience for you?" I nod, not wanting to say more than that.

"Have you ever heard of the Ace spectrum?" he asks. I shake my head slowly, trying to recall if I've ever heard the phrase. "That's okay. Do you know what the A stands for in LGBTQIA+?"

"Asexual?" I ask after a second, not super confident, but I've been friends with the Caldwells for long enough to have attended a few Pride events, and I think I've heard that word used.

"Yeah," he says, his whole face lighting up. "Do you know what that label means?"

"Sorry, no." I'm sure my confused expression is making it clear that I'm not following this conversation, but Adrian just keeps smiling at me.

"I'm no expert, but there's a whole umbrella of labels and

identities that fall under the Ace spectrum, and I think what you just described might fit," he says. He's tucked his feet under his legs on the chair and is bouncing a little as he talks, like he's excited to tell me more. "Asexual people don't experience sexual attraction. There's also gray asexual, when someone does experience sexual attraction, but only rarely, or under certain circumstances."

I'm staring at him with my mouth hanging open in shock, my confusion starting to morph into relief with every word out of his mouth. I've been so lost trying to understand what's been going on with me for the last few months, unsure why I was suddenly so attracted to Oakley after all of this time, wondering if I was broken. I've considered that I might be bi, or gay, but I didn't think to consider the other orientations. What Adrian is describing certainly sounds closer to what I've been going through than anything else I've heard of.

"I'm probably about to piss you off, so I'm still not going to say names even though we both know you and a certain friend of yours have been acting weird around each other for *months*," he says dramatically like he's about to share juicy gossip. I'm not confirming anything, but I don't stop him either.

"If my hunch is correct, then I think the term you might want to start looking into is demisexual. It's when someone only experiences sexual attraction after there's an established emotional connection. There aren't rules on when the attraction changes, my understanding is that it's different for everyone. But, if my guess is right about who your new-found attraction is to, then there could be a deeper emotional connection," he says, raising his brows and giving me a smug grin.

Then it's like he remembers something because his expression falls and he moves again, sitting properly in the chair and pulling it in closer so that he can grip my hand where it's resting on my desk. He meets my gaze, expression serious. "Those aren't the only identities in the spectrum, and there are a lot of people who don't need a specific label, but if any of that sounds familiar, I hope you already know there is absolutely nothing wrong with you."

I still have questions, but this feels important, like for the first time those questions might have answers. His confirmation that there isn't anything wrong with me makes my throat tighten, and his words feel like they're starting to untangle the knot in my chest.

"Just so you know, I'm respecting that we're not talking about it, so I'm *not* going to tell you how happy the two of you together makes me. I'm definitely *not* going to tell you that it's about damn time," Adrian teases.

I give him a sad smile though, because I know whatever he's picturing isn't our reality. "It's not like that," I say with a shrug.

"What do you mean?"

"We're not together," I explain. I know that's not exactly the truth, even if it's true we aren't dating. We did agree to continue hooking up, but I also don't think we're supposed to tell anyone. If our friends do find out, they would assume it meant more, and that's not what Oakley's agreed to.

"Oh," he says sounding disappointed and his whole body visibly deflates. "Well, now I really want to ask questions."

"That wasn't the deal," I tease, shaking my head.

"But, but, but," he splutters, blinking up at me with big puppy-dog eyes.

"Nope, sorry that won't work on me. Plus, there's nothing more to tell," I lie. Then I act like my sandwich requires all of my focus until he finally sighs in defeat and takes out his own lunch.

"Well, if you're truly done talking, I suppose I *can* update you on my hockey player," he says with another huff. But I know he's actually dying to talk about Hudson, so I laugh.

"Is your dream man ruined now that you're sharing a space with him?"

"Ugh, I wish! It's somehow worse. He's fucking perfect: He's clean, polite, and always offering to help me."

"That sounds awful?" I say like it's a question because I'm not sure where the "worst" part comes in.

"It is awful!" he insists. "Because he's hot as fuck, and he walks around half-naked all the time. Plus, he has more muscles than you! It's obscene. And then there's the teasing. You know I flirt with all of the Werewolves players in my over-the-top, obviously joking way. Well, Hudson has always teased me back, it's *our* thing. Now that we're living together, he's still doing it! And he's straight! I don't think my little gay heart can take it for much longer!"

"So ask him to stop," I suggest.

"Stop what?"

"The teasing and the half naked thing. You're helping him out by letting him stay with you, so you should still be comfortable in your own house."

"Ugh, you're one to talk," he scoffs, rolling his eyes. *Fair point.* "But there's no way I could ask him to stop. I'm loving every second of it," he says, sounding exhausted.

"Sorry, Adrian," I offer, wanting to support him, but unsure what he actually needs from me.

"Thank you! It's really hard living with the perfect man," he deadpans.

And I know he's still joking about Hudson, but I can't help but feel like I know exactly how difficult it really is.

23

OAKLEY

October

With everything that's been happening with Parker, I'd almost forgotten that we'd agreed to go to a Halloween Party with the girls tonight.

I love Halloween, and normally I'd jump at the chance to dress up. Parker and I have had some amazing coordinated costumes over the years. But tonight, no part of me wants to go out. It's a work night, we have a ton of stuff to catch up on in the office after our Bora Bora trip, and I haven't been able to focus on anything other than hooking up with Parker again.

I'd much rather stay home and keep exploring our new physical relationship than be paraded around some party with a bunch of people I don't know. Plus, these costumes are ridiculous. I loved the *Wicked* movie as much as the next person, but I don't understand why I need actual straw on my costume. It's so uncomfortable. Sage and Aspen wanted to be the good and bad witches, which left us as the scarecrow and tin man. At least I don't have to cover my face in silver makeup like Parker. He's usually a good sport and wears whatever I get for him, so I guess

I shouldn't be surprised that he agreed to the paint, but I didn't expect him to look so hot in it.

"Is my makeup messed up? Why are you staring at me like that?" he asks, eyes wide. He turns, probably to go find a mirror, so I grab his arm to stop him while I laugh.

"No, I was just thinking about how hot you look."

"With full silver face makeup?" he asks, tone full of disbelief.

"Yeah, it makes your bone structure pop or something. I don't know. Don't make it weird," I tease.

"You're right. *I'm* the one making it weird," he says dryly.

I pat his shoulder, nodding in agreement with a huge grin on my face. He rolls his eyes, twisting his mouth to the side, obviously trying to hide a smile. At least we get to spend *this* holiday together. Ever since we decided on separate Christmases, I can't help but question why he's still even doing the whole fake relationship thing with Aspen.

I know that Parker agreed to it to help her because he's a good person, and he seemed fine with the holiday plans, but I've never spent Christmas without him. I don't want to start now. But, he already committed to be there and the girls told their families they'd be coming, *so I guess I'll be fine with my awesome family.*

I know that helping Aspen makes Parker happy, and I want him to be happy. I would do anything to make him happy. So, I need to get over myself and stop worrying about a few days apart. It'll be fine.

"Ready to go then?" he checks, and I gesture for him to lead the way. Definitely going to be doing that a lot tonight because following him gives me the perfect view of the silver jeans Aspen got him. They fit like a glove and his ass looks incredible. I've always considered myself to be an ass man, and I can't believe it took me so long to appreciate how spectacular Parker's is. I know he puts in a lot of work to get his bubble-butt, and I would really like to become better acquainted with it.

He seemed surprised the other day when I brought up rimming and anal, but I hope he warms up to the idea soon. I'll volunteer to be on the giving or receiving end of whatever he's willing to do. I want to try it all. Especially after discovering how hot it is to blow him.

What else I've been missing out on?

"OAKLEY, CAN YOU COME IN HERE?" Parker calls out from his bathroom. As soon as we got back from the party, he said something about getting the "stupid makeup off of his fucking face" and disappeared into his room.

"What's up?" I ask as I round the corner to enter, but I bust out laughing when I see his pissed off expression. He's holding a washcloth and it seems like he might have tried to use it to get the paint off because it's wet, but whatever makeup he's wearing must be waterproof because there's very little on the towel and his face is still completely silver. "Oh, no," I finally get out in between laughter.

"This isn't funny!" he insists, sounding alarmed. "It's everywhere." He really did commit to the look. There's silver makeup covering his ears, neck, and even the top of his chest so that it went under the collar of his shirt.

"I'll call the girls and see if we can borrow makeup remover or something," I suggest and he visibly relaxes at the idea.

"Okay."

I call Sage on my way down to their apartment and luckily Aspen has a ton of whatever she used to get the green off of her own face, so after they calm down from their own laughter, they give me a whole bottle of the stuff and I'm back upstairs. Keeping them as friends is actually really nice. I was worried that things would be awkward when we ended things, but knowing that we're all still close and there for each other is cool. Even the party tonight wasn't as bad as I had been expecting. Aspen introduced Parker as her boyfriend to a few people and we took some pictures together, but there wasn't any fake PDA or anything to be uncomfortable with. I mostly just hung out with Parker while the girls socialized. Not a bad night.

"This will probably be easier in the shower," Parker suggests when I show him the bottle.

"Trying to get me naked again?" I tease, waggling my eyebrows suggestively.

"Is everything always sexual for you?" he asks with a laugh.

"Obviously," I say with a wink before slapping his ass. *Fuck* it feels even better than it looks.

"Come on brat, strip for me and get in the shower."

"Yes, Daddy," I tease.

"I'm not your fucking daddy, " he scolds, unable to stop himself from laughing at the title.

"Well, you keep calling me a brat and bossing me around, Park. What would you like me to call you?"

"Literally anything else," he deadpans.

"Hmmmm. What's something that's fun but still implies authority?" I called him babe in Bora Bora. It just slipped out and he didn't seem to even notice, but that's not the type of nickname I'm going for right now.

"Can't you just call me Parker or Park like you normally do?"

"Not when we're both naked. Where's the fun in that?" I think about it for another moment before the most obvious option comes to me. "Ranger! Like a park ranger, get it?"

Parker just blankly stares at me for a few seconds. "I get the name reference… But I don't understand how that's better than my name?"

"It's fun!" I insist, looking up at him with big eyes. I start to slowly unbutton his shirt as I use the most over the top sex voice I can manage. "Come on, Ranger. You're all dirty. Do you need some help getting cleaned up?" I wink as I run my hands under his shirt and over his pecs, grazing my thumb over his nipple. "Not that a big, strong man like you probably ever needs help with anything," I continue, batting my lashes.

Parker rolls his amber eyes, the almost golden color shining in contrast against his silver skin, but he's smiling. "I want to tell you that you're ridiculous and that this isn't doing anything for me, but I'm going to need you to cut that shit out before I say fuck the makeup and strip you for a much less practical reason," he says in a dark tone, as if he's trying to warn me against something I wouldn't enjoy.

"Don't tempt me with a good time," I respond, quickly pulling my shirt off, ready to get off now and deal with the makeup later.

"Fuck, Oak, orgasms after this itchy shit is off of my face. I want to be able to focus," he says with a playful slap to my ass that has me grinning even more.

"Will there be more spanking, please, Ranger?" I taunt, totally okay with that idea.

"You really are a brat, aren't you?" he asks fondly, and I just shrug, stripping down the rest of the way before I grab the bottle Aspen gave me and a couple extra wash clothes to bring into the shower. Parker joins me and it isn't easy,I definitely don't think he could have done it all by himself, but eventually I get all the makeup off. I barely even groped his muscles as I was soaping him up too. I feel like I deserve a reward for being so good, ignoring my hard cock the entire time was almost impossible.

"There's your handsome face!" I say, cupping his cheek with my hand after the last of it's gone.

"I'm glad my face is still there after all of that scrubbing. Earlier I was hot, but now I'm only handsome, should I put the makeup back on?" he teases.

"Ha-ha. You're always hot, you know that," I say, stroking his cheek with my thumb. His eyes are wide though, like he's surprised by the compliment, so I step forward, going up on my toes to bump my hard cock into his to show him just how attractive I think he is. "See."

"Fuck, even that feels good," he groans, grabbing my hips, bending down to line up our cocks as he holds me against him. Then he wraps his large hand around us both and strokes. A surprised moan escapes my lips at the sensation of our dicks rubbing together inside of his tight grip. *How did I not know how amazing that could be?*

But this shower isn't meant for multiple people, especially when one of them is as massive as Parker. We've had to switch off who was under the stream of water as we washed up and I know we'd be more comfortable if we got out. "Want to move to your bed?" I force myself to suggest, not wanting to stop.

"Yeah," he says, but his hand doesn't slow its movement on our cocks.

It feels so fucking good, but I also want to try something else tonight. "Come on," I say laughing, finally stepping back and turning off the water.

"Fiiine," he groans and we quickly dry off.

I don't bother wrapping a towel around my waist and head straight to his bed, sitting down on the edge, not-so patiently waiting for him to follow.

"Any bets tonight?" he asks, and my smile gets even wider. He also skipped a towel and hasn't bothered to reattach his pump yet, so obviously we're on the same page. He looks so fucking hot, his muscles on display, hard cock straining toward me.

"I bet…that you'll like rimming," I say with a smirk.

His eyes widen and his cheeks darken. Seeing this giant man blushing because of me is such a turn on. "Okay, get on the bed," he says, gesturing toward it. It takes me a second to realize what he's implying.

"No, I was trying to be the one eating you out," I explain with a laugh.

"Oh. Really?" His cheeks get even darker. "You want to?"

"Hell yeah, I haven't been able to stop thinking about your ass all night. You can do it next time, but if you're okay with it, I'd really like to."

He's still staring at me hesitantly, so I stand up and grab his hands, pulling him to sit down on the edge of the bed next to me. "We don't have to. I don't want you to be uncomfortable," I assure him.

"It's not that I don't want to," he says with a laugh. "It's just surprising. I mean, a few months ago we would laugh at anyone who thought we were dating, and now you're casually asking to stick your tongue in my ass."

I laugh too. "So, is that a yes?" I ask, trying not to sound too excited in case he isn't up for it.

"Oak, I think I'd let you do anything you want to me," he admits with a sigh.

"Only if you want it too," I emphasize, making him smile. Then he takes a deep breath and nods before crawling onto the bed on all fours. He rests his head on some pillows, hugging them with his arms, his ass sticking up toward me.

Holy fuck. If I thought he had a nice butt before, I can now confirm that Parker has the best ass I've ever seen.

I might have checked out some gay porn in the last few months as a part of questioning my sexual orientation, and as much as I never really understood the appeal when I'd heard Beck and his friends mention it, actually watching someone feasting on an attractive guy's hole was absolutely hot as fuck.

Now that I think about it, my lack of interest probably had

something to do with talking about sex stuff with my brother and not the acts themself.

"I'm feeling extremely exposed right now and you just standing there, not saying anything is freaking me out," Parker says quickly.

"Sorry, I was just admiring the view," I hurry to say. Then I get on my knees on the bed behind him and take each of his round cheeks in my hands, squeezing and massaging them. "Fuck, Parker. Your ass is perfect."

He lets out a short laugh. "Thank you?" he responds, his tone going up at the end like he's asking a question. I'm not sure if he doesn't believe me or just doesn't know how to respond to compliments, but I want to drive all of the doubts out of his mind.

I move my hands to spread him slightly, debating if I should warn him before I actually touch him, but before I can even think it through, I'm leaning in, licking a strip right over his exposed hole. He whimpers. *Fucking whimpers* and it's the greatest sound I've ever heard. I want him to do it again. I want to record it and listen to it whenever I'm sad. Because Parker making that noise somehow both brings me immeasurable joy and is the sexiest thing I've ever heard.

Just like that, I'm addicted. I immediately move my mouth back to his rim, licking and teasing him, completely insatiable in my desire for him. At first, I think he's attempting to hold back any more noises, but eventually he must give in because the sounds coming out of his mouth are completely pornographic.

He eases back into my hold, even shifting his hips to meet my eager mouth, and his hole relaxes enough that I can slip my tongue inside. "Ohmyfuckinggod," he gasps, rocking onto my face more confidently now. "Holy shit, more. I need more," he demands, voice straining. I feel consumed by the high I'm riding from having him squirming and begging for me like this.

I don't want to stop, but I need to ask what he's okay with, so

I reluctantly pull back. His hips chase me, and I can't help but smile. "Do you want me to add fingers?"

"Yes, anything, just keep going."

I chuckle and grab the lube from the nightstand as I suck on my finger, making sure to get it coated in spit before moving my mouth back to his hole. He moans, and the sound goes straight to my balls. But I ignore my own desire and focus on Parker. I bring my finger up to his entrance and slowly circle his rim, earning a muttered "brat" from him before I finally slide it in with my tongue, trying to give him time to adjust to the new size.

After a few moments, he's rocking his hips again, pushing my finger deeper inside of him, making more of those addicting noises. "More," he commands again in that firm, confident tone I'm not used to hearing from him, and I repeat the process, using a generous amount of lube before adding a second finger. Once he's adjusted, I move them around a bit, making sure it's still nice and wet. Spreading them just a little, I fantasize about how amazing this will feel when it's my dick instead of my fingers. I curve them, and brush against something softer, so I rub against it more intentionally, wondering if it's his prostate.

"Fuckfuckfuck," Parker shouts, hips jerking forward as his ass clenches tightly around my fingers, pulsing like he's trying to pull me even deeper.

"Sorry! Are you okay?" I ask quickly, worried that I hurt him. After he relaxes, I'm able to slowly remove my fingers, and I hurry to his side so I can see his face.

There's a few quiet moments where he seems to be catching his breath, then he collapses onto the bed and starts laughing.

"What the fuck is so funny? Are you okay?"

"I'm great," he gets out in between laughter. "You didn't hurt me, Oak, I just wasn't expecting to finish without anything touching my dick," he says.

"Wait, that's a real thing?" I ask, perking up again, trying to look at his cock even though he's laying on it. I want to see the proof that he already came.

"Apparently. The prostate is as amazing as Cody's been going on about," he answers, still chuckling.

"Do me next!" I say, flipping around so that I'm on my hands and knees with my ass facing Parker.

Moving to kneel behind me, he grabs my hips and gives me a firm smack. Tingles of the lingering pain spread turning me on even more. "How about you ask nicely?" he taunts, rubbing the cheek that he spanked.

"And if I don't?" I tease, looking back at him over my shoulder with a raised brow, shaking my hips back and forth slightly in invitation.

"Brats don't get tongues in their asses," he promises, landing another smack to my other cheek this time. It isn't hard, and I doubt there's even any redness. Parker isn't trying to hurt me, but this teasing and punishing, combined with the light pain on my ass has my already-hard dick leaking like crazy. This whole exchange has been so hot, I kind of don't want it to end, but I do really want his mouth on my hole, so I decide to play nice-ish.

"Please, Ranger? I promise I'll be good for you," I say in a sugary sweet tone.

He mutters, "fucking hell," before bringing his mouth to my hole like he's a starving man offered his favorite meal.

I feel like nerve endings that I never knew existed are shocked to life. "Fuck!" I grunt out. No wonder Parker was so vocal because this is unlike anything I've ever experienced before. The intense pleasure that's building inside of me is too much to handle. I was already so desperate to finish from being on the other side of this, so there's no way I'm lasting long enough to add fingers. I need to come right now. That's the only thought in my head. I shift my weight to one arm, and move my hand to my cock, desperately stroking, chasing my release.

I must relax enough for Parker's tongue to push inside of me, and I don't know if it's the feeling, or if it's knowing that *Parker's tongue is inside of me* that tips me over the edge, but my cock is jerking, covering his sheets in my release as I enjoy the high of my orgasm.

Eventually my breathing returns to normal, and I glance at where Parker's now leaning against the headboard, a small disbelieving smile on his face.

"I'm going to be an awesome bottom," I announce confidently. "I don't even think my prostate was involved there, and I came in like two seconds."

He bursts out laughing, and I join him. "What if I wanted to bottom?" he asks with a raised brow.

I move my gaze to where his cock is resting between his thighs, even though it's soft now, it's still intimidating. "Hmm, on second thought, maybe I need some toys to ease into bottoming before you try to split me in half." *Toys would be great to add to our list of things to try. I'm sure there's a ton of them.*

"I will buy you all the sex toys you want," he promises. "But I am also definitely volunteering my ass. I did not expect that to be so good."

"Right?" I agree. "Want to go wash up again and stay in my room with me? I think your sheets are ruined."

"Yeah, let's go."

I jump out of bed. "First one in bed gets to pick out the first sex toy!" I taunt, running toward my room.

"Fuck," he mutters, chasing after me. When he catches up, he grabs me from behind and lifts me up, tossing me over his shoulder in a fireman's carry. We're both laughing hysterically by the time we make it into the bathroom. We quickly get clean and ready for bed. I wait for him to get his insulin pump hooked back up, which was still in there from before our first shower, not wanting to win on a technicality. We end up making it to my bed at the same time, with me diving onto it for a photo-finish, and after more laughter, we eventually settle with Parker spooning me.

"I really like this," I whisper after a while, unsure if he's still awake.

"Me too," he mumbles. Then he places a kiss on the back of my neck, and I feel my cheeks heat.

I know that we're just having fun, and that Parker isn't looking at our arrangement like the long term thing I'm hoping it will be, but moments like this, where we can switch from silly to tender and still manage to feel like *us*, even when so much has changed, have me desperately wishing he wanted more with me.

Maybe even forever.

24

PARKER

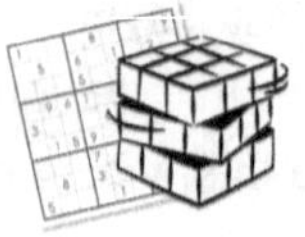

November

I'm trying to focus on this meeting

Not on how hot Oakley looks in his suit. I swear, every time we hook up it's like it unlocks a new level of attraction I didn't know was possible. I'm officially obsessed with my best friend, and I don't want to ever go back.

We're meeting with the event coordinator that we've hired to plan all of the weddings and parties at the Bora Bora resort, as well as the general manager, one last time before they officially move there after the holidays.

"I was thinking we also need to offer more fitness classes," Oakley suggests. He is full of new ideas for things we should provide for the guests. Just in today's meeting, he's suggested expanding the menu, the spa treatments available, and now the group exercise options. And that's only what Bella, the manager, has to worry about.

"Oh, Theo." He shifts his attention to the highly recommended events specialist, Theodore Tyler, before our manager can even respond. "I was watching a wedding video today where they had different performers in each space. How many live music options do we offer?"

He's also questioned the number of linen and plate varieties there are, the different uplighting, projectors, and flower options. They're both excitedly agreeing with everything that he says, but throwing me anxious glances when he looks away. They know how expensive every item he lists off is and that I'm the one they'll have to talk to about it.

It'll be fine.

Working with my best friend has never been a problem. Despite what some of the board members like to whisper about, I've never let our friendship compromise my ability to do my job well. If anything, it motivates me to do even better, because I know I have to prove myself. I know I'm the right person for this position I've been training half of my life for, some people just need convincing.

Making Oak happy is just a bonus. If he did something irresponsible or was pushing for something that didn't make sense, I wouldn't hesitate to shut it down.

In fact, I'm growing quite fond of putting Oakley in his place when we're alone.

I know our new dynamic won't change any of that at work, though. Oakley and I have always motivated each other to be better, and hooking up doesn't mean I'll suddenly start bending over backwards to give into all of his demands. *Even if I'm happy to bend over at home.*

I also know this won't last forever either, so not having to publicly defend our situation will make everything a whole lot easier. When the time comes that Oakley decides he's bored with me sexually and wants to go back to being just friends, we can do so without anyone else's concern. I know we won't let anything come between our friendship. But other people would assume it would affect our jobs.

Since I met him, Oak's always been the most important person in my life, and that's never going to change. Maybe there's always been something *more* between us, at least to me, and I just never recognized it as attraction because we never acted on it.

I'm trying not to dwell on my feelings for him. We've always loved each other as best friends. No need to start wondering if he could ever be *in love* with me when it wouldn't change anything. He's going to move on once he's comfortable physically being with a man. *No use thinking about my own feelings and if I'm in love with him either.* I should focus on the fact that I get to feel sexual desire and connection in a way that I never have before.

"So, when can we visit again?" Oakley asks them, drawing my attention back to our meeting.

"Well, we won't be moving in until the second week of January, and we have some time set aside to get settled. By the end of January, all of the construction should be completed, and we'll move into the design phase," Bella says.

"I've already scheduled all of the shipments for that first week of February for our event staples that we had previously agreed on. But, keep in mind, the larger selection we offer, the more storage we'll need for when they're not in use, and we're working with limited space," Theo reminds Oak gently.

"True. Okay, I trust your judgement. If you're happy with the selection then I'm sure it's fine," Oakley agrees, and Theo's smile relaxes. "Sorry, I'm just excited. I love weddings so much and I want this resort to be the perfect venue," Oakley says for probably the fifth time today. It really is sweet how invested he is. "I don't want to get in anyone's way, but I know I'll be way too hyped to wait until the soft launch with our family and friends to arrive with them all. Parker and I will probably come out a week early if you don't need us before then."

"That sounds perfect," Bella says, sharing a relieved look with Theo, who nods his agreement.

"Well, unless you have anything else to address, I think we'll say goodbye and safe travels," I say as I stand. We all shake hands and wish them luck with their moves, leaving Oakley and I alone in my office.

"Was there anything else you wanted to do before we head out?" I ask.

"Nope, let's go. I have somewhere for us to stop on our way home!" he says, sounding far too excited.

"New restaurant?" I guess.

"Better than food," he assures me. Except it has the opposite effect. Because I have no idea what would have him so excited that he's practically jogging down the hall ahead of me.

"What's better than food?" I finally ask when we're alone in the elevator.

"Sex, duh," he answers, flashing me a huge grin that brings butterflies to life in my stomach.

"You want to stop somewhere…to have sex?" I clarify, and he laughs in response.

"No. We're going to a sex shop," he explains, basically bouncing off the walls. "Someone promised to buy me all the sex toys I want." Those butterflies seem to multiply as I remember saying something along those lines after he offered me his ass.

"What if someone sees us?" I whisper, even though it's still only us on the elevator. I've never been to any sort of adult store, and I have no idea what to expect.

"Then they'll think we're getting a sex toy. Who cares?"

"What are we actually getting?"

"Lots of lube for sure, butt plugs, and maybe a dildo or two that's smaller than you so I can practice," he says casually, like he's talking about his grocery list and not preparing for me to fuck him. I let out a surprised laugh although my cock starts to thicken at the thought. I quickly adjust myself so that I'm not walking out of the elevator with an obvious tent in my pants. *How am I supposed to get through shopping with him?*

THE ADULT TOY store isn't at all what I was picturing when Oakley said where we were going. I have no idea why, but I thought it would be some shady dungeon-type setup where we needed to go down a sketchy alley or into a creepy basement behind some hidden door. Nope, Ecstasy Emporium is a storefront right on State Street with a large Pride flag in its normal window. There's bright lighting, colorful dildos everywhere, and even ads for events and parties.

The friendly staff member who offered to help us out probably took one look at my bright red cheeks and knew I was a sex-toy virgin, but Oakley is acting surprisingly chill here. "Have you been here before? How are you so fucking calm right now?" I hiss at him under my breath as he admires a shelf of butt plugs in a variety of sizes.

"Ha, no. When would I have come here without you? I'm just excited. I'm glad you think I look calm. I feel like a kid in a candy store right now thinking about everything we could do with this stuff," he says, smirking at me, and I feel my cheeks grow even hotter.

"Have you ever done anything like this before?" I hesitantly ask, not sure that I really want to know his answer. Thinking about him with anyone else makes my stomach churn.

"I've hooked up with a few girls who wanted me to use their toys on them, or had handcuffs, shit like that, and I'm a big fan of spanking, but I've never bought anything for myself," he says with a shrug.

"Fuck, I've never even done any of that," I admit. I never saw the appeal, and none of my previous partners ever brought it up.

"See anything you want to try?" he asks, waggling his eyebrows at me.

"I thought I was buying whatever you wanted?"

"Well, sure, but if you want to try anything, then you should get it too," he encourages. "I want us both to figure out what we like."

I think about it as I look around at the various options on display. There's a leather section with collars, harnesses, even full outfits. Lace lingerie, some specifically labeled for men. A whole bunch of stuff that seems BDSM related that I wouldn't have the first idea how to use. Then my gaze focuses back on Oakley, and my anxiety eases. "I don't think I need anything," I say. Getting to be with him is already so much better than anything I had ever dreamed of sexually. I don't need anything extra.

If he asks me to try something, though, I won't say no. I'm hoping to keep his interest for as long as possible. If that means we try out every kink under the sun, or buy a toy in every size and color…as long as we're doing it together, then I know I'll love it.

"Well, I sure as fuck will. There's no way I'm taking your monster cock as the first thing in my ass."

"I think my tongue has that honor," I remind him, and he smirks, shoving my shoulder. It's so easy to relax around him, to slip back into our comfortable dynamic that I almost forget where we are and why we're here.

"You know what I mean. So, which one do you think is the closest to your dick size? I want to get a few that are smaller than it," he says at a totally normal volume.

And just like that, I'm back to being embarrassed. I try to be subtle as I point to one that seems about the same width and length as my hard cock, trying not to draw any more attention to us than Oakley already has. He eagerly picks it out and adds a few smaller dildos and plugs to the baskets he's carrying. Then he looks back at them all again and adds another one to the basket. "I think you need a matching one," he says, throwing me a wink.

He adds some cleaning supplies for the toys and an obnoxious amount of lube to the basket as well—promising different flavors, temperatures, and toy compatibility. Then he hands me the basket, blinking up at me innocently, saying, "Thanks, Ranger," with a shit-eating grin.

"Don't be a brat or we're not getting anything," I warn, rolling my eyes.

"So strict," he teases, but I can't say I really hate the nickname. It's ours, something he's picked out just for me, so I could never hate it. Plus, the implication that I'm in charge of this man —my brilliant, charming, gorgeous best friend—is a rush.

I pay for everything, and thankfully, they put it all in discreet bags so we're not flashing our plans to the world after we leave.

I can't imagine running into anyone in our building and being able to keep a straight face if it had Ecstasy Emporium on the packaging.

OAKLEY

November

"I'll order us some food while you drive," I offer.

Now that we're no longer in the sex store with the threat of a public erection clouding my thoughts, all I can think about is using the toys we got. Using them on him and him using them on me to prepare for his giant cock. I shift my thickening erection again as I get into my car, trying to find a position that will be comfortable enough to last the entire ride home.

Parker usually likes driving me around. I prefer to look out at the city and people, be on my phone or messing with the music, while he insists he's content focusing on the road. I think it's a control thing after he lost his dad to reckless driving. Not that he doesn't trust me to drive him. I've always interpreted it as more of a wanting to protect me thing. He usually drives us to work or when we go out if we don't use a driver, and as we head back, I'm really glad I'm not the one having to think about operating a moving vehicle, so I can give my full attention to the man beside me. I'd much rather focus on how hot he is.

"The food won't be here for a while," I say when we finally walk into our condo.

"Okay. Wanna throw on the Werewolves game?"

"We could do that. Oooooor we could open our new toys and get everything ready," I suggest with a smug grin.

"Well, obviously that one," he agrees with a laugh.

I dump out the bag right on the kitchen counter. "Let's open them all and get everything clean so that we don't have to worry about it each time we want to use a new one," I say, already tearing into the box that's closest to me. I take it over to the sink with the toy cleaner we got, and Parker works on taking out the rest, giving each of them to me to clean as we go. Then I lay them all out on some paper towels in order of their size.

It's all very domestic, like we're an old married couple washing the dishes as a team, and not preparing butt plugs to prep for fucking each other. *I love it.*

"Should we shower first?" he suggests.

"Yeah. We should probably do it separately, though, so we don't get distracted and miss the delivery guy."

"Fair. I'll be quick," he promises.

We both manage to get cleaned up, and are back in the kitchen by the time the concierge brings our food. I opted for just some loose grey sweats, and Parker did the same.

"Fuck, grey sweatpants really are like male lingerie," I say, obviously staring at the visible outline of Parker's cock, ignoring the bags of takeout on the table. "Do you wear those in public?"

"Why? Don't want anyone else to see?" he taunts.

"I can't decide what's hotter, me being the only one who can look at you in those, or the idea of everyone seeing while I know that I'm the only one who gets to touch," I answer, still staring at his crotch the entire time. I'm sure my cock is also making itself known as it thickens, the sweats definitely don't leave anything up to the imagination.

Then I have the horrible realization that we never discussed exclusivity. "Wait, it is just me, right?"

He chuckles, shaking his head a bit before answering simply, "Only you."

"Okay, good. I'm not very good at sharing," I say on a very relieved exhale before quickly adding, "Obviously, I'm not going to be with anyone else while we're hooking up either." He smiles at my comment, and the panic I'd felt moments ago vanishes. I can't wait any longer, I need to touch him.

"Want to wait to warm up the food later and get started with our new toys?" I ask hopefully. I intentionally ordered things that'd reheat well because I hoped we'd have some fun before eating.

"Sure, who goes first?"

My gaze snaps up to meet his. "You want to use one tonight too?" I clarify, trying not to get too excited, but I can't help the giant smile stretched across my face.

"Isn't that the plan? I thought you wanted us to have matching butt plugs," he teases, even though I know him well enough to see that he's still nervous. After having my tongue in his ass, and showing him just how amazing that could be, you'd think he'd be more excited to put a silicone toy up there, but I can also tell that he doesn't want me to call him on it, so I take him at his word.

"Fuck yeah, it is," I agree, hurrying to put away the food and move toward the selection of plugs on the counter. I'm really glad the guy from our building didn't bring the delivery all the way in because our kitchen looks like we're ready to host a sex-toy party.

"Can you do mine first?" I ask, finding the two matching plugs that are smaller than the other ones we got, but still have wider bases than the fingers we've used so far. Then I grab the next biggest size too, just in case.

Maybe if we start with me, I'll get used to the size and can upgrade to a slightly bigger one after his is in. I know we need to be careful and get used to things, especially as we're starting out, but I'm eager to have Parker fuck me. I love the idea of fucking him too, but thinking about his impressive cock somehow fitting inside of me is way hotter than I anticipated.

"Are we staying in the kitchen again, or do you want to ruin some more sheets?" Parker asks me with a smirk, picking up one of the bottles of lube we bought.

"Let's do your bed again for sex and mine for sleeping," I suggest eagerly, making him laugh as I head toward his room. I strip off my sweats and get on my hands and knees on the edge of the bed. His sheets have since been changed, but I like the idea of ruining them again.

"Fuck, that's a pretty sight. Can you always be waiting for me like that?" he asks lightly.

I know he's only joking, but my stomach flutters, and I kind of love the idea of surprising him like this, maybe already with a plug in, waiting for him to wreck me. *We have plenty of time for that, more things for the list.* I need to calm down before I get too excited. My cock is aching with how hard I already am, and Parker hasn't even touched me yet.

I move my hips side to side, taunting him a little. "Are you planning to stand there all night, or are you going to actually touch me?"

"Definitely touching," he says, and he finally places his large hands on my outer thighs, sliding them around to my hip. His touch feels amazing, but it's like he's intentionally avoiding my hole to drive me crazy.

"Stop torturing meeee," I whine. *Have I ever whined before being with Parker? What the fuck has he done to me?* I guess it doesn't matter. I'm desperate for him and I'm not ashamed of it.

"Can I start with my mouth again?" he asks, rubbing a finger gently over my rim.

"Yes, please." I shift my hips back toward him, seeking more, and am rewarded with his mouth on me in the most satisfying way. We may be new at this, but Parker isn't holding back. His enthusiasm makes it obvious that he enjoys prepping me like this as much as I loved doing the same to him.

I focus on the overwhelming pleasure he's giving me, trying to consciously relax for him. Each swipe of his tongue is incredible. I could stay like this for hours, but it doesn't take long to feel like I'm ready for more, like I need it. His tongue is easily fucking into my hole now, and my aching cock is already leaking. We need to keep going before I repeat how quickly I came the first time he ate me out like this. "Go ahead, try the plug," I say, my voice breathy and nearly unrecognizable.

I hear the cap of the lube bottle pop before he spreads some over my hole, pushing in slowly with a finger and making me moan. I can't believe I wasted all of these years without putting anything in my ass, it feels incredible. Then his finger is replaced with the soft tip of the toy at my entrance, and I try to force myself to relax. I've done my research since I started questioning my attraction to Parker, so I bear down and take deep breaths.

His slicked-up hand wraps around my cock and my head swims at the feeling of being surrounded by him. Sex has never been this all-consuming. I don't know if it's because I'm with a man for the first time, or if it's just that my best friend is inside of me, but I'm quickly confirming I don't ever want this new aspect of our relationship to end. I can't imagine wanting to be with someone else when being with Parker is this good.

I hope that he feels the same way, but I don't think him working a butt plug into my ass is the time to bring up any sort of promise of commitment to each other. We've agreed to be exclusive, so for now, that will have to be enough. He strokes my cock as he slowly advances the plug, never quite fast enough to tip me over the edge, but enough to distract me from the new sensation of being stretched with the toy.

It's different than his fingers were, the feeling of fullness so much more intense and constant. *I think I love it.* Eventually, he gets the plug seated and sits back. "I'm going to need you to hurry up with mine," he says, voice deep and gravely in that way I'm obsessed with.

"Okay," I say on an exhale as I go to stand. The change in position causes the toy to shift over what must be my prostate. "Oh fuck, holy shit. I think I almost just came just from moving. This thing is incredible," I say, laughing.

"My turn," Parker reminds me sternly. He's already removed his insulin pump and pants and is now in the same position I'd been in.

I don't hesitate, I place a hand on each of his perfect round cheeks, squeezing as I bring my tongue to his hole. I've never been religious, but this moment—with my tongue ravaging Parker's ass, and a toy he put in me rubbing against my prostate—feels like a holy experience to me. When he's eventually rocking back to meet my tongue, I add a finger, which he easily accepts, and use some lube to add another before I reluctantly pull away to get his plug.

I add more lube to his hole, pushing it inside before I slowly start to work the toy in. The noises coming from him are completely pornographic and I love them all. He's soon rocking his hips back again, forcing the plug deeper, much faster than I had intended. In no time at all, it's fully in, and I'm fucking him with it.

The sight is indescribably sexy.

He keeps saying "more" which makes my cock leak and my brain go fuzzy, focused solely on chasing my orgasm. Parker is still on his hands and knees, and my hips are at the perfect height to line up with his. My dick is still slick from him stroking it so I slide my erection between his round cheeks, rubbing over the toy's base.

A deep moan escapes from him. "Fuck me," he says firmly, and at first I think he's just swearing at how amazing this feels. But then he repeats himself and I freeze. "Take out the toy, I need you to fuck me."

"Are you sure?" I manage to ask, proud that my voice only cracks a little.

"I've never been more sure about anything," he states, almost matching my own desperation.

Not going to argue with that level of confidence.

"Do you have condoms in here?" I scramble to remember how to function while I'm wrapping my mind around what's about to happen.

"Nightstand."

I open his nightstand drawer and see the double XL condoms in there. "These aren't going to fit me," I say with a desperate laugh. "Don't move."

I'm already running from the room to my own, ignoring my swinging dick as I go. I almost rip out the entire drawer from my nightstand with how quickly I try to open it and grab a handful of condoms, just in case.

Thankfully, Parker is right where I left him. I pull the plug out slightly before pushing it back in a few times and rub my other hand up his back. "Tell me if you change your mind or want me to stop, okay?"

"Uh huh," he grunts, nodding. I slowly pull the toy completely out and watch in awe as his hole clenches. "Fuck, I feel so empty now. Hurry up," he demands as his hips squirm.

"Bossy bottom," I tease, wishing I sounded a little more confident with my taunt, but I can't help how breathless it comes out.

"I'm going to pull you onto this mattress and hold you down while I sit on your cock if you don't move in the next two seconds," he promises. My smile grows with every word and as tempting as that sounds, I don't think it's actually what he wants.

I put the normal sized condom on, quickly add more lube to his hole, then cover my dick in more than I probably need and grip the base, guiding it to his entrance.

"Okay, deep breath in and bear down on the exhale," I instruct in case he hasn't done his own research. But with how well he took the plug, and how eager he is for me to fuck him, I'm wondering if he hasn't been doing some practicing of his own.

I ease in my tip as slowly as possible. As much as I want to give in to how fucking incredible it feels, I can see the muscles in his back tense at the intrusion, and I want this to be great for him. I shift to move my free hand around his waist to stroke his cock and he immediately relaxes. Eventually, I ease the tip in enough for him to start working himself back onto my dick and I try to stay as still as possible so that he can control the movement. His ass is so warm and tight, *has sex ever felt this good?* His body is gripping my cock like we were made to perfectly fit together in this way, and the plug in my ass feels unbelievable rubbing against my prostate every time I move. I already feel like I could come, but I never want this to end.

When I'm fully inside of him, I grip his hip firmly with my free hand and try to take a moment to appreciate that my dick is inside of my best friend. The thought seems so wild, and yet so normal all at once. Then he picks up the pace, truly fucking himself back onto my cock, sliding his dick through my fist with each motion. Any ability I have to rationally think is lost. I feel wild, an animal only capable of chasing my own release.

I meet his thrusts with my own, unable to worry about being gentle as I completely lose myself to the pleasure. The plug is hitting the perfect spot inside of me as I move, my balls are drawn up, ready to explode, and my muscles are tensing.

"Parker—" I try to warn him as I give in, tipping over the edge into bliss, but as soon as I say his name I feel his cock twitch in my hand, and his ass clenching around my dick, somehow sending me even higher.

I try to keep up my rhythm as we both ride out our orgasms, and eventually collapse next to him on the bed. We're both covered in sweat, but I'm not complaining with how each contour of his muscular body seems to be highlighted.

"Best. Sex. Ever," I manage to get out between labored breaths.

"Agreed," Parker says before we both burst out laughing.

"Give me a minute and I'll grab some wipes to clean you up," I say when I calm down.

"I'm not going anywhere," he says softly and I look over to see his eyes are closed with a completely relaxed expression on his face. He looks so handsome, so happy and my heart stutters in my chest, overwhelmed by how privileged I suddenly feel knowing that I was the one who made him look like that.

I just hope that he keeps letting me.

PARKER

November

I'm in no hurry to move.

I'm awake first this morning, spooning Oakley in his bed where we slept last night as I think about how much has changed this year. I've taken some time at work while I'm alone in my office, which is pretty much the only time I'm ever not with Oak, to look up a little bit more about the terms and labels Adrian told me about. There's still a lot for me to learn, and I'm not sure if I'll ever *need* to label myself, but since discovering I'm attracted to Oak, I always want him. Even thinking about him turns me on and has me daydreaming about sex. *Definitely not something I'd ever done before.*

Based on how much sexual attraction I feel for him, and the little I've learned of the Ace spectrum so far, I think the demi-sexual label rather than the gray asexual label is what I'll try to focus more of my research on. But even knowing the spectrum and the different labels exist has made me feel a sense of belonging I wasn't expecting.

I don't think I'd fully accepted just how broken I'd felt when I realized that I hadn't been attracted to anyone before turning thirty. Or that I finally did feel attraction and it was to someone who's always been there. I've always been drawn to Oak, wanting to spend all of my time with him, so maybe some part of me has always known he was different. Still, I felt like a complete idiot for not realizing it sooner.

But knowing there are labels for my experiences, and that other people are just like me, has allowed me to snap out of that weird-kid-who-doesn't-fit-in mindset I sometimes slip back into. My experiences and feelings are valid. *I just need to remember that.*

Everything with Oakley has been great, we still spend almost all of our time together, just like we did before that kiss all of those months ago. Sex hasn't changed our friendship dynamic, which is a huge relief.

I can't imagine not having Oak at my side for everything. Sometimes when we're alone, our usual competitive teasing and taunting has a more flirty edge which is definitely new, and we almost always end the night exchanging orgasms, but we're still *us*. He's using bigger plugs now, but I'm in no rush to top him when I'm enjoying him fucking me so much, plus all of the other ways we can use our hands and mouths to enjoy being together. And if he's working off some sort of "first times" list, then I'm fine to keep delaying so that we can still be together.

Today will be a test though. Going to our families' large Thanksgiving party will be the first time since we've started the new arrangement that we'll be in front of our closest friends and family. Hopefully, no one will realize if we are acting any differently, but I'm hoping the amount of people there will be enough of a distraction that we can carry on with minimal stress and just enjoy the holiday.

"You're thinking pretty loudly back there, Parker," Oak says, surprising me and drawing me out of my thoughts.

"Ha, yeah I guess I was. I hadn't realized you woke up," I admit, squeezing him tighter to me. I really don't want to get out of bed.

"Anything you want to talk about?"

"Nah, I was just thinking about today," I answer vaguely.

He makes a noncommittal grunting sound and turns toward me in the bed so our faces are right in front of each other. "Are you ready?" he asks, wearing a very somber expression and my gut drops in response. *What could possibly have him looking so serious?* "All of your energy and focus needs to be on beating Beck and Cody today in our football game," he deadpans.

"What the fuck man?" I say laughing as I shove his shoulder jokingly "I thought something was seriously wrong!"

"Not yet, but we need to set the tone! I'm the defending champion and this is Cody's first Thanksgiving with us. They're engaged now, so we need to properly welcome him to the family by beating his ass in flag football."

"I'd rather you stay away from his ass, thanks," I tease, and he finally ditches the serious expression to laugh with me.

Oak rolls his bottom lip into his mouth, and the mischievous glint in his eyes has me bracing for what I know will be a bratty comment.

"He does have a nice ass though," he comments in a serious tone, slowly blinking at me with false innocence.

Okay, even I wasn't prepared for that.

"Oak, he's practically your brother!" I shout. But I can't stop myself from laughing as I scold him. "You can't say things like that about your brother's fiancé."

"My family's treated you like a brother for years, and I'm constantly thinking about your ass," he says casually.

He did not just call me his brother. I roll on top of him so that I have him pinned to the bed, staring at him seriously as he grins up at me with wide eyes. "I am not, nor have I ever been 'like a brother' to you. Shut the fuck up with that shit. You've always been my best friend and it is perfectly normal for people to have sex with their best friend, *not with their brother,"* I insist, grinding my hardening cock down into his.

"Calm down, Ranger. Obviously, I'm joking," he says rolling his eyes, but the smug look he can't quite hide makes it clear his comment was meant to get a rise out of me.

"Brat," I mutter, moving off of him. "We should get ready. We need to leave soon."

WE MAKE a lap when we arrive at Oakley's grandparent's house, saying hello and making sure we see everyone before we focus on our game. The Turkey Bowl has been happening since I met Oakley. Even before I was included in the festivities, I remember him talking about how excited he was for it, and him bragging about winning to his brothers who were on the losing team. There's an actual gold trophy they engrave every year with the team captain's name and the brothers all fight for the prime spot. His grandfather no longer plays, but his dad takes it just as seriously as Oak.

"Okay, everybody listen up!" Gregory yells, immediately getting the attention of the crowd that's gathered in the giant backyard. "We have some fresh blood here today, so we need to make sure our teams are evened out and everyone knows the rules. Anyone who wants to play, please line up over by the treehouse there, spectators please move onto the back deck for your own safety. From this moment on, if you're in the grass, we'll assume you're playing. This is *flag* football people, but we all know how rough things can get! You've been warned."

A few people move to the back deck where our moms are

already set up with mimosas petting Spot, and Beck's new rescue, Duke. All of Oak's brothers—plus Cody, Jordan and Adrian—are gathered by the tree ready to play. The crowd also includes a few cousins, some of Oak's brothers' friends, and even Jordan's dad, the only other person who's Greg's age and is still willing to participate instead of drinking on the deck.

"Last year's winning team captain, Oakley, please step forward with your selection of which family member will be the second captain," his dad dramatically announces.

Oak wears a cocky as fuck smirk as he walks forward to face the crowd. "Cody, as an official welcome to our family, and as a congratulations on your recent engagement, I would like to nominate you as our second team captain. Beckett, don't think that means I'll go easy on you," he warns.

"Who says I'm picking Beck?" Cody teases as he bounces to Oakley's side and everyone laughs. Cody tends to have that effect on people, leaving everyone around him laughing and smiling no matter the situation. When we were kids, I used to wish I could be more like that, the way that Oakley was, but I'm glad I've let go of those thoughts and can appreciate that it's okay to not be the person everyone is drawn to. Especially on a day like today where I don't want anyone looking at my relationship with Oakley too closely.

Cody chooses first and *does* pick Beckett, surprising no one. Oak chooses me like he always does and then it's a mix of the three other Caldwell brothers and their friends and family. The dads act offended when they're chosen toward the end, but Cody picks them both for his team and they're happy to be together.

The game starts out with Oak acting as our quarterback, throwing an easy pass to me. I'm able to quickly dart around Lincoln's attempts to pull off the flags clipped around my waist, he's probably way too short to be covering me, and we score the first points. Cody congratulates us, but Beck and Lincoln look pissed. Their frustration only grows as Jordan's dad fumbles an easy pass, and we regain possession without them scoring.

"Wow, I thought we might have to try this year with Cody joining your team, but it looks like you'll be the one's singing yet again, Beck," Oak taunts as we get ready for the next play.

The losing Caldwells have to perform a holiday carol on the ice before the national anthem during a home game in December. The bet's been going on since Oak's grandpa was playing with his own siblings and it's become a fan favorite, blasted all over social media. The stakes are definitely high since none of them can sing, and Beck hates cheesy public displays. I know the players love it when he loses, though.

"Fuck off, Oakley," Beck fires back, and as competitive as I am, I can't help but laugh to myself at how into the sibling rivalry they both get. And not just them, Lincoln looks equally pissed as he gets ready to cover me, and Harrison and Dominic on our team are throwing their own taunts at the opposition. As the two eldest, Beckett and Oakley always seem to be the ring leaders though.

Oak gets the football, and turns toward his younger brothers looking for an opening. They're both being covered, so I raise my hands, not needing to do any more to draw his attention. His throw is a little long and I rush to get under it just in time. As soon as I have possession, I'm knocked to the ground by a heavy weight colliding into my side. The fall is more disorienting than painful, and I do a quick check to make sure my pump and monitor are still in place, but I'm good. Before I can even get my bearings to figure out what happened, Oakley is dragging Lincoln off of me and shoving him away with both hands.

"What the fuck are you doing? This is flag football, you fucking asshole!" Oakley's yelling right in Lincoln's face, shoving him back again.

Lincoln looks just as surprised as I feel at Oakley's outrage, muttering, "I tripped. It was an accident," as he backs away.

I've never seen Oakley yell at anyone. Even when he's fought with his brothers in the past, it was never like this. Everyone seems to be frozen in place, unsure of how to handle his unusual reaction. Sure, it's flag football, but there have been years where people get way too into it—I've seen Oakley himself trip or push his brothers in his efforts to win. I might know exactly what happened just now, but the fall felt awkward enough that I'd believe it was accidental.

But even if it wasn't, this reaction is extreme.

"You could have fucking hurt him!" Oakley scolds, face turning red now as he continues to glare at his brother. Beckett seems to be the only one who can move, rushing to Oakley's side. He grabs his hand and mutters something to him about calming down, but I don't think Oak's even noticed Beck's there because he still looks about ready to swing at Lincoln.

"It was an accident, man," Jordan insists, stepping in front of Lincoln so that Oakley can't push him again. Jordan was on our team, so if he's on Lincoln's side, Oakley *really* has no reason to be freaking out like he is.

I finally shake myself out of whatever shock I'm in. Cody and Adrian are here now too, offering to help me stand, and I walk over to Oakley's other side.

"Oak, I'm fine," I say gently, putting my hand on his arm. I feel his shoulders drop as he physically relaxes, turning to meet my gaze. "I'm okay," I repeat, hoping to settle the anger and concern I see shining in his eyes.

He takes a deep breath, his gaze pinging between Lincoln and me, before he finally mutters, "Sorry for freaking out. Just be more careful."

Lincoln apologizes to me, but I wave him off. I really am okay. Oakley's reaction left me more shaken than the fall itself.

"Well, let's get back to it then," Oak says, laughing awkwardly as he picks up the discarded ball and tosses it to Beckett.

I exchange a concerned look with Beckett, both of us unsure about how to handle Oak's outburst. Eventually, he shrugs and the game resumes. It's more subdued than before, and it takes quite a few plays before any of the taunting begins again. Oak stays pretty quiet, but after another hour of play without any further incidents, our team ends up winning by one touchdown. Oakley will get to keep the trophy for another year, but he isn't even bragging about it.

It's too cold to be outside for much longer, so we all head in. Oak's grandparents have a huge meal catered, but most of it's prepared early in the day so that the staff can make it home to spend time with their own families. Oak is still being quiet and I overheard Beck taunting Lincoln about beating him in pool, so I think everyone else was headed to the large game room in their basement.

I grab Oaks's arm before he can follow the crowd downstairs. "Hey, why don't we hang out with Duke and Spot in his room for a bit." I don't love being in huge crowds of people all day, so the Caldwells are used to me excusing myself to spend time with their dog, but I also just want a minute alone with Oak to see if he's okay.

Spot has his own full-sized bedroom. There's a queen bed, a doghouse in the corner in case he wants the privacy, a TV to watch dog videos, and a huge bin full of toys for him to play with. Oak's grandparents don't mess around. Spot is one of their children and they treat him as such. I don't remember his grandpa being such a softie when we were younger, but in his retirement he's become obsessed with their dog, and I know Beck and Cody are very similar in how they've been spoiling Duke.

Oak sits on the edge of the bed, patting his lap for Spot to come and join him. Duke is still warming up to everyone here, so he heads for the little doghouse. Oak's super focused on petting Spot, not talking like he normally would be. He doesn't even look my way when I sit right next to him so that our thighs are touching.

"So, do you want to tell me what happened out there?" I ask, gently bumping our shoulders together.

He huffs out a big breath. "No."

"Okay, but will you?" I push. If he really didn't want to talk about it, I'd give him space. But Oakley and I don't know the meaning of that word. He always wants to talk things through with me, and his silence is kind of freaking me out. *Has today been too much already?* We've barely had to interact in front of other people, I don't think we've been different than we normally are, but maybe after his outburst he's worried about his family suspecting something between us. Adrian already knows. Maybe we're being more obvious than I thought. *That doesn't explain the freak out, though.*

Spot jumps off to join Duke as Oak lays his upper half back on the bed with his feet still on the ground, rubbing his face as he lets out a deep groan. "Fuck, Park, I don't even know what happened. One minute I was passing the ball and the next I was screaming in Lincoln's face. I don't think I've ever wanted to punch someone more."

"Was pretending we've never hooked up in front of your family too stressful?" I ask. I don't know what would happen if Oak decides to change his mind now.

His eyes widen in both shock and defense. "What? No. I've barely even thought about what they would think."

"So, why did you freak out?"

He sits back up looking me right in the eyes. "You really don't get it, do you?"

"Get what?"

"I freaked out because I thought he hurt you!" Oak stands up, running his fingers through his hair as he paces in front of me. "I saw him on top of you on the ground and I just saw red. I've always been protective of you, but… I don't know." He huffs out a big sigh and I feel helpless, wanting to fix whatever is causing him to look so tortured. "If I'm being honest Parker, my first instinct was to drop down to the ground, check you over and then if you were okay, to kiss you. To ignore all of the people around and be able to feel for myself that you were fine and that my fear was unfounded."

I suck in a sharp breath. He wanted to kiss me to make himself feel better? Because he was so worried that I was hurt? That's not what we are. That isn't best friends just fooling around with a guy for the first time behavior. Obviously, we've kissed a lot by now, but other than the first one in front of the girls, the kissing has always led to more. It's foreplay, we don't casually kiss.

He sits back down, avoiding my confused gaze, taking my hand in his and focusing there. "I think I was upset that I couldn't do that, that I can't just kiss you whenever I want, and I lashed out at Lincoln instead."

Kiss me whenever he wants? What is he saying? Could he feel the same way for me that I do for him?

Stop. He said kiss, not marry, calm down. He doesn't mean anything by it.

Fuck, would it even matter if he does?

Even if Oakley decided that he was okay with giving up that traditional wife and kids daydream that he's always talked about, even if my search history might include information on surrogacy, adoption, and fostering, would we really be willing to risk over twenty years of friendship to start dating? What if we tried to actually date and broke up? Would I be willing to give up my career I've spent half of my life building? I could lose everything: my job, my house, his family that I consider my own.

I don't even want to think about what I would do if I lost Oakley himself. My job is all about calculating risks and planning accordingly with the company's finances. There's just no need to risk everything when I already have so much that makes me happy just the way things are.

Being with him in private is already so much more than I ever thought I'd have for myself.

I try to focus back on the conversation we were having, making an effort to keep my tone light. "So, why have you been all mopey still if you know that I'm okay?"

I squeeze his hand and he finally looks up at me before muttering, "I guess I've been doing a lot of thinking today." He sits up a bit straighter. "I'm already bummed you won't be here for Christmas."

See he isn't saying he wants more with me. He's just upset we'll miss our tradition with his family's Christmas.

I squeeze his hand again, earning a sad smile. "I'll only be gone for a few days and that isn't happening for a whole month. Let's try to just enjoy this holiday, and we can stress about the next one another day."

He rolls his eyes at me. "Fine."

"Stop with the eye rolls, brat," I tease with a smile, and he finally perks up for real.

We spend a few minutes playing with Spot and Duke and the food is quickly announced as ready. Oak's grandparents have a large formal dining room that's off their living room, and for the amount of people that are here, they've added tables extending the dining table into the other rooms in order to fit everyone.

I sit with Oakley to my right, Adrian to my left, and Oakley finally returns to his normal happy self as we chat with his family and their friends. The food is delicious. I try not to overindulge in the carb-heavy options, but the turkey was prepared perfectly, and there's a ton of veggies to choose from. We all go around the room to say what we're thankful for, Adrian makes everyone laugh when he announces that he's thankful for hockey butts, and

I nearly choke when Oakley says he's thankful for new experiences. I manage to find my voice in time to give my standard answer that I'm thankful that the Caldwells have always treated my mom and I like family, and she echoes the statement.

Other than Oakley's little outburst, it's a picture-perfect holiday.

And really is it a family holiday without some sort of drama anyway?

OAKLEY

December

What is wrong with me?

Christmas is tomorrow and I should be wrapped up in blankets with hot chocolate after ice skating in Millennium Park. I should be enjoying the snow everywhere, walking through the city to take in the beauty of the lights twinkling on every tree and building. I should be watching Christmas movies or buying last minute presents for my family. I'll have to go to my grandparent's house soon, but I don't even want to get out of bed. Parker would probably tell me that I'm acting like a brat with how dramatic I'm being, but it's his fault I'm even acting like this.

Parker isn't here.

He left super early this morning in a huge rush, so I didn't even get to say a proper goodbye. Aspen actually woke us up, storming into my room in a panic after not finding Parker in his. Once she knew we were both okay, she muttered a very smug "I knew it," before telling Parker he had one minute to be out the door. We must have both slept through his alarm and somehow she got into our condo.

I'm trying to suck it up and follow through with our plan without throwing some huge temper tantrum, but I'm only barely succeeding.

I miss my best friend, dammit.

But helping Aspen is making him happy, I try to remind myself. I take another deep breath and attempt to ignore the unwelcome thoughts about Parker.

What's he doing with Aspen? Will he always want to be with me behind closed doors? What would he say if I told him I wanted to be more than a friends-with-benefits situation? If I admitted to wanting to publicly date him instead?

The final thought has been consuming far too much of my time over the last month. Before Thanksgiving, I had been happy enough going along with their plan. I liked the idea that Parker was making things easier for Aspen. I just didn't realize that when he'd agreed to meet her family, it would mean I had to be away from him for Christmas.

But even finding that out, he's seemed so all-in with publicly dating Aspen, and I can't really wrap my head around why. How much longer does he plan to do it? He's the one always confirming our plans with them, offering to include them in things we're doing. He's talked about how much they'll like Bora Bora when we visit for the opening, but every time he brings it up, I want to stomp my foot and pout, "but Bora Bora is *our* thing!" and find an excuse to not invite them.

When I almost punched my brother for accidentally hurting Parker, I knew I had to stop ignoring my own feelings—that it was probably time to admit that I care about him in a way that I've never cared about anyone before.

I just don't know how to tell him that.

But sitting here, alone, I can't stop thinking about who isn't here. I can't stop my thoughts from spiraling, questioning what I should do. Being away from him now has made it really difficult to pretend it isn't so much more than that.

Maybe there's a reason that I've *always* been so drawn to Parker. Even when we were younger, he's always meant more to me than any of my other friends. He's always been my person. Maybe I've always wanted him to be more.

Is that love? Am I in love with him?

Why am I even pretending like I don't know the answer to that? I obviously am.

I feel incomplete when I'm not with him, like a part of my soul is missing. I constantly crave his calm, steady presence at my side to set me at ease. I love how strong he is. Not physically, although I definitely enjoy that too, but how he hasn't let the shitty hand he was dealt in life break him. Between his diabetes diagnosis and losing his dad at such a young age, it's a wonder that he isn't ever bitter or resentful.

I love everything about who he is as a person. The small things like his fascination with numbers and patterns, how he lights up when he solves a puzzle or finds a way to bring my latest vision to life at work without sending us over budget. I love his kindness and desire to help others without expecting anything in return, which is the whole reason we're apart right now as he helps Aspen.

I have no idea when exactly I fell in love with Parker, but I'm done lying to myself about it.

I love him, and I have no idea if it even matters.

If I was confident that he felt the same way, then I wouldn't hesitate to tell him. To stop pretending like our arrangement is purely physical and date for real. We already live together, work together, do everything together. There are married couples who are far less attached than we are, and I know that dating Parker would be serious. There would be no casual dating for the two of us, but I don't want that from him anyway.

The time I've spent fooling around with Parker has been the best of my life, and if he'd agree to it, I'd marry him tomorrow.

But I have no idea what he wants when it comes to me. I'm usually so attuned to him that I know how he'll react to something before he even gets the chance to do it, but this is different. He hasn't given me any indication that he would want more with me. He hasn't once hinted at wanting more, even at Thanksgiving when I admitted to wanting to kiss him in front of everyone, he brushed it off.

So, I haven't said anything more. I've ignored the times I've wanted to kiss him outside of sex, and I've held back from pushing about his motives for wanting to continue to help Aspen for so long. I'm ignoring the fact that all I can think about as I picture future Christmases is what a little Parker would look like calling me dad.

I think this is the first time in my life I've ever really been afraid of something. Like, truly, paralyzed by my fear. I'm usually so confident, so sure that things will work out, that I don't hesitate to go after what I want and deal with the consequences later. I've always been popular, I've always had my family's money to fall back on. Even at work, I have my dad on the board to support me if I suggest something not everyone agrees with.

But the fear of losing Parker if I do or say the wrong thing—that is fucking terrifying. I don't think he would ever intentionally cut me out of his life, even if I did royally mess something up between us. But what if I told him how I really feel, and he doesn't feel the same way? What if this really has just been fun experimenting for him? Or a convenient hookup for someone who's never loved dating? What if I tell him and he feels sorry for me? He could put distance between us, or knowing Parker and how important I am to him, he might try to force something he doesn't really feel in an attempt to make me happy.

There are so many ways our relationship could change, hurting one or both of us, and I can't seem to find my usual courage to ignore them to go after what I want.

So here I am, stuck alone on Christmas Eve, wrapped in a blanket that smells like Parker, wishing that I was with the man I love instead, but too afraid to do anything about it.

PARKER

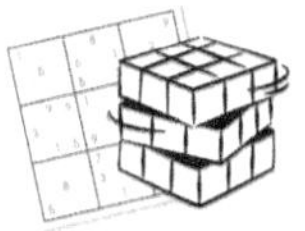

December

Today is an absolute mess.

It was pretty jarring to be violently woken up by Aspen when I'm so used to Oakley's face being the first thing greeting me, it completely threw me off. Especially because she was truly concerned and her fearful expression immediately triggered my fight-or-flight response.

I'd jumped out of bed, looking around for Oak, who was still half asleep and seemed very confused by what was going on. Once Aspen and I had calmed each other down enough for me to realize we were already running late, she said something under her breath about finding Oakley and I in bed together, but at that point I was rushing to throw my toiletries into my bags and running out the door, I didn't have time to really care that she'd caught us together. Of all people, Aspen knows what I'm going through. Except her situation actually worked out really great for her. *If only.*

Apparently, she got into our place by begging the doorman

because she was worried I might be passed out from low blood sugar.

She's been around me, and Oakley's constant worrying about me, enough to know the basics about my diabetes, but I was still a little surprised that she's been paying that much attention. It's nice to be reminded how great my friends are, even if I feel really bad about stressing her out.

I'm still wearing the sweats I slept in last night, so I'm really hoping her parents don't pick us up from the airport themselves. I doubt they will because from everything she's said about them, they don't seem the type to go out of their way to greet us, but they definitely seem like the type to judge me for sweatpants. *Why am I doing this again?* I really hope Aspen figures out a way to get her dad out of her company while we're there.

I've also never been a big fan of flying.

There are so many things that can go wrong and derail even the most carefully laid plans, and today it seems like anything that can go wrong, will. I'm so mentally exhausted trying to deal with it all that I've given up any hope of enjoying this trip.

Not that I've been particularly excited about it because being apart from Oakley and our families for Christmas is going to suck.

Mom was scheduled to work Christmas this year anyway, so she and I will do something next week. I told her I was going to Atlanta with a friend to help them deal with their unsupportive family, not giving too many details because I didn't want her getting any ideas that I'm dating anyone. She isn't on social media, so she wouldn't have seen any of Aspen's posts, and I'm hoping to avoid the full explanation since the arrangement should be over after this anyway. She said that she'd want more details after the trip, so I can tell her everything then.

It took forever to check our bags, and the security line we're stuck in is way longer than I'm used to with it being Christmas

Eve. I'm starting to get worried we're actually going to miss our flight.

After what feels like hours, it's finally our turn to load our carry-ons onto the belt so we can go through security. Of course, for me, that means requesting additional screening to avoid the body scanner that could mess up my insulin pump, which means even more time on top of whatever time it takes me to explain my insulin and supplies and for them to wipe it all down to check for illicit materials. I'm allowed an extra bag for medical supplies, but I hate carrying extra stuff around the airport, so I always have it in the backpack I use as a carry-on.

Except when I go to remove my insulin and extra supplies from the insulated pocket where I always put them with a TSA-approved ice pack to keep them at the correct temperature, the pocket is empty.

Fuck.

I must have forgotten to add them this morning with how distracted I was.

Fuuuuck. Fuck, fuck, fuck.

I take a deep breath. No need to panic, it'll be fine. I changed everything last night, so my pump's reservoir has a good amount of insulin, which I usually only change every two to three days anyway. If I avoid carbs, I can stretch that even longer, and we're flying home first thing on the 26th. I put in a new sensor then too, and those only need to be changed every week or two, so I won't actually need anything.

Aspen must see the panic on my face. "Everything okay?"

I take one more deep breath willing my features to calm. "Yeah. I meant to add my phone charger to my bag this morning and forgot. No big deal, I can get another one when we land." I actually did forget my phone charger, because of course I did with how today is going, and I decide not to worry her further with the news of my missing supplies. She eyes me skeptically but drops it, and we eventually make it through security.

"Do we have time for coffee?" she asks hopefully, looking longingly at the coffee shop we hurry past.

"I'm sorry, but I don't think so, they've already called our flight overhead to start boarding," I remind her apologetically as we continue to our gate. We're not the last to board, but rushing around this morning has been so stressful that I feel like we've accomplished something amazing by the time we're both in our seats on the plane.

The flight is only about two hours, so our first-class seats are two wider ones that make a row near the front. Aspen takes the window and gives me the aisle. After the drama of this morning, we both try to distract ourselves. She has a book and I listen to my favorite financial podcasts while playing with the Ghost Cube Oak got me last Christmas.

The first hour of the flight is blissfully uneventful. We're offered snacks and refreshments, and I almost start to believe the day could be redeemed. But then, there's unexpected turbulence. The seatbelt sign isn't even on when the cabin jolts, violently sending the flight attendants who are attempting to finish their rounds to scramble for balance.

The one nearest me is pushing a metal cart full of different drink options up the narrow aisle when it happens. Luckily, they weren't pouring hot coffee or anything, and no one is spilled on. Unfortunately for me, the whole cart is jerked into my arm, snagging on the raised edge of my continuous glucose monitor and ripping it right out of my tricep.

Fan-fucking-tastic.

My insulin pump relies on my continuous glucose monitor to constantly check my blood sugar levels, and the newer pump I have now can adjust the amount of insulin it gives me based on those numbers.

I can tell when my blood sugar is too high or too low depending on what symptoms I experience, but it's been years since I went more than a few hours without a confirmed blood sugar reading. My pump will still give me the continuous rate of insulin, and I can still tell it to give me more or less based on how many carbs I eat, but part of the supplies I left at home included the back up machine I could use to manually check my levels, as well as another continuous glucose monitor sensor.

So now I'm left without any way to actually check my levels.

I'm less sure this will be fine.

ASPEN'S PARENTS send their driver to pick us up. He assures us that her parents are at a church event and that the house will be empty when we arrive, so I'll be able to change into more respectable clothing. I might not actually care what they think of me, but it kind of defeats the point of our whole arrangement if they don't approve of me.

We enter the property down a long driveway surrounded by old trees, passing an elaborate fountain before pulling up at the grand entrance; the mansion has to be worth millions. Once inside, the over-the-top luxury feel is complete with a curved staircase seeming to wrap around the grand piano featured in the large entry space.

"It's obnoxious, I know," Aspen says, rolling her eyes as I take in the detailed moldings and polished marble floors.

"I've been around the Caldwells' wealth enough that I'll be able to feign a polite, unimpressed expression at your parent's stuff if that's what you'd prefer," I offer through a smirk.

There's a mischievous glint in her eyes that I've never seen before. "Yes! That will be perfect. Act underwhelmed and indifferent, it'll quietly piss them off, and they'll respect you more for it."

"Sounds good," I agree with a laugh.

Aspen leads me up the stairs and down a long hallway as she pulls out her phone, showing me a text from her mother that looks like instructions explaining where we're sleeping. "Oh, good. Our room assignments, just in time," she says sarcastically. "Obviously, I've talked about how antiquated my parent's beliefs are when it comes to relationships. That's basically the entire reason we're supposedly dating in the first place, but in case you were doubting just how strict they are, they have us staying in not only separate rooms, but in separate wings of the house."

"Oh darn," I tease, not minding that I won't need to sleep on the floor in a shared room with her to maintain our ruse. Even though we've slept in the same bed before, and I'm confident we could do it again without it feeling awkward in any way, I wouldn't want to.

If I'm being honest, the only person I ever want to share a bed with again is Oakley. "Do we have time to shower before they get back?"

Opening the door to what I assume is my room, she waves me in with an expression that tells me she's already exhausted. "Yeah, just text me when you're ready and I'll come find you so we can do formal introductions."

I nod and enter my room. I take a second to unpack my things, wondering if there's an iron in here anywhere, but I settle on hanging my clothes in the bathroom and hoping for the best. Oakley's been blowing up my phone all day, and I've been trying to keep up with his conversation without completely ignoring Aspen.

OAKLEY

Seriously, this is bullshit. It doesn't feel like
Christmas at all when you're not here.

PARKER

Aren't you with your brothers?

OAKLEY

It isn't the saaaame.

I laugh aloud as I picture him rolling his eyes.

OAKLEY

So, how was the flight? Did you have any
trouble getting there on time after getting up
late?

I'd sent him a quick update on our way to the airport, but didn't have time for details. I hate lying to him, but the truth is, there's nothing Oak could do to help me with the forgotten insulin and other supplies. You're not supposed to put insulin in checked luggage because the temperature can't be maintained as well as in a carry-on, but I confirmed I didn't have any back-ups of my other supplies as well.

It's not like I could walk into a pharmacy and get more. You need a prescription, and even if I tried to call my doctor now, it's Christmas Eve, their office is closed, and I'd hate to bother whoever is on-call to attempt to get one sent here where the pharmacies are probably also closed. On our drive from the airport, I was reminded it's normal for businesses in the south to just close down on Sundays and holidays, even gas stations, so I'm sure the drug stores have similar hours.

I'll be fine. I still have the insulin in my pump. So, I don't tell Oakley about forgetting the medical stuff, but that does remind me, I need a phone charger.

Fuck. Those three words make my heart race. Ever since he casually mentioned wanting to kiss me on Thanksgiving, I feel like I've been reading into his every move, every word, trying to figure out if he's acting and speaking like we're just best friends who hook up or if there's a chance he could be feeling the same way about me that I do for him.

I know we couldn't publicly date without me risking everything, but I can't help it. I want to know if Oakley might reciprocate even a sliver of the love I feel for him. It took me over twenty years to find out I was attracted to my best friend. I'm all but convinced that he's the only one who could ever make me feel like this.

Every moment of my life that's been spent with Oak is better for it. He's added so much sunshine to even my darkest days. Since the first conversation we had when we met, I've been happier, felt less alone in the world, and it's entirely because of him. There's no one else on Earth who could make me feel safer, more secure in who I am, and more appreciated than Oakley does.

Add in how fucking turned on he makes me now that I know I'm attracted to him. How the moment we're alone, I want to tear off his clothes and kiss every inch of his body, how I want him inside of me, connected as much as physically possible. Even if we're destined to be with other people, I know I'm lucky to have experienced this kind of connection with someone at all.

PARKER

Miss you too, have fun with your family. I have to shower and get ready to meet the parents.

OAKLEY

Fuuuuck, don't tell me you're about to be naked when I'm not allowed to sneak away and video chat.

Damn, that sounds hot. Oak and I are always together, so there's never been a need to video call or send each other dirty texts, but the idea has blood rushing to my cock.

PARKER

Next time.

I have no idea how long Aspen's parents' church thing is, so I end up rushing through my shower and get ready quickly. She comes back to get me and offers a tour of the house, and I appreciate that it's a very practical tour meant to help me get around the place, rather than focusing on any of the expensive decor or design. After it's done, we decide to sit outside by the pool.

We grab some water to drink, and she tells me more about what to expect with her parents. She doesn't have any siblings, but she does have a few cousins who will be joining us for the formal Christmas brunch tomorrow morning. She doesn't get along with any of them, explaining that her dad and his brother always pinned them against each other, trying to always have their kid be the best. The cousins are also the ones who would get more money from the trust if Aspen is cut-off, and she hates that her money will likely end up in their ungrateful hands.

When her parents get home, it's nearly dinner time. Between the travel and the time change, we skipped lunch, and I'm starving. Her family has a personal chef who we met on our tour. They've been inside preparing dinner, but they left as soon as it was ready.

After introductions, we all sit down in a very formal dining room, and my stomach makes an obnoxious sound, letting everyone at the table know just how hungry I am. Dinner is a meatloaf with asparagus, so the main source of carbs would be whatever sauce they're serving with both, and if they used bread-crumbs in the loaf. I should have asked the chef for an ingredient list before they left, but I have a headache, probably from how little I've eaten today, and it's made me a little foggy mentally.

The food tastes great, though, and I'm tempted to ask for more when I finish, still not really feeling full. I make an educated guess on the amount of carbs. Since I've been diabetic for so long, it's second nature to me, and I program my pump with how much insulin I need.

"Young people and their phones, I swear, Mary. The men at the office can't stay off of theirs for an entire meal either. They don't even realize they're being disrespectful," Aspen's father says to his wife, presumably about me using my pump. Apparently, checking a phone would be rude, but he's allowed to talk with a mouth full of food.

"That's his insulin pump, Father. I told you that Parker has diabetes," Aspen defends, sounding as exasperated as I feel.

Both of her parents seem like shitty people in general, and it's clear they think their money makes them more important than other people. I expected having to come here as Aspen's fake boyfriend meant I wouldn't get along with them, but still, I had underestimated just how much patience I would need to have during one meal in their presence. I'm trying to play my part and not rock the boat, but they're making it difficult.

"Parker, what is it you do again?" her father asks, turning his full attention to me with what is probably meant to be an intimidating glare. The conversation during the meal was mostly about the plans for tomorrow, but I guess we've moved onto interrogation time.

"I'm the CFO of Caldwell Hotels," I say, kind of hating that I know these people will be impressed by my title, but at least I'll be playing my role of acceptable boyfriend well.

They both give approving hums, nodding like I've passed a test. *As if they didn't know exactly what I do already.* Then her father launches into more complaining. "I'd bet you deal with a lot of bullshit from your employees too. Just last week we were expecting a shipment of new supplies and had another delay. The office manager, this gay Latino kid who's probably way too young to be in charge of anyone at like twenty-five, no doubt a diversity hire, had the audacity to blame the weather. If you know your supplies are coming from the north in December, make a fucking plan for that, don't come crying to me that now we're going to be over budget and behind our timeline."

Aspen cuts in before I get the chance. "Father, that man's race, age, or sexual orientation have no impact on his ability to do his job. They were completely unnecessary details to include in your complaint."

He rolls his eyes. "I was just describing him so you could have a visual. There's nothing wrong with that."

"There actually is something wrong with it. You sound racist, homophobic, and like you're discriminating based on his age. If you talk like that at work, I'm shocked you haven't had HR complaints."

I love that Aspen isn't afraid to put him in his place, even if she isn't comfortable living her full truth with them. Her father humphs out a big sigh, rolling his eyes again. "I swear, the more time you spend in that city, it's like I don't even know you anymore."

"Honestly, darling, you should know better than to talk back to your elders like that," her mother adds in a sugary tone that's probably intended to mask her poor attitude.

"Well, as much fun as this has been, I think we're ready to call it a night," Aspen announces, dramatically pushing her seat out from the table. I hurry to follow her, giving her parents a quick nod goodnight, and her mother calls out something about making sure we sleep in our own rooms.

It's still pretty early for us to actually go to bed, so we decide to watch a Christmas movie in their home theater. Aspen has somehow never seen *Christmas Vacation*, so we put it on, attempting to distract ourselves with fake family holiday drama that is far more entertaining than our own.

Even though I went during dinner, I have to go to the bathroom again before we can start the movie, which of course has me worried that my blood sugar is already climbing because frequent urination can be a symptom.

But I've also had a lot to drink today. I jumped at the offered coffee on the plane, and the dry air usually makes me thirsty, so I had a few cups of water as well. I'm not sure how much, though, since the flight attendant kept refilling my glass. And I've had more since being here.

Being thirsty is another symptom of a high blood sugar level.

I check my pump for what feels like the hundredth time since my monitor was pulled out and confirm that my continuous insulin rate appears to be delivering properly.

Then why do I feel like my blood sugar is high? Am I just psyching myself out?

I stick to water during the movie, not wanting to deal with more carbs, especially because I'm worried I might have underestimated how much insulin to give myself for dinner. I'm feeling dehydrated, and my muscles are feeling tight, which happens when my levels get high, so I program the pump to give myself even more insulin, confirming that there's still plenty of the medication in the reservoir, and try to relax.

The movie is one of my favorites. Oakley and I usually spend Christmas Eve watching it while we wrap presents, and when I send him a picture, he sends a similar one back that he's also watching it. I like that even in different states, we're still in sync. But after the stress of today, I'm having trouble focusing.

When it's over, Aspen walks me back to my room so I don't get lost, and we stop for more water on the way. My mouth is really dry, and my muscles feel like they're being squeezed to the point of pain—*my blood sugar is definitely high.*

I give myself even more insulin, but at this point, I'm worried there might be a problem with my connection site. I've given myself way more insulin than the amount of food I've had today should have called for, but I don't think my level has gone down at all. As much as I'd like to say I'm just being paranoid and that my symptoms are a result of me being worried, I can't keep ignoring that I'm also nauseous, another concerning symptom.

Even though it's getting to be pretty late, and I'm exhausted. I know I won't be able to sleep with my blood sugar so high. When we make it back to my room, I can no longer deny that something is seriously wrong. I have to jog the final few feet, rushing into the en suite to throw up.

"Holy shit, Parker. Are you okay?" Aspen rushes into the bathroom, apparently undisturbed by seeing me getting sick. "What do you need?"

It's time to admit defeat.

When I'm sure I can answer without anything else coming up I take a deep breath and say what I probably should have hours ago. "The hospital."

OAKLEY

December

OAKLEY

This movie isn't as funny without you to say all of the lines with me

OAKLEY

I don't know how I'm going to sleep tonight without you in my bed.

OAKLEY

Was that weird to admit? I know we haven't really been talking about what hooking up means, but I'm getting sick of filtering myself to you—I never have before

OAKLEY

Fuck, why did I say that over text. Ignore me, I'm just being overly sentimental about us missing out on our Christmas traditions

OAKLEY

I'm choosing to believe that your phone died and you haven't found a new charger yet, not that you're ignoring me…

OAKLEY

Also, did the plane mess up your monitor or something? I got the alert that it went offline in my app when you were on your flight but it never turned back on. Can you at least reset that so I know you're okay?

OAKLEY

Fuck it, I already sound really clingy, I might as well go all in. I really miss you. Merry Christmas, Parker

OAKLEY

Charge your damn phone.

I'm staring at my unread texts from last night, refreshing the screen like that will somehow change the fact that Parker hasn't even opened them. He has read receipts on, but the last message he saw was the picture I sent of my brothers and I watching *Christmas Vacation* too.

Logically, I know that means his phone must have died and he couldn't find another charger, but emotionally, I feel like something is wrong. My anxiety is already through the roof being away from him, add in not getting any responses, and I'm worried I might have some sort of outburst soon. I'm sure I'll be anxious for a whole other reason when he actually does read those messages, because I did sound more lovesick than I intended, but for now, my focus is on making sure he's okay.

I had trouble falling asleep last night with his lack of response, but I had tried to reassure myself that he didn't bring a phone charger, and that he'd find a way to charge it in the morning.

Yet here we are, *and it's well past morning.* It's nearly two PM on Christmas day and still no response.

Aspen also isn't responding. I texted Sage, and she hasn't heard from her either. I'm staying at my grandparents' house for the holiday and none of my brothers or any of the other friends we've texted have heard from Parker either. I tried to hold back from texting his mom, not wanting to worry her if he's just without a charger, or if I said something wrong and he's ignoring me, but I gave up on that a few hours ago. My heart sank when she said she also hadn't heard from him, and we promised to update the other when we do.

My brothers know I'm distracted and they've been trying to cheer me up, but there's no use. I'm sitting on the couch with Spot, waiting for dinner to be served, ignoring my relatives. Trying to put on a happy face for the sake of my family is rough since I don't actually know what, or if, anything is wrong. But if Cody's worried expression as he stares at me from the opposite couch is any indication, I don't think I'm doing a very good job of hiding my worry.

"Still nothing?" Beck checks. I shake my head, my leg bouncing uncontrollably with my pent-up nerves.

"Aspen must have forgotten her charger, too," Cody offers, again.

We've all speculated why they would both be ignoring me because they stopped responding around the same time late last night. There's no reason either of them would be leaving the house at midnight on Christmas Eve, so a car crash seems unlikely. *Unless they left to find a phone charger.* But the stores would be closed so that doesn't really make sense either.

I've also been checking any Atlanta news channels I can find. Surely if there was some sort of tragedy, someone would be reporting on it, even if they didn't include names. *So if they're okay, why aren't they responding?*

Finally, my phone vibrates, and my entire body seems to soar with hope when I go to answer, assuming I'll see Parker's name on my screen.

But it isn't him.

It's Aspen.

Which means something bad happened to Parker.

My gut drops and I go cold, like the blood has been drained from my body, stealing any sign of life from inside me. I'm sure I look like I've seen a ghost as I jump up from the couch, leaving the room as I desperately pick up the call. "Aspen, what's wrong?" I demand.

I know without a doubt that something is wrong with Parker if she's the one calling me back after all this time. He would understand how anxious his lack of response would have left me. He'd be doing everything that he could to get a hold of me, to reassure me that he was okay.

"Parker's fine," she chokes out, attempting to reassure me, but the words do little to calm my racing heart.

"Aspen, tell me what the fuck is wrong!" I shout.

I know I'm way too loud and that the whole family can hear me yelling from where I ran into the hallway. I do try to calm down as I take deep measured breaths. Still, it's hard not to keep yelling at Aspen, because clearly something is wrong with Parker, and she didn't stop it from happening. *Probably not her fault.* I remind myself of that but logic and reasoning can only go so far when my anxiety over Parker's well-being has been so high all day. It's poisoned my every thought with intrusive, worst-case scenarios. I know I won't be able to calm down until I can physically see for myself that he's okay.

It's only been a moment, but it feels like an eternity before she finally answers. "He's in the hospital, but he really is fine! They said his blood sugar was high. He stopped throwing up—"

My eyes widen. "He was *throwing up?*"

"—*but* they gave him fluids to replenish his electrolytes. He's in good hands, Oakley."

Even though she says it, I don't believe it. There's so many things that could go wrong here. If it was bad enough that he needed to be hospitalized, I can't just stay here and do nothing.

I take in another deep breath, trying to level out my breathing before I respond. I don't want her to think I'm angry, but *fuck me*, she could have called me sooner. "Thank you for calling."

She sighs over the other end of the line, guilt written in her tone. "I'm sorry I couldn't call sooner. We just found a phone charger—"

"It's okay," I rush out. I don't mean to interrupt her, but I don't care to hear anything other than information that will get me to Parker. "Please give me the address."

"Okay," she says through a small tremble. She rattles off the address of the hospital they're in. Before I can hang up, she stops me. "Oakley, I really am sorry."

"Thanks, Aspen. See you soon."

When I hang up, I'm shaking, adrenaline racing through my body with nowhere to channel it as I pull up a rideshare app to request a car to the airport.

"Is Parker okay?" Cody asks as he enters the hallway. I'm assuming he and Beck probably waited to give me privacy, but they both look alarmed when I flash the rideshare app.

"He's in the hospital with diabetes complications. Aspen said he's okay, but I'm going to Atlanta. He needs me."

"I'm glad he's okay and in the hospital with professionals who can help him," Beck says with a loud exhale, obviously relieved by the news. "I get that you want to be with him, but are you sure you want to leave without even saying goodbye to our parents or grandparents?" Beck checks, following me as I put on my shoes and walk outside.

"I can't wait, I need to be there." I insist, pacing as I check the app again.

"Oak, he's going to be okay," Beck tries, reaching out to place a hand on my shoulder, but I shrug it off.

"You can't know that!" I insist. "I never should have been away from Parker to begin with, this never would have happened if I'd been there," I point out, voice cracking as I spin to face him. "I promised. All of those years ago, when he first got diagnosed and almost died. It was the scariest moment of my life, but his dad promised me he wouldn't let anything happen to Parker. And then his dad died, and I took on that promise. I swore to him he wouldn't end up back in the hospital, that I would be there to make sure it never happened again."

"Oakley, you have to know it's not your fault," Cody tries to reassure me but there's no use.

Any sense of a filter I had is gone with all of the stress, and I can't stop the thoughts flying through my mind from spilling out of my mouth without my permission. "I love him. I'm in love with Parker and I should have been with him today. Not just because it's Christmas, or because he was struggling and I could have made it easier on him, but because I want to be with him all the time. Every moment that we're together is better than when we're apart. His presence settles something inside of me that I can't explain. It's like a part of me is missing when I'm not with him. And I'm an idiot for not realizing it sooner, for not seeing what was right in front of me."

Beck looks a little smug at my confession, and Cody is beaming at me, but neither looks surprised. I've probably gotten my point across already, but I keep going. "I don't want to wait until we're alone to be able to touch him. I don't want to hide the fact that I'm in love with him from my own family." My voice is calmer now, each word seemingly loosening the imaginary chains I've felt tightening around my chest, slowly suffocating me the longer I went on pretending Parker and I are just friends.

"Keep us updated. Go get your man," Beck says with a smirk as my driver pulls up and I promise I will.

By the time I'm at the airport, I've booked a seat on the next flight to Atlanta. Luckily, there was a flight because if driving had been faster, I was prepared to pay my Uber driver an exorbitant amount of money if it meant getting to Parker sooner.

Other than the wallet that was in my pocket, I didn't bring anything with me since I walked right out of my grandparents' house and came straight here. I get through security quickly, and learning from Parker's mistake, I buy a phone charger before I get to my gate. I make a quick call to Parker's mom, updating her on what I know and that I'm on my way to him. She asks if she should come too, but I assure her I'll make sure he's okay and that I'll call with any updates. I can tell she's hesitant to agree and that she wants to see for herself that he's okay, but she admits that Parker would hate it if she made a fuss and makes me promise to video call as soon as I can.

The flight feels like it drags on forever, but eventually I'm pulling up in another rideshare at the Atlanta Hospital. I guess it's only been a couple of hours since I first heard from Aspen, but in a way, I feel like a different person than I was when I answered her call. I have new priorities, a new perspective on what's important in my life, and I'm finally ready to fight for it.

I've spent the entire time thinking about what to say to Parker. Aspen texted that she left while Parker was still sleeping to get some sleep herself, so I shouldn't have an audience at least. I need to be honest and tell him how I really feel, but as I enter the lobby to check in, it's like my mind has gone blank.

"I'm here to see Parker Leighton," I tell the security guard, who already looks annoyed.

They type something into their computer before turning back to me. "Intensive care visiting hours ended over an hour ago. You can come back at eight AM."

Yeah, that's not happening.

I take a deep breath and flash my most charming smile. I'm fully prepared to yell and throw my name and money around, barge my way past this guy if I need to, but I'll try to be nice first. "Listen, I don't know what I need to say to get in there, but I need to see him. I just walked out of my family's Christmas party without saying goodbye, and jumped on the first flight here to see the man that I'm in love with because finding out that he was in the hospital and I wasn't there for him when he needed me nearly broke me. I need to see him for myself, to make sure he's okay, and that he knows we never should have been apart for Christmas, for any day. I spent the entire flight planning speeches, picturing a dramatic reunion where I can confess my feelings after putting in all of this effort to be here *today,* and none of that is going to work if I have to wait another twelve hours to do it."

The guy looks amused now, smirking as I keep going. "I don't care who I have to bribe, or if I need to claim to be family, or his partner, or his husband. I want all of that to be true anyway. So just tell me what to say and I'll say it, but respectfully, I will be seeing him tonight. So how can we make that happen?"

He eyes me for another moment before finally smirking, holding up one finger as he picks up the phone in front of him to make a call.

"Hello, are you the charge nurse tonight for the ICU? I've got the husband for 2108 who just flew in requesting permission to visit after hours. He seems pretty desperate, but I don't think he'll cause any trouble." He laughs at whatever she says, before ending the call. "Apparently, his girlfriend was with him all day. Lucky for you, the nurse is intrigued enough to want to hear more about your drama, so she'll let you visit after hours."

He gives me a pass and wishes me good luck before directing me on how to get to Parker's room. Exiting the elevator onto his floor, it's like I'm eleven years old again, scared and desperate to see for myself that my best friend is okay, only now I know he's so much more than that.

When I enter the room, I'm frozen for a moment as I take him in. He's laying in bed in an ugly hospital gown, with wires connected to his chest that I think are showing his heart rate on a monitor next to the bed. The soft steady beeping assures me that even though his eyes are closed, he must be alive—sleeping and not in a coma again like my anxiety has been trying to convince me he would be. There are tubes coming out of both arms, connected to bags of fluids and medications hanging from the pole on the other side of his bed.

The scene is peaceful, and there's no staff in the room. Logically, I know that means he must be stable, not fighting for his life like I kept picturing on the way here. But he looks so sick, so vulnerable in a way that my strong best friend never should. It breaks my heart that I wasn't able to prevent this from happening. My guilt is threatening to consume my every thought. I know Parker won't blame me, but I don't know if I'll ever forgive myself that he ended up back here.

I need to get over myself, though, and focus on being there for him in the future, and that starts with telling him the truth now.

I finally shake off whatever fear had me hesitating and rush to his bedside. I don't want to wake him up.

I know that I should let him rest, but I can't stop myself from leaning in and placing a soft kiss right on his lips.

PARKER

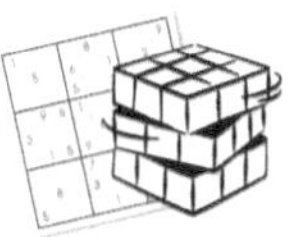

December

Soft lips brush against my own, rousing me from sleep.

Oakley. His mouth on mine is the most comforting feeling I've ever experienced—a sense of belonging, of home that I've only ever associated with him. I chase his lips as he tries to pull away, my eyes aren't even open yet, and I'm ignoring the soft beeping that must be his alarm. I'm not ready to be apart from him.

There's stubble on both of our faces, and I love the rough scratch of it rubbing together as we deepen the kiss. He's firmly cupping both sides of my face, tongue licking into my mouth desperately, like he wants to be inside of me in any way that he can. I alternate fighting him for control of the kiss and letting him take the lead.

I try to move my hands into his hair, but my arm is caught on something, preventing me from reaching him. I pull back to see what it is and he lets go as I finally open my eyes and take in my surroundings. We're not in our condo like my half-asleep mind had assumed. I'm laying in a hospital bed and the thing tugging my arm is an IV.

Shit. How did I forget I'm in the hospital?

The events of the last few days come rushing back to me all at once, and I'm suddenly much more awake.

"Oakley, what the fuck are you doing here? This is still Atlanta, right? How long have I been out if you're already here?" I'm so confused by his arrival that I just keep asking questions without actually giving him any time to respond. I'm pretty confident I hadn't even had the chance to tell him where I was or what had happened yet, but somehow he's already here.

I'd been panicking over telling Oakley everything. I begged every nurse, doctor, lab tech—really anyone who's come into my room—to lend me a phone charger so that I could talk to him, but no one had.

I glance around the room, wondering if Aspen came back, but Oak and I are alone.

"This is still Atlanta," he confirms with a smirk. I'm glad to see that he's smiling. He was so concerned about being apart, and I had to go and end up in here. I expected him to be pissed. "I'm not sure when you fell asleep, but Aspen called me a few hours ago. I think a nurse gave her a phone charger, and she told me what happened. I left right away. I didn't actually bring anything with me. I just walked out of my family Christmas party..." he admits, trailing off like he isn't sure he should have been so honest about dropping everything to be here.

"Won't that worry them?" I point out.

"Beck and Cody saw me leave. I have a feeling my entire family knows exactly where I am," he says in a strange tone that makes me think there's more to that story.

Did something happen? Maybe he ran into an ex while I was gone, or met a man he's interested in and wants to date? Maybe the time apart was all he needed to decide he was done experimenting with me, and now he's ready to find someone to settle down with. Did he come here to end things with me in person so that he could properly date this new mystery person?

One of my monitors starts beeping loudly, pulling my attention away from the dark spiral my thoughts have turned into.

"Woah, Parker. What's wrong?" Oakley's eyes are wide as his gaze pings from me to the monitor. "You're breathing really fast and your heart rate just jumped up."

I try to calm down and force myself to breathe and ask him rather than making assumptions. "Did you come here to end things between us then?" I choke out, not sure I want to hear his answer.

"What? No! The opposite actually. Why would you think that?" he rushes to reassure me, and the monitor stops alarming. It's embarrassing to have such obvious proof of the effect he has on me.

"I just thought that maybe you met someone while I was gone…" I trail off.

"No. We were apart for less than forty-eight hours. Jesus, how am I fucking this up already?" His eyes are wide, pleading with me for something I don't yet understand as he runs a hand through his hair, messing up the usually styled strands. He only manages to look hotter the less put-together he is, though, and I have to force myself to ignore my lust for him and focus on his words as he continues.

"Parker, I came here because I never should have been away from you in the first place. We should both be in Chicago right now, enjoying Christmas with our families *together* like we always have. And you sure as shit shouldn't be in the fucking hospital! I don't know exactly what happened to land you here, but I should have been there to prevent this from happening. I broke my promise. I wasn't there when you needed me, and I'll never forgive myself—"

"Hey, calm down. It's okay," I hurry to interrupt his rant before he can continue any further with that completely wrong line of thinking. "I'm fine, and you didn't do anything wrong. There's nothing you could have done." I don't want him to feel guilty in any way. I think we're both struggling not to assume the worst right now, so I try to reassure him and explain what actually happened. "It's no one's fault that I'm here but my own. There were a lot of things that went wrong; forgotten supplies, my continuous glucose monitor got ripped off, and I guess my pump's insertion site was in scar tissue so I wasn't absorbing any of the insulin it was trying to give me. But I ignored how bad it all really was until it was too late. You couldn't have fixed any of that."

"Well, if we were together, I would have packed extra supplies like I always do and you would have been okay," he insists.

My jaw drops in shock. "You do what?"

He looks away, biting his lip, clearly hesitant to expand on his admission, but after a moment of me staring at him expectantly, he goes on. "I've never said anything because I don't want you to think it's a big deal, or like I don't trust that you can take care of yourself, but whenever we travel, I bring an extra glucose monitor and a backup of all of your supplies."

"Always?" I ask, completely surprised by the quiet support I've never known he's given me. *What else has he done for me without expecting any acknowledgment or thanks?*

"Um, yeah. It's not a big deal. I asked your mom for extra supplies, the first trip we took together back in high school when you came with me to visit Beck at college. I've been to doctor's appointments with you before, and Dr. Martin loves me. She wrote a note for me to carry explaining why I would have insulin with someone else's name on it just in case, but no one's ever questioned it before. They always have to go through your stuff anyway at the airport, you've never noticed them going through mine?"

"No, I have not." *Apparently, I haven't noticed a lot of things.*

"Well, I'll be there next time. I won't let this happen again," he says seriously, taking my hand in his and holding my gaze.

"Oakley, it isn't your job to take care of me," I try to point out.

He rolls his damn eyes again, and I'm not sure what I've done to frustrate him this time. Even though a part of me wants to scold him, I can't get past how much I hate the idea of being a burden.

His expression grows more serious before he finally softly asks, "What if I want it to be?"

I think I'm lost again, not following what he's really trying to say. "What do you mean?"

"What if I want to take care of you?"

"Oak, you already do. You're the best friend anyone could ask for. I had no idea you were that prepared to help me if I needed it. I just don't want you to feel obligated—"

"Fuck, Parker, just let me talk," he interrupts. "The whole way here, I was preparing a big declaration, and I feel like I'm just making it worse. I don't feel obligated to help you because you're my best friend. I *want* to help you because I want to be so much more than that!"

He's squeezing my hand now, like he's afraid I'll pull back or try to break the connection with him, but I'm gripping him back just as tightly.

Could he really be saying what I think he is?

His shoulders rise as he inhales deeply, seeming to hold his breath for a moment as he continues to stare at me, searching my face for something. Whatever it is, he must find it, because he nods sharply before finally letting it out. He continues, his voice more confident than before. "I can't keep pretending like I'm not in love with you, Parker. It's alright if you don't feel the same way, and I really hope that I haven't just ruined everything by telling you, but you're my person, you always have been. I've never had to filter myself around you before, and I can't do it any longer."

I feel like someone's replaced my IV fluids with helium, like if Oakley let go, I might just float away. I'm overwhelmed by the different emotions racing through me: happiness, disbelief, fear. I can't believe he's really telling me this, that Oakley could actually feel the same way about me that I do him. I've been so convinced that this thing between us was purely physical for him, that he still saw me as his best friend, and that I was just a convenient experiment—someone he was comfortable exploring his sexuality with.

He's always been so excited about the idea of getting married one day, of having a wife and family, and maybe I have some ingrained homophobia or biphobia or something else that I was ignoring, but I had just assumed that meant he would still want that exact situation in the future. That he would never consider anything more with me than what we've already been doing.

"It's okay if you don't feel the same way," he murmurs, sounding defeated. "But I needed to tell you how I really feel. I can't keep pretending you aren't everything."

He looks so sad as he tries to pull away, but I don't let him. I use my grip on his hand to tug him even closer, and at the horrible angle, his upper half practically falls onto me. He steadies himself with his other hand on my chest, a questioning gaze in his eyes as he finally looks at me. I want to kiss the wrinkle of worry that's in-between his eyes, smooth it out so that he never looks so unsure again.

"Of course I'm in love with you, Oak. How could I not be?" I can't help my smirk at the way his entire body seems to light up at my confession.

Before I can say anything else, he's leaning in and his soft lips are back on mine. He moves one hand to cup my jaw, the other to tangle in my hair, controlling the angle of the kiss as he deepens it. There's something so freeing about kissing him like this, knowing that it isn't leading to sex, that we both just want the connection. I feel so content just kissing him, finally being together in this casually intimate way that started it all so many months ago, but that we've only allowed ourselves in the private moments of our hookups more recently.

He nips at my bottom lip when he finally pulls back for air, only to move down my jaw, covering it with kisses and continuing down my neck like he wants to claim every inch of my skin with his mouth.

As much as I would love for him to keep going south, I'm in a hospital bed, and I'm shocked we've gone this long without a nurse to come in here to check on us with how erratic my heart rate has probably been over the last few minutes.

"Oak, we should probably cool down. The nurses definitely didn't sign up to walk in on what I want to do to you right now."

He smirks at me with a wicked challenge in his eyes, like that only makes him want to keep going, but I laugh and tug his hair until he's back to being seated upright in the bed next to me. I take his hand in mine once again, interlacing our fingers this time, and I force myself to ignore the lust coursing through me.

I know there's still a lot we need to talk about.

"Oak, what changed?" I hesitantly ask, afraid that he might still be unsure, but I need to know. "I thought that you wanted us to fool around until you were confident enough to start dating men."

"I agreed to keep things physical because I thought you wanted me to, Parker. You mentioned a checklist when we agreed to it, and I was just trying to make you happy," he says softly.

Is he joking? "Fuck, Oak. I only did it for you."

He lets out a sharp, disbelieving laugh. "So, you're telling me we've both wanted more, but because we thought the other one didn't and were too afraid to actually talk, we've both just been pining after each other for months?" he clarifies.

When he spells it out like that, it makes me feel like the world's most oblivious person.

"Apparently," I chuckle.

"So, I didn't fuck up twenty years of friendship by telling you I'm in love with you?" he asks, his smile stretching wider than I've ever seen it.

"Definitely not. Oak, I think you're the only person I could ever feel this way about. I'm so in love with you in a way I didn't know existed until the first kiss changed everything," I agree, mirroring his expression. "What do we do now then?" I ask, unsure of what my own answer would be.

"I do still want a big family like you said," he admits slowly. "I just don't want to do that with anyone who isn't you. I want to be living together as partners, in the same room, eventually I'd love to raise kids that call you dad, too."

I'm struggling to take a full breath with how tight my throat is. I love the sound of the future he's suggesting, one I'd never considered before we kissed. It sounds perfect. It's a future where there's no need for anyone else, and I want it more than anything.

Oakley isn't done talking, though, so I try to stop my thoughts from running away and focus on what he's saying. "You've never really talked about wanting to marry anyone, or have kids. So if that's not what you want, then we can talk about it and figure something out. I don't want to pressure you into anything. The last few months when I've gotten to be with you physically, but had to hold back emotionally, have made it very clear to me that all I really, truly want, is to be with you in every way that I can."

To me, his words are everything, because it's what I want too. I want to keep sharing a house with him, I've always dreaded the day he was no longer my roommate, but now he's saying that day might never have to come. I want to give him the big family that he's always dreamed of having, to be his kid's other parent, to raise them together.

The image of that future seems so clear in my mind, even if this moment is the first that I've ever allowed myself to truly see it as a real option.

I've always known Oak will make a great father. After losing my own so unexpectedly, it hasn't been something I've really focused on for myself, but being a parent with Oakley as my partner sounds like the best possible outcome.

Is this really happening?

Or am I actually in a coma and my swollen brain is providing me with the perfect fantasy of everything I've never known I wanted Oakley to say to me?

He looks at me expectantly, and I decide I need to go along with what's happening as though it's real until proven otherwise. "Oak, you're the only person I've ever loved. I'm fairly certain you're the only person that I could ever be in love with. The whole reason I agreed to the friends-with-benefits thing is that I wanted whatever relationship you were willing to give me," I admit.

"Does that mean we're officially together?" he asks, and the pure joy shining in his eyes as he stares at me like I'm the greatest thing to ever happen to him is equally as intimidating as it is satisfying. I'm ecstatic that, somehow, Oakley loves me back. But I also don't want to disappoint him, and I don't think it will be as easy as deciding we want to date each other.

As much as I hate myself for bringing it up and being the one to potentially upset him, I know we need to stop filtering our thoughts and concerns from one another. That's what led us to being with the girls for so long instead of each other.

"What about our jobs, though?" I point out. "One of the major benefits I saw to dating Aspen publicly was that no one at work would question my qualifications and ability to do my job well if they suspected we were together. You're technically my boss. What if they think I only got my promotion because we're together? What if the board calls to fire me?"

I didn't mean to throw all of my concerns at him at once, but I guess it's good that they're out there. Oakley's eyebrows are pulled together again, and his eyes are unfocused as he looks around the room like he'll somehow find a solution to all of our problems there.

"Then I'll quit," he says simply, like it's an easy decision.

"What the fuck, Oak? You can't quit. Your whole life has been about taking over the Caldwell Hotel brand," I point out.

"I don't think you get it," he says seriously. He's smiling softly, staring right into my soul. I'm captivated by his eyes. They remind me of the endless shades of blue we saw in Bora Bora, the place where this new phase in our relationship truly began. I'm still sort of in shock about everything that's happened today, that he not only loves me, but that he would be willing to put our relationship above literally everything else. Before I can formulate a response though, he's continuing, making me somehow even more emotional. "You're my whole life, Parker. The thing that makes me happier than anything else. I could be happy without my job, but I don't think I could ever be truly happy without you."

My heart is racing again, and he chuckles as he glances at the monitor. I try to take steadying breaths as I think of a way that he wouldn't have to risk his career. "What if we don't tell anyone yet? We could take some time to figure out a better plan," I suggest.

"About that..." he says slowly, looking guiltier than I've ever seen him. "You know how I said Beck and Cody saw me leave?" he hesitantly asks. I nod and he bites his lip before continuing quickly. "Well, I might have blurted out that I'm in love with you and that I was coming here to fight for you."

"Oh," is all I can get out, shocked by his confession, my mind racing with what that means for us if people already know.

"There's a good chance he's already told my entire family in explaining my sudden disappearance. I'm so fucking sorry, babe. I never meant to out you."

"Babe?" I repeat with a smirk, getting hung up on the nickname he's only ever used during sex.

"Can I call you that now? Are you mad Beck and Cody know?" He sounds so concerned, and I never want to be the cause of his worry again, so I quit my teasing.

"You can call me whatever you want, my love." My responding nickname has him looking at me like I hung the moon. I can practically see the hearts in his eyes and I wish I could somehow freeze this moment so that I had time to properly appreciate that the man of my dreams is somehow looking *at me* like that. I don't know what he sees in me that's so special, but I vow to never take it for granted.

"And I'm not mad that they know," I continue. "I'm not upset that you think you outed me. Plus, we don't even know for sure that they've told anyone. Adrian has known about my feelings for you for a while, and I don't think he's told anyone."

"Adrian knows?" Oak asks, tone full of disbelief.

"And Beck and Cody know," I remind him with a smirk as a nurse comes in to check my blood sugar again. She adjusts my insulin drip accordingly and lets us know that my glucose level is almost back to normal, so I should be able to get out of the ICU and into a regular medical room soon if the rest of my labs are also improved. She warns Oakley that the charge nurse approved him to stay overnight, but that if he causes any trouble, she won't hesitate to have security escort him out, so he promises to stay out of her way.

He moves back to the edge of the bed, taking my hand in his. "I know we don't have all of the answers right now, but we love each other, and that's really what matters in the end, right? If we get back and find out that people already know and we need to be public about it right away, can we promise to find a way to work it out?"

Of course I want to find a way to make it work with him. I just wish there was a way for us to move forward without there being so much risk involved. His eyes are filled with so much hope as he waits for me to respond, and I know this isn't truly a decision at all. Oakley said that I was his everything. Well, he's mine, and there's no way I'm about to turn him down, no matter how complicated what he's offering may be.

"So does this mean you're my boyfriend?" I ask, and the joy that replaces his previous worry makes every risk worth it.

"I sure fucking hope so."

OAKLEY

December

*M*y *boyfriend* gets moved into a regular medical room first thing the next morning.

We called his mom last night after things settled down and again this morning with updates. I still can't believe he agreed to date me. When I rushed to see Parker in the hospital, I was really hoping he might admit to having feelings too, but I hadn't dared hope for what that could mean for us.

Honestly, I hadn't given much thought to the consequences of that for us professionally until Parker voiced his concerns about it, and I don't know how exactly we'll get around the things he's worried about, or if they even matter at all, but I'm sure we'll think of something.

Even though I hate that Parker is here and I never want him to have to go to another hospital again, things are definitely looking up for us. *Parker is my boyfriend*. The smile on my face might be permanent at this point with how fucking happy I am.

That is until Aspen waltzes into the room with her own smile aimed at me as she sets down luggage before handing me a coffee. My gut drops. I had kind of forgotten about the fact that she's still technically publicly dating Parker. I don't know if her parents are about to follow her into the room expecting their daughter's boyfriend, or how she'll take the news that we're together.

Aspen takes one look at my conflicted expression and bursts out laughing. "Calm down, Oakley. I caught you two in the same bed and then you rushed across the country to be at his bedside. I know you're together." Then she turns to give Parker her attention, pulling up another chair to join me at his bedside. "I wanted to come and tell you in person that you're officially off the hook." She's still smiling as she continues, so I guess she's happy about how things have turned out so far. "We'd always intended for this arrangement to work out for us temporarily."

Parker doesn't look nearly as nervous as I feel about this conversation. Aspen doesn't seem mad at us though, and assuming this coffee isn't spiked with anything unpleasant, I think she seems to be handling their arrangement ending gracefully.

Parker gives Aspen a soft smile before asking in a teasing tone, "Aspen, are you fake breaking up with me?"

I relax a little, sinking back down in my chair when her expression doesn't change. Then he sits up a little straighter in the hospital bed, looking very serious as he continues. "Aspen, I really hope you got what you needed while I was in here, but even if you didn't, I would just like to wholeheartedly say, fuck your asshole family. Fuck what your evil parents say. You deserve to be happy with Sage."

I'm kind of surprised he said that so bluntly, even though I wholeheartedly agree with him. *What happened before he ended up in here?* Aspen's eyes are watering like she's trying to hold back tears as he continues.

"You're one of my best friends and you'll always be important to me. I want you to be happy. I know it isn't always that simple to be with the person you want to, especially when your family is against it. Oakley and I have had Beckett as our example of queer relationships, and how easy they can be when the people in your life love and support you. But I know that wasn't the case for you growing up here. No matter what you work out, I hope you find a way to be happy, and I would love it if the four of us can remain friends even though our arrangement is over."

I nod along, not wanting to interrupt their moment, but also trying to show my support. Aspen stands up, clearing her throat before leaning over Parker to leave a kiss on his forehead. "I hope you two can find that happiness too," she whispers before straightening again. "I think I got what I need and I'm planning to go straight from here to the airport, so hopefully I won't be seeing anyone I'm related to any time soon. Don't worry, I'm not going anywhere. You're stuck with us as your friends. I've brought the rest of your stuff too," she says, motioning to the bags she left near the door. "Will you head back to Chicago when you're discharged?"

"I haven't gotten that far, but I assume so. Thanks."

"Sorry you ended up in the hospital," she says quietly, like she's also felt some of the guilt I've been dealing with since I found out he was here.

"Eh, I think it's worked out pretty well for me," Parker says, winking at me.

How is a wink so fucking hot? And how much longer does he need to be in here before I can jump him?

The rest of his hospital stay is a blur of nurses, doctors, and lab techs in and out of the room at all hours. The medical floor has more relaxed visiting hours, and they don't care that I spend the night again.

Rationally, I know that Parker is fine now, and if I had to go to a hotel for a few hours, he'd be okay. He's already in the hospital for fucks sake, the people working here wouldn't let anything bad happen to him, but the part of my brain that's always worried about him is still relieved I'm able to spend the night.

He's discharged the next day and we get a suite at the Caldwell hotel in the city so we can both shower and get some actual sleep before heading back to Chicago in the morning. As much as I wish we had the energy for a more exciting night full of orgasms to celebrate our new official relationship, sleep in the hospital was nearly impossible with how often the staff had to come in to check his blood sugar or vitals, not to mention how loud it was with all of the machines and people, so we're both exhausted.

We pass out as soon as we're in bed, but it's okay, because we're together. It doesn't matter if we have sex, or just spend the night wrapped in each other's arms, having him sharing my bed again makes everything better.

When we finally get home, though, I'm practically buzzing with anticipation. Parker is my boyfriend and it's about damn time that he fucks me. I've loved every time we've gotten off together—topping him, exchanging blowjobs, even just using the toys together—and it truly has been the best sex of my life.

But during all of that, we weren't *together* together. We hadn't admitted how we really felt about each other, and I was delaying checking off such a big sex act from the nonexistent list that I assumed Parker was working through. Now that I know he loves me, that there's no end date or limitations on us being together, I want nothing more than for him to claim me in every way that he possibly can. We've been using condoms up until now, I think mostly to avoid any discussion of what not using them would mean, at least that's why I never brought it up, but I don't want there to be anything between us if there doesn't have to be.

I slam the door to our condo as we walk in and spin to face him. "I haven't been with anyone other than you since I ended things with Sage. I've been tested since then and everything was negative. Did you get tested at your appointment last month?"

"Yeah, also negative," he says with a small laugh.

"Well, boyfriend," I say, grabbing his bag from him and tossing it aside. "I think it's finally time for you to top me, and I'd like to skip the condoms if you're comfortable with that."

His smile lights up the whole room. "I've never fucked anyone without one before. You want to be my first?"

"Your first, your last, and every time in between." I know it sounds cheesy when I say it like that, but I really do mean it. I'm so glad he's already agreed to date me, because I have a feeling I wouldn't have lasted long without trying to officially claim him as mine.

He steps in closer, wrapping his arms around me to squeeze my ass, leaning in to talk lowly near my ear. "Let's go shower the plane germs off. I want to taste you. I want to take my time stretching your hole and getting you ready for my cock before I fill you up."

"Damn, Ranger. Bringing out the dirty talk already?" I tease, definitely not complaining. My dick is already thickening as I tug him toward the bathroom, eager to live out what he's promising.

"I don't need to hold back anymore. You've already agreed you're mine, so now I don't have to second guess my every word and action when it comes to how desperately I want you," he answers seriously.

The thought of him doing that, that he's had to filter himself like that around me, is so wild to consider when I've been doing the same exact thing.

I hold out my pinky for him. "Let's make another promise— no more holding back. I hate that we were both so afraid to be honest about our feelings when they changed. We probably ended up hurting each other and ourselves with all of the stress and tiptoeing around. From now on, let's promise to go back to telling each other everything, even if we're not sure about how the other will react. Does that work for you?"

He lets out a soft laugh, wrapping his finger around mine. "Yeah, Oak. I pinky promise, no more hiding from each other."

Then he uses our connection to pull me to him, stepping in until he's close enough to lean down for a quick but passionate kiss. His mouth on mine reminds me of expensive champagne, leaving my lips tingling and my head a little fuzzy as he wraps his arms around my hips to grab my ass once more.

But then his hands keep moving and he's using his grip on me to hoist me up until I'm over his shoulder in a fireman's hold.

I burst out laughing. "What the fuck are you doing?"

"Taking you to be fucked."

"And I couldn't walk there myself?" *Not that I'm complaining, I have a great view of his ass from here.*

"Nah, you said I shouldn't hold back, and this is what I want. To throw you over my shoulder and have my way with you," he teases. His voice is strong, and he doesn't seem to be struggling with the effort to hold me. *Why is that so hot?*

"I could get used to this, ya know. You carrying me around."

"Say the word and I'll have you wrapped around me all day," he promises.

I love the sound of that, and how easily he agreed, but that might not be the most practical plan. "Maybe not at work," I concede. "Or before we tell everyone about us."

We're in the bathroom now, so he sets me down gently on the counter before turning on the water to warm up the shower for us "So, when it's just the two of us then?" he checks. "No more walking for you?"

I smile up at him, blinking in an exaggeratedly innocent way as he walks up to me again, legs between mine. He leans into my space, resting an arm against the mirror behind me.

"I meant it. I think you're the only person I could ever love." He runs the tip of his nose up mine, closing his eyes and just breathing me in as he explains. "I've been talking to Adrian about all of the different labels that are out there, and I think I'm on the Ace spectrum, maybe demisexual."

It's hard to focus with him surrounding me like this, but I also think that this conversation might be important, so I try to work on steady breathing as I meet his gaze, managing to ask, "What does that mean?"

"Well, it can mean a lot of different things for different people, but for me, I think I need to already have a very deep emotional connection with someone before I can be physically attracted to them. When we kissed that first time, it was like it woke up something inside of me that I'd never experienced before. That was the first time I was ever truly aware of being physically attracted to someone in my life."

Fuck, ever? I've heard the terms he's using before, but I've never given them too much thought. "But you weren't a virgin. You weren't attracted to any of the women you've hooked up with before? Or any other guys?"

"Not like this. It was never like it's been with you." He's still running his hands all over me, tracing the muscles of my arms, up my neck, into my hair, as he continues talking, a determined expression on his face. "I'd had sex before because the physical stimulation still felt good, and mostly because I felt pressured to fit in, not by you specifically," he quickly adds before I can panic that I'd failed him somehow without realizing it. "But just by our society in general, so I went along with it. I really had no idea that it could even be like this until after we'd kissed."

I can't help the growing smile on my face as he explains. "So, I'm the only person? Ever? I must be really fucking awesome."

"Without a doubt," he agrees smoothly.

"For what it's worth, you're special to me, too. I've always been drawn to you, wanted to spend all of my time with you. I've been wondering lately how much of that was just us being such great friends, or if a part of me has always wanted to have more with you."

He leans in to claim my mouth with his, and I can't help but groan at how amazing it feels to be able to let go and be with him without worrying about giving away how much I care for him. His lips are soft, dragging against my own in the most teasing way, and I lean back against the mirror so I can give myself completely over to the kiss.

His hands move to my abs, pushing my shirt up, and I hate having to break our connection even for a moment to push it over my head. I help him out of his clothes until we're both naked. He removes his insulin pump, pausing to take a moment to appreciate my body. At least, based on the hungry look he's giving me, that's what I'm assuming he's doing, because I can't take my eyes off of him either.

PARKER

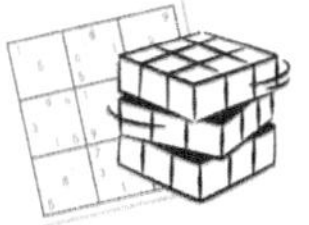

December

I want to do this right.

I want Oakley's first time bottoming to be perfect, for him to enjoy having me fuck him as much as I've loved when he tops me. But I am also struggling to remind myself of that when he looks so fucking sexy, draped across the counter, all of his clothes gone, looking so eager for me as his eyes roam my naked form.

Shower first, then sex.

I quickly scoop him up again, worried that if I allow myself any time to think that I'll change course and take him straight to my bed. But we were just on a plane for a few hours and traveling is dirty, so I need to *focus*.

I check the temperature of the water, making sure it isn't too hot, before putting Oakley down under the warm spray. His body visibly relaxes, and I try not to get too distracted by his hard cock as I grab the body wash. I take my time washing him, rubbing into his muscles, tracing every inch of his body with my fingertips, appreciating as much of him as I can with my touch.

"I could wash myself, ya know," he points out, but his eyes are closed and his neck is rolled to the side. He's completely relaxed, and I love being the one who makes him look so happy.

When he's been thoroughly cleaned and massaged, I quickly wash his hair and my own. He tries to help me with my soap, but I playfully swat his hand away. "Don't be a brat, you promised me your ass and now you're making me wait," I say firmly, raising a brow at his smirk. I help him get a towel, and once we're both dried, I bend down to pick him up and carry him right to my bed, laying him down gently with his head on a pillow while he sports a very smug grin.

"I want to taste you," I say as I move down his body on the bed. "To use my mouth to relax your unused hole before it's finally time to stretch you wide open with my dick."

"Please do," he agrees eagerly, rolling over and presenting his ass to me.

I take a moment to massage his firm cheeks, running my hands over the tempting curves before spreading them and leaning in to lick his hole. He moans at the touch and I don't let up, holding him in place as I eat him out like I'm a starving man and his ass is the first sign of food I've seen in days.

His hips shift, squirming, like he can't help but push back into me, demanding more. I feel high off the fact that my tongue alone is enough to make him so desperate. I pull back slightly, massaging his rim with my finger as I speak. "Stay still, my love. I want to take my time, to enjoy this for everything it is before I add any fingers."

He moans again at the mention of more, and I chuckle as I resume my feasting. Eventually, I ease the first wet finger in, savoring each and every one of the beautiful moans he's making just for me. I'm able to add two as he relaxes. He's shown me which plugs he's been using, and they're much larger than the one he used on me. I know he enjoys the sensation of being filled, and

I'm slightly less concerned over the possibility of hurting him if I rush things than I would be if he'd never used the toys, but I remind myself that I still need to be careful.

"Where're your plugs?" I ask, my voice sounding deep and gravely in a way that even I don't recognize.

"I should still have one in your nightstand."

I scramble to the nightstand and remove one of his largest toys, along with lube, and get it slicked up. To be sure he's nice and relaxed, I start once again with my fingers, making sure his hole is properly lubricated, exploring and stretching him until I have three fingers inside of him.

I've only been teasing his prostate, wanting to really draw this out. I want him ready, needy, and desperate for my cock to fill him, but I also don't want to make him so eager that he rushes things and ends up hurt.

He's squirming now, shifting his hips back, trying to take me deeper.

When I remove my hand, he lets out a desperate moan. "Don't stop," he pleads. He's practically whining now, and I fucking love it. He's looking over his shoulder at me with an arched brow, probably wondering what I have planned next, and as much as I would love to replace my fingers with my aching cock, I force myself to pick up the plug instead. "Sure you don't want to skip the toys and give me your dick already?" he taunts, but there's a bit of an edge to it, like he's trying to convince me to do just that.

I slap his ass, and although I'm sure it wasn't hard enough to feel like more than a light sting, the sound of the smack and the resulting jiggle of his butt from the motion are *very* satisfying. "I'm trying to do this the right way, you brat. Shut up and let me stretch you out properly."

Adding more lube to his hole, I guide the toy to his entrance, slowly pushing it inside of him. His groan is like a hit of a drug. *Not that I've ever done any,* but the high I experience with each sound of pleasure coming from Oakley is what I'd imagine a drug would feel like, and I'm completely addicted. I try to focus on taking deep breaths, ignoring my own desperation to focus on him. "Fuck, baby. You're so beautiful right now," I praise as I fuck the plug into him slowly. "You're taking this so well for me."

"I bet I'd look even better if it was actually your cock inside of me."

I smack him again. "Every time you taunt me, I'm going to wait even longer to actually fuck you," I promise.

He moans and shifts back into the toy more forcefully. "That sounds like a punishment for you too."

"True."

"Seriously, babe. I'm ready." His voice still has the high-pitched tone of a whine, and knowing I'm the one driving him to this point of desperation fulfills some part of me I never knew existed. I feel important, special, powerful. This is Oakley Caldwell, he could have anything or anyone that he wants, and he's begging *me*. "Please. I don't think I'll last much longer if you don't fuck me and I really want you inside of me when I come."

That is an excellent argument, so I finally give in to his request, slowly removing the plug. He's deliciously stretched out for me now, and his hole attempts to clench around nothing as I lube up my cock. I'm harder than I've ever been, but I still hesitate.

"Flip over onto your back," I command, grabbing a pillow to prop his hips on as he reluctantly follows my direction.

"Baaaabe, stop stalling. Please just fuck me already."

I laugh as I get him positioned how I need him. He's on his back now, and I help support his legs as he holds them up to expose his hole to me once again as I kneel between his legs. This isn't a hookup. I don't want to be staring at the back of his head as I enter him. *This is Oakley,* my best friend, the love of my life. I need to face him; I need to be able to kiss him as I finally slide my cock inside of his tight hole.

I'm not a virgin, but there have been women in the past who didn't want to attempt penetrative sex because of my size. It never bothered me before, since I wasn't invested in any of them, but I really want this with Oak and I know he does too, so I hope I don't hurt him.

I guide my swollen tip to his opening and he takes a deep breath, exhaling slowly as I begin to cautiously push inside of him. The feel of his warm, tight body wrapping around my shaft is so much better than I had even dared to hope it would feel. I have to grip his hips, practically pushing him away to prevent myself from chasing more of this pleasure and slamming into him faster than I want to.

I try to hold as still as I can, allowing him to slowly work himself to take more of me. "Damn, Ranger. I know you're big, but this stretch is so good. Fuuuck, I'm so full. I don't know how I could possibly take more," he says with another moan as he shifts further.

"Just wait until you top me without a condom. This is unbelievable. You feel so fucking amazing."

"More. Keep going, keep moving, urgh—" he moans, and I do. I work the final inches of my cock in until I bottom out, my hips meeting his ass, and I finally lean in to bring his lips to my own. I try to pour all of my love and appreciation and desperation for him into the movement of our mouths and the dancing of our tongues.

I can't hold back any longer, grinding my hips to fuck into him, and he meets the motion thrust for thrust. I blindly search for the lube next to us on the bed, refusing to separate from his mouth. When I find it, I'm able to add some to my hand, moving it to work his weeping cock, and another whimper escapes his throat.

Each movement of our hips is driving me closer and closer to the edge, the pleasure building at the base of my spine so intense, it's a wonder I didn't finish the moment I was inside of him.

I move my mouth to trail sloppy kisses along his jaw, shifting down his neck. "Perfect, so good, love you so much, I'm so lucky." My praise mixes with his cries for "more, harder, yes, right there," and it's the dirtiest, most satisfying soundtrack I've ever heard.

My muscles are straining, my balls high and tight, ready to burst, but I need Oakley to finish first. "Come for me, Oak. Fuck, I can't last any longer. I'm going to shoot any second now, going to fill you up."

He must like the sound of that because he finally shudders in my hold, dick thickening and twitching in my hand before warm, white ropes of cum cover our chests between us. His ass clenches around me as he continues to come, squeezing and forcing my orgasm to crash through me. I struggle to support myself above him as pleasure overwhelms me, spreading throughout my limbs as I continue shooting inside of him, as it seems to go on and on.

When I finally finish, I slowly pull out of him, fascinated as I watch my release leaking out of his used hole. "Fuck, Oak. That's the hottest thing I've ever seen."

He laughs, "Parker, that was fucking amazing." He's got a dazed smile as he stares in my direction, eyes unfocused. "I don't think I'll be able to move for a week, but that was so damn good."

I lean over him to place a softer kiss on his lips before standing from the bed to get some warm washcloths to clean him up and draw a bath. When I return and am satisfied I've gotten most of his cum off him, I scoop Oak into my arms and carry him back into the bathroom. After verifying the temperature is okay, I carefully climb into the large bath, positioning Oak so that he's sitting in between my outstretched legs. He relaxes into me, resting his head back on my shoulder.

"You okay?" I check, running a hand through his hair.

He laughs. "Parker, I'm so fucking great right now."

"I love you," I say softly.

"Love you, too. So glad we get to do this forever."

"Me too." I place a soft kiss on the top of his head, thinking about that word. *Forever.*

I can't believe I almost settled for a future of hiding this, or worse, not having it at all. I know nothing is public yet, but I know we're both all in. There's no going back to the way things used to be, and I would never want to. Even if we both have to quit our jobs, *and I really hope it doesn't come to that,* but even if we do have to completely start over, we'll be together, and that's all that really matters.

Oakley has always been the most important thing in my life, and I'm so fucking grateful that he somehow feels the same way about me.

AFTER THE WATER COOLS DOWN, I help get Oak out of the tub, taking longer than I probably need to drying him off before we head back to his clean bed. Even though it's been a long day between traveling and finally having sex for the first time as an actual couple, it's clear Oakley isn't ready to go to sleep yet. He practically skips into his room, and he's got a faraway look in his eyes, obviously distracted about something.

I'd pulled on some sleep shorts with pockets so my pump can go in them, but Oakley is still completely naked when he whirls to face me, excitedly asking, "So is the concern at work that if people knew we were dating, they'd worry we might break up and cause drama that would affect our job performance?"

"Or that we would compromise the quality of our work to

make the other happy," I add, a little confused by the topic change, but rolling with it.

He barks a laugh at that. "You're the first one on the upper management team to shut down my unrealistic ideas, and you're constantly keeping me on task and within budget."

I shrug giving him a guilty smile. "True." *Guess I'm not as subtle with my persuasion as I thought.*

"So that shouldn't be an actual problem," Oak adds excitedly. "We have evidence that we've never let our relationship interfere with work if anyone actually questions it. There's a huge paper trail of you keeping me in line, and everyone has seen it in our meetings. Think about all of the couples who already work there, it's okay because they're married right? If the biggest concern is us breaking up, we'll just prove to them that we won't break up."

He sounds so confident and proud of himself that I feel like I must have missed something. "They've all also proven they can do their job impartially. I don't think promising we're committed to each other will be enough to ease their concerns," I gently point out.

"It will if we do it right," he insists, practically bouncing where he sits now. "Would you promise that? We've already proven we can be impartial with our work over the years. I know we've only just confessed our feelings, but this isn't actually new. You said you think I'm the only person you could ever love? Well, I feel the same way. We already spend all of our time together, live together, and the sex has been the best of my life."

I can't help but laugh at that, but I agree with everything he's saying. "Yeah, Oak. I'd promise you anything. I just don't want either of us to give up the career we love and have worked so hard for if we don't have to."

"I don't want you to have to give up anything either," he assures me.

I didn't think he would, but it's still a relief to hear he understands the risk I'd be taking by announcing a relationship with him. He's the heir, he won't be the one people expect to leave if something did happen.

He rushes forward to stand next to where I'm sitting on the bed, taking my hand in his. I arch my brow in his direction, silently questioning what he's doing.

"Parker, I'll be honest, this isn't how I pictured tonight would end," he starts, fully beaming at me now, and his smile makes my heart soar. I always want him to look like this, want to understand what's making him look so damn happy so that I can make sure it never stops.

"I can barely remember a time when you weren't my best friend, my person, and now, I've finally realized that you're the love of my life. Promising to be with you would be the easiest thing I ever do."

I'd never imagined that Oak would say any of this to me. It's almost too much to process. I feel like we're moving in slow motion, frozen in this moment where we can finally be honest about wanting to be together. My chest feels ready to burst with how much I adore him, and I know my smile is just as big as his.

He drops to kneel on one knee, still holding my hand, and the move distracts me from his declaration enough that I look away from his handsome features, down at where his knee is now touching the floor.

"What are you doing down there? Come to bed so we can cuddle."

"I'm trying to be romantic, dammit," he laughs. My eyes widen as they snap back to his, and I realize what position he's now in.

"Oak…" I trail off, unable to form any thoughts, let alone say anything else, as he continues to smile at me.

He shifts his hand so that only our pinkies are wrapped around each other, and I'm reminded of him doing the same thing when we were much younger. Reminded of the promises he's made me over the years, always so serious while I laughed at his silly displays.

But I'm not laughing right now as my eyes fill with tears.

"Parker, I've always wanted a family of my own," he says confidently. "I know you thought I wanted a wife and kids, but the only thing I've ever really dreamed about having was a love like my parents do. I want to grow old with my person, and still be as in love with them in our nineties as we are on our wedding day. If you're open to it, I want to have a bunch of kids, and I want them to be embarrassed by how in love their parents are. I don't have a ring yet, but I can make you another promise—to do everything that I possibly can to make you happy for the rest of our lives as your husband, if you'll let me."

Is this really happening right now?

Is Oakley actually proposing to me, completely naked with a pinky promise? It's fucking perfect.

He's got the biggest smile as he says, "The more I think about it, it's like we've already been together for a really, *really* long time. I don't want to date you, I don't need to. I already know everything about you and I know that I want you to be my forever. Let's skip to the good part. Will you marry me?"

I don't want a ring. This is so much better than any piece of jewelry. This is over twenty years of friendship and support, of being there for each other through the best and worst moments of our lives. *Aren't those the wedding vows? For better or worse, through sickness and health?* Oakley has already been by my side through all of that.

I think I'm nodding, but I still can't get my voice to work as I picture him standing in a tux, in front of all of our friends and family, promising to choose me as his partner. Could I really be that lucky? Is there any way being married would actually help our case at work and I could get to not only keep my dream job, but also get to be with Oakley forever? Obviously, that's the ideal ending here. Even if I end up unemployed, being presented with the option to actually claim Oakley as mine—to marry him—is enough. *How could I say no to that?* No looming end date to being roommates. No women to publicly date while we hide our true feelings.

It really does seem too good to be true. I'm not convinced there won't be consequences at work. But even if there are, marrying Oakley will be well worth it.

"Okay," I finally choke out, wrapping my finger around his. He stands to cup my face in his hands once more, claiming me with a kiss full of love and passion and everything I thought I would never have in life.

I pull back after a moment. "You do actually want to get married though, right?" I clarify. "You're not just suggesting all of this thinking it will make things easier with our jobs?"

"Fuck yeah, I want to marry you," he says quickly. "I'd marry you tomorrow and not tell anyone if you'd like."

As nice as getting married with just the two of us there sounds, I don't think it's what Oak would really want. "I think we can do better than that."

OAKLEY

December

After a relaxed make out session post engagement, we're lying in my bed.

My head is resting on Parker's chest and we're both on our phones, sleep schedules completely thrown off by the time in the hospital and all of our travel the last few days. I've been showing him different pictures of men's wedding bands and what I want ours to look like—flashy with diamonds—when Parker suddenly shows me his screen that's pulled up to a page on what looks like French Polynesian marriage laws.

"What if we got married at the resort launch?" he casually suggests.

I sit up quickly, spinning to face him with the biggest smile. His entire body is relaxed and full of joy in a way that I haven't seen from him in a while. I'm immediately all in, practically shouting "Yes! The resort launch! I can't believe I didn't think of that! It'll be perfect. All of our friends and family and the important people from the company are already planning to be there. You and I have been coordinating everything, so the details for the event are already things that we like. We can surprise everyone once we're there! Like an 'ask for forgiveness, not permission' sort of thing with the company."

He laughs, obviously loving my enthusiasm for the idea as I continued to voice everything he was probably already thinking. "That way if anyone at work is actually as concerned as you think they might be, we'll already be married. I'm sure HR would rather be the first to know, but we can point out that we've always been close. Everyone knows that, and we'll explain that when we decided to become more than friends we didn't see the need to date, and went right to marriage."

"It'll be good PR for the resort too," he pointed out.

"Hell yeah, it will. We're hot. Our wedding pictures are totally going viral."

"So, should we tell anyone? Or are we even going to surprise our families?"

I pause for a moment to consider what he's asking. I'm the one with the huge, super-close family. Even though I know a lot of them consider him to be an honorary member already, I'm the one who will end up facing their wrath when they find out we kept the truth of our relationship from them.

"Maybe tell our immediate family that we're dating now. I think we can trust them to keep that a secret, but I love the idea of a surprise wedding."

"Perfect. You know that means we'll both be coming out to the people who don't know as we walk down the aisle though?" he points out.

My eyes go wide and my smile turns a little wicked. "This is going to be the best wedding ever."

"When you made the suggestion that the two of us secretly get married, knowing how much the idea of it being something special for just the two of us would appeal to me, I couldn't help but think about the type of wedding you'd prefer to have," he explains. "One that would have gorgeous photos with over-the-top decor, every detail meticulously planned to your liking. I figured nothing could top the event we've already been working on. You've practically been planning your dream wedding for almost the last year," he points out and I laugh, a huge smile on my face as I stare at this perfect man. How could I ever have thought there was someone out there for me who would be a better partner than my best friend?

"I considered not even telling you about the surprise," he admits. "I knew you'd agree the moment I suggested the idea, but there are legal aspects to getting married outside of the United States, and though it is legal for same-sex couples to get married in French Polynesia, all marriages have to be at a town hall in French. The ceremonies on the beach and at our resort will technically be commitment ceremonies after couples take care of the legal bit if they choose to go that route," he reminds me.

"So, I was thinking that maybe we could have the best of both worlds—a small, maybe courthouse, wedding in Chicago like you'd suggested—something for just the two of us, followed up by the big, flashy, surprise island wedding of your dreams witnessed by everyone we know."

"That sounds perfect," I agree, and I can't hold back from kissing him any longer. We're going to have the best wedding ever.

I'M ABRUPTLY WOKEN from a peaceful sleep by loud banging on what I'm guessing is our front door. Parker is wrapped around my naked body, and other than the incessant knocking, I'm quite comfortable. I tap my phone screen to check the time and see a bunch of missed calls and texts from both Beck and Cody. *I wonder who's at the door?*

It's almost one PM, so at least we were able to catch up on some sleep before my brother interrupted us. I decide to call Cody back, choosing the nicer option, not convinced I really need to get out of bed yet.

"Hey!" he answers after the first ring.

"Hey, Cody. Can you tell my brother to kindly shut the fuck up," I say in a cheery tone.

He laughs. "Yeah, I'm not saying that." Then his voice gets quieter like he's pulled away from the phone. "It's Oak. He asked you to stop knocking, please." Then there's some shuffling noise, and Beck's voice is coming through the speaker.

"I've given you more than enough time. I want details if I'm going to keep lying to the family for you. Let. Us. In." Then the line goes quiet, so he must have hung up.

Lying to the family? Maybe he didn't tell everyone about my love confession then.

"Cody and Beck are here to interrogate us after my abrupt departure at Christmas, but it sounds like they might not have told anyone else about my big speech," I tell Parker as I get out of bed and hurry to put on clothes. I rush to open the door while Parker heads to his own room to get dressed.

Should we combine closets? Get a different condo? Move to the suburbs? We have so many decisions to make and I'm so excited for them all.

"Can I help you?" I say in a sugar-sweet tone as Beck pushes his way past me, making himself comfortable on our couch. "Come on in," I huff sarcastically.

"Where's Parker?" he asks, sounding concerned as he looks around the space to find it empty. I'd updated my family that Parker was doing okay and when we'd be coming back, but I guess I didn't give any other details, too distracted by finally getting to be with him for real.

"He moved out," I say, attempting to keep a straight face so I can fuck with my brother. I sink onto the armrest of our other couch, trying to look defeated while wondering how long I can keep this up before Parker comes out here.

"What?" Cody croaks out in alarm. "We were so sure that he was in love with you too…" he trails off, and I feel a little guilty for not telling Cody the truth, but Beck rudely woke me up, and he didn't stop him, so they can both deal with me messing with them for a minute.

"I do love him. He's just being a brat because you woke us up," Parker guesses correctly as he joins us in the living room. He sits down on the couch right next to me, before surprising me completely by pulling me onto his lap.

"Hi," I whisper, turning to sit sideways on top of him with my legs stretched out on the couch so that I can look at both him and our uninvited guests.

"Hello," Parker responds in a soft tone, sounding amused before gently cupping my chin to guide my mouth to his.

"Well, it looks like you two finally figured your shit out," Beck comments in a smug tone, but he also looks genuinely happy for us.

"Sorry. I couldn't resist," I say, looking at Cody.

"I'm just so excited that you two are together," he replies.

"Took you long enough," Beck teases.

"Have you told anyone else?" Cody asks, bouncing on the edge of the couch now.

"We haven't even left our place since we got back from the airport. I had assumed that you guys would have told the family when I ditched Christmas, though," I say looking back at Beck.

"I would never out anyone," he says firmly.

I smile warmly at him in response. I really have the best family.

"Our other brothers and parents are all still staying at our grandparents', you know how they like to pretend like we aren't all local and have us spend the week there. We actually came here as a well-being check and to see if you'd be up for coming back there since you left before everyone exchanged presents. Which you would know if you'd checked your phone," Beck informs us.

"Perfect. We can tell everyone at once. Want to see if your mom can meet us there?" I ask Parker and he nods, smiling as he pulls out his phone.

PARKER

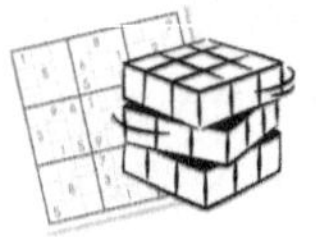

December

We text Adrian and Jordan too to see if they're available to join us.

We pick them up so that the four of us can follow Beck and Cody back to the suburbs, since they live in the same neighborhood as Oakley's grandparents now.

The whole car ride over, Adrian updates us on everything that's been going on with Hudson living with him. We still catch up pretty regularly, but it's been a while since he and Oakley have had time to really talk. It's pretty clear to me that Adrian is obsessed with him, but as far as I know, Hudson has only publicly dated women.

"In the beginning, all the poor man would talk about was wanting to be a dad," Adrian explains. "It was never 'I miss my ex-wife,' or 'I hate being alone,' it was always, 'I'll be so old now if I ever become a father,' or 'what am I going to do with my life if I can't be a dad'. I was sick of him complaining without taking any action, so one day I printed out a bunch of information for him on surrogacy, fostering, and adoption, and reminded him that you don't need to have a partner to be a parent. He seems to be doing much better now that he's working with the adoption agency."

Adrian might sound put-out by Hudson, but I know he loves helping other people solve their problems, and a "hot, broken hockey player" as he's called him, is probably his ideal man. Adrian casually mentions all of the things he's been doing with Hudson as a part of the adoption for "moral support" and it sounds like he's just as involved with the process as Hudson has been.

I'm grateful for how chatty Adrian is so that we don't feel obligated to tell him and Jordan that we're together before we get there. When we arrive, I hang back with Oakley to talk to him about how he wants to do this.

"So do we work up to it, or announce it when we walk in?" he whispers as we're walking up the drive.

"How about we just walk in holding hands?" I suggest as I take his hand in mine, pleased when he smiles up at me adoringly and nods.

With it just being immediate family here today, we're the last to arrive. My mom is chatting with Oak's parents near the kitchen island and his grandparents are talking with his three other brothers in the attached living room. Beck, Cody, Adrian, and Jordan all say their hellos before sitting at the kitchen table. Their house has an open concept, so we're all able to essentially be in the same space which makes this easier.

It's Adrian who notices our hands first. "Oh my fucking god!" He stands from his chair so quickly that he almost knocks it over as he slams his hands onto the table in front of him. "Sorry, Grandma Caldwell, but Oakley and Parker are holding hands and if that doesn't call for some swear words, I don't know what does. Are you seriously telling me that you let me rant for the entire car ride when you two were hiding that?" he asks, waving both arms in the direction of where we're joined. I can't help but smirk at him, and when I glance at Oak, he's got a giant smile spread across his face.

He lifts our joined hands before casually asking, "Have you guys met my boyfriend?"

The room erupts in a chorus of questions and congratulations, and people claiming to have always known that we should be together. In all of the chaos, Oakley and I are pulled apart into different hugs. My mom manages to find me in the Caldwell commotion and we step off to the side.

"I'm so happy for you, honey. It's always been him, hasn't it?" she asks, pulling me in for a warm embrace.

"Yeah." I nod, laughing at how we seemed to be the last to figure that out. "It has been."

"Your dad loved him, you know," she adds, and suddenly my vision is blurring at the edges. "He was always saying how good Oakley was for you. How glad he was that we moved here because you'd finally found a home." My throat is tight, and tears are silently spilling down my face as I hold her even closer as she continues. "I've always tried to look for the light that manages to shine through life's darkest moments. Whenever I wanted to regret moving here, wondering if things would be different, if we would still have him, I would see you with Oakley. I've always wondered what would have happened if we hadn't moved before you were diagnosed, if you were alone when you lost conscious-ness. He saved you that day, but it was more than that. I would hear you both laughing from the next room, see how much happier you were because of him, and I would know that your dad wouldn't have changed a thing. I know that you haven't had the easiest life, but Oakley has always been your light. And I see how he looks at you, like you're the center of his universe. I'll always be so grateful that you two found each other."

We're both attempting to wipe the tears from our eyes when

Oakley comes over to wrap his arms around us both. The rest of the Caldwells continue to joke around and talk as the three of us enjoy our quiet moment. Just as we suspected, no one cared that we aren't straight; they're just all happy to see us together, even if they're probably going to tease us about how we were the last to know for the rest of our lives.

I've always felt so privileged to be included in this big, supportive family, and I love that I'll no longer have to be an unofficial member.

In just a few months, I'll be married to a Caldwell, and I can't wait.

EPILOGUE ONE-OAKLEY

March

Sure, most people might assume I'm the more spontaneous and "fun" one in our relationship, but Parker has also been my best friend for over twenty years now, so I think he's learned exactly what sort of elaborate, over-the-top displays bring me the most joy.

And really, making each other happy is all that we've ever cared about. Now we just get to do it as partners, and soon publicly as *husbands*.

We're finally in Bora Bora for the resort launch. Our guests, aka our friends, family, and coworkers, are all here, though Parker and I got here a few days before everyone else. We wanted to get here first to work with the resort's event coordinator, Theodore, in person. We did warn him ahead of time, but I felt better being here early, just in case. He's gladly signed an NDA, so we're confident he's kept quiet that the soft launch is no longer just a party to celebrate the opening, but our wedding.

Our surprise wedding that no one but him knows about yet, even though it's going to happen any minute now.

Back in Chicago, we couldn't go the very next day to get married like I had hoped because you need to get a marriage license the day before going to the courthouse. When we filed for the marriage license, we realized it would be public record, so after some debate we decided to warn our heads of HR and PR. We assumed they might have search engine alerts for our names, and figured it would be better to hear from us. We scheduled an emergency video meeting to explain our plan and see if they might agree to hold off on telling anyone else. Neither of them are on the board of directors, and they loved our plan.

After getting the license, we agreed to wait the couple of days until NYE so that we could have an excuse to celebrate that night without telling everyone about exactly what we were celebrating. We both put on our nicest suits and waited in line to be married. It was perfect.

I probably could have bribed our way through the process more quickly, but there was something really nice about going through it without drawing any extra attention. Just two men in love who finally got their shit together enough to get married. Especially when our commitment ceremony today has the exact opposite vibe, with everyone we know in attendance on a very difficult to get to island resort, with every flower and seating chart meticulously planned by Theodore and I.

Everything looks absolutely gorgeous. The huge all-glass indoor reception area is arranged with tables for dinner, a dance floor, and DJ for later in the evening. The outdoor deck is set up with open bars, and cocktail tables are spread out through the space while appetizers are being passed around. Elaborate local greenery mixed with flowers and candles compliment the romantic island vibe, and there's torches surrounding the space as live local music plays.

All of the guests are showing up in their best island formal wear, and everyone seems very impressed by the resort and with how their accommodations have turned out.

"Is everyone here yet?" I ask Parker as I look around the room one more time. I've confirmed that all of our relatives are outside on the deck, along with all our friends, and even Aspen and Sage made it. We were only waiting on a few coworkers for the last headcount we did, but I think they've all arrived.

"Yeah, I think Bob from the board was the last one we were waiting for," he confirms.

"Okay, I've got the microphone. Are you ready?"

"As long as you do the talking," he mutters, making me laugh.

"Obviously," I agree with a wink.

We both approach a small stage that has the band on it, asking them to please pause their playing. They also know there will be a ceremony today, but not who it's for. "First of all, I want to say a huge thank you to everyone for joining us all the way out here to celebrate the latest resort to join the Caldwell Hotel family! This really is a family company through and through, and I am honored to continue the legacy my great-grandparents started many years ago."

I pause for the polite clapping from the audience and look at Parker beside me before continuing. "I do have a slight confession to make, though. This isn't just a launch party to help prepare the staff for opening to the public, and the photographers aren't just here to take pictures for our website..."

I pause again because I can't help it. I love building the suspense as people begin to murmur amongst themselves. Parker laughs next to me, raising a brow and motioning for me to get on with it.

"Today will also be the first wedding at this new venue!" I announce dramatically, and the whispered murmurs grow louder as people look around in confusion, probably looking for someone in a wedding dress. As hot as I'm sure Parker or I would look in one, we've opted for tan linen suits.

"Who's getting married?" someone finally asks loudly enough for me to clearly hear them.

I plaster on my biggest, brightest smile before answering, "I am."

My mother is toward the front of the crowd, and it's her voice that I hear cut through the crowd next. "You're doing what?"

Then Beck, who's standing next to her, says in the cockiest fucking tone I've ever heard, "Who are you marrying, Oakley?" as he stares directly at Parker.

Damn him. Of course, Beck knows and is just trying to ruin my fun when I'm attempting to be all dramatic and surprise everyone. At least he isn't mad that I'm getting married first when he beat me to the whole engagement thing.

Then Parker surprises me, stepping forward to take my hand before answering, "Me." He's loud enough that he cuts through the chatter, and everyone falls silent at once to face us again as he goes on. "Well, legally, we're already married. But today will be our commitment ceremony and reception."

"Welcome to our wedding!" I announce again. "If everyone could please make your way to the beach to find a chair, we've got everything set up. Family will probably want to sit up front, but fight amongst yourselves if you must. The ceremony will begin in ten minutes."

There's more murmuring, and I hear a few phrases like "I didn't even know they were gay," and "Are we supposed to give them a present if we didn't know this was a wedding?" No one seems particularly upset. Glancing back toward my mother reveals Parker's mom is now huddled with both of my parents, and they're all smiling, looking excited as they talk.

Parker squeezes my hand, pulling me closer to him. "Was that everything you'd hoped it would be?"

"Honestly, no one yelled or seems mad or anything, so it was kind of more chill than I was expecting,"

"And that's a bad thing?"

"No… I just thought maybe someone would be devastated that I'm officially off the market for good and might object," I joke.

"There's still the actual ceremony," he offers, making me laugh.

Beck and Cody approach us, interrupting any response I might have had. "So, you just had to show me up," Beck directs at me, the smirk on his face assuring me he's teasing and isn't actually upset.

"You had a pretty dramatic year with the whole cult thing. I figured I could draw some of the attention away from you."

"We're so happy for you both," Cody cuts in, his permanent smile even wider than it typically is.

"Thanks," Parker replies, returning his offered hug, and I do the same.

"I *am* really happy for you guys," Beck reiterates.

After another round of hugs with him, Parker and I promise to talk to them after the ceremony and rush to catch up with our parents, asking if they'll walk us down to the beach. My mom is already crying, and even my dad's eyes look misty as they all eagerly agree telling us how happy they are for us, and that they can't believe we kept it a secret.

No one is upset though, and as Parker's mom walks down the aisle created on the beach with her arm through his, I have this overwhelming feeling that I know his dad would have been happy for us too.

Parker turns to face me with all of the love and joy I feel for him shining back in his eyes, and I can't help but feel like we were always meant to end up here.

I might not have known to what extent when we met all of those years ago and I pointed out that we had similar nature names, but even back then, it was obvious Parker and I were always meant to be.

EPILOGUE TWO-PARKER

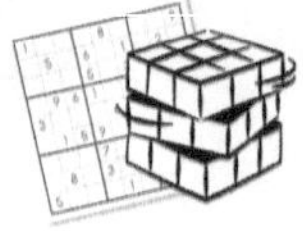

A Few Months Later

*T*urns out we had nothing to worry about at work. Our wedding was a huge success and did in fact go viral. Our professional pictures of the day, along with all of the videos from the guests blew up on social media, and the resort quickly booked all open dates for the next two years. Everyone at the company was thrilled, and if anyone had anything negative to say about the relationship, Oakley's dad shut it down before we could even begin the first board meeting after the ceremony.

He had loudly congratulated us on our marriage before launching into a speech about how proud he is that his family's companies continue to be such safe and accepting places for queer relationships. The Caldwell Corporation has been able to successfully launch the resort with a same-sex wedding in the same year that the Werewolves have had their first player come out.

It was all really dramatic and over-the-top if you ask me, but no one was going to dare question the validity of our working relationship after that. HR had already helped us complete the necessary paperwork, so we didn't need to worry about that. I think it also helped avoid drama with the other board members when they saw that nothing changed as far as our work dynamic goes.

That was a few months ago now, and I'm still the first to rein in Oakley's wild ideas and keep him on budget, and the financial success of our first major expansion since I took over my position hasn't hurt either. We're already exploring other places to revive exclusive destination venues, and Oakley is very excited about the possibilities.

I'm more excited about the things that have been happening close to home, though. We were able to come to an agreement with the owners of the house next to Cody and Beck's in Oakley's grandparents' neighborhood before they even listed it. They casually mentioned wanting to sell to Beck, and Oakley and I were touring the place a few hours later.

It's perfect. Six bedrooms with a large office on the main floor that we can both work out of since we still don't like to spend much time apart. We've converted the finished basement into a large home gym, but a few of the rooms upstairs remain unfurnished. Oakley and I have talked about both wanting to have kids sooner rather than later, and he's made a few offhand comments about waiting to decorate until they can be nurseries. I know he probably wanted to come across like he was joking, but I don't think he was, which is fine by me.

We moved in quickly and the best part has been that we finally adopted a dog from the same shelter that Beck and Cody found Duke at. Buddy is a scrappy little thing, probably only half the size of Duke or Spot, but he clearly hasn't caught on about that. He's a pretty chill dog most of the time. He enjoys our walks and loves fetch, but he's also content to hang out in the office with us if we're working. But get him around other dogs, and it's like he wants to prove that he's the biggest and baddest. It's adorable to see him try to bark louder than them, or try to chase after something like he could possibly be faster when his legs are half the size.

We still have our condo in the city for when we need to work super late, and Buddy seems happy enough there, but we usually have him hangout with Duke next door if Cody and Beck are around, and we've been watching Duke when they can't bring him with them to Montana with all of the work they're putting in there.

They're watching Buddy tonight so that we can stay in our condo after our dinner with Aspen and Sage. They're finally officially together. Aspen's family unfortunately did cut her off from her trust fund. But her company is hers, and she's assured us that she has no regrets. They really do seem happy together, and from what they've said, it seems like Sage's family has been more accepting, even if they were surprised and confused by the announcement of their relationship.

We try to see them at least every other week, and they've asked us to dinner at their condo tonight. It's wild to be walking up to their door, hand in hand with Oakley, coordinating wedding bands and all, when just a few months ago we were walking into this same apartment to find our girlfriends cheating on us with each other.

The road we took to get here was definitely messy, but with how happy we all are now, I wouldn't change a thing.

"Think they'll be decent this time?" Oakley jokes, clearly remembering the same night that I am.

"We'd better knock," I suggest, just in case.

Aspen answers the door with a huge grin, rushing us inside. Sage is finishing setting the table, bouncing around like she's excited about something. *Maybe she tried a new recipe?* She's gotten really into cooking lately, and most of what she's had us taste has been pretty good, but there was a night with some very overcooked salmon that we ended up having to order in.

"You guys seem happy," Oakley comments with a grin of his own as we sit next to each other at their table.

The girls exchange a knowing look before turning back to us. "We wanted to talk to you both about something," Aspen starts.

"We don't want you to feel any pressure at all," Sage jumps in to assure us. "We just wanted you to have all of the information and present the option."

"But obviously the decision is yours," Aspen adds, nodding seriously.

I look at Oakley out of the corner of my eye, and he's looking at me with the same confused expression I'm sure is on my face.

"Okay…" I say slowly. "What decision?"

The girls join their hands over the table, exchanging another smile before Aspen turns to us. "We've decided we don't want to be parents."

Not sure how I'm supposed to react here. "Congratulations?" I try, completely unsure if that's the response they're looking for.

"That's a totally valid choice. Not everyone needs to be a parent to be happy and to live a full and fulfilled life," Oakley adds.

The girls both laugh at his response before Sage looks at him seriously. "But you do, Oakley. You've talked about wanting to be a dad since we met you, and now that you guys are married, I'm sure you've talked about your options to become parents."

"We wanted you both to know that we think you'll be the best dads, and we wanted to offer to donate eggs, if you want to go that route," Aspen adds. "We can't be surrogates because we've never completed a pregnancy before and neither of us loves the idea of being pregnant. This way, if your kids had questions or ever wanted to meet their donor mom, we'd be around. Again, if you'd rather it'd be anonymous, or you want to take a different route, no pressure."

I am stunned speechless by their offer. I've been looking into adoption, fostering and surrogacy since before Oakley and I were even officially together. I look over at Oak, and he doesn't seem to be processing this any more quickly than I am. His mouth is hanging open, and his eyes are wider than I've ever seen them.

"We're so grateful to both of you, not only for your friendship and support, but also for the part you played in encouraging us to finally be together. We're happier than we've ever been and we want to share some of that joy with you in this way, if you'd like that," Sage continues.

Oakley finally snaps out of his stupor, turning to me, eyes full of hope and questions. He's obviously fighting a smile, trying to hold back how excited he is by this offer until I can weigh-in on it. But he should know by now that I want the same things he does, especially when they'll make him happy. So I smirk as I give him a small nod, and it's like his joy explodes out of him all at once.

He's out of his seat, rounding the table to hug the girls before my brain can even process he's moving. "Thank you so much! That would be amazing! I can't believe this is really happening! We're going to be dads!" He's rambling loudly as he continues to hug them both, alternating between them before rushing back to me and practically jumping into my arms.

I catch him easily, and we laugh while I hold him in the embrace for a long moment. I know that these arrangements aren't easy and can take a long time to work, if they do at all. But everything else has worked out so well for the four of us so far, I have no reason not to hope for everything they're offering us. We've all been through so much together, but we're all better off for it. Now that they've made the offer, there's no one else I would trust more to be the biological mother of our child.

When we first started seeing the girls over a year ago now, I had hoped dating someone who was best friends with Oakley's girlfriend would be the solution I'd been looking for, a way for me to remain close to him while he still got the happily ever after he's always wanted.

I'm so glad we didn't settle for that version of ourselves. Our actual happily ever after is so much better.

THE END

AFTERWORD

Thank you for reading!

Want Aspen and Sage's side of the story? Check out the story early on my Patreon

Keep reading for the first chapter of Accidentally Falling For Her an AFFMBF companion novella! Chapters releasing weekly to paid Patreon members, coming to KU later this year.

The following is unedited and subject to change.

ACCIDENTALLY FALLING FOR HER

FF COMPANION NOVELLA

CONTENT WARNING: INCLUDE SPOILERS

- Cheating, homophobic and racist comments by secondary character
- threat of being cut off for being LGBTQIA+
- Bi-erasure
- Fetishization of queer people kissing by secondary characters- main characters are encouraged by friends to kiss each other "because it's hot"

Chapter One

ASPEN- 18 YEARS OLD - AUGUST

I'll never forget the first time I saw a bride. I was seven years old, my uncle was getting married, but all I really cared about was the pretty new dress I'd gotten to pick out for the occasion. I'd always loved playing dress up and covering myself in sparkly things, but that day felt different. There was no pretending that I was in a castle, no using my imagination to create a fantasy world of wonder. *It was real.*

The venue was gorgeous, in an old church with stained glass windows that bathed the room in rainbows. There were flowers in every direction. Colorful fabrics draped across the back of the pews and down the length of the aisle. I was convinced that I'd entered a real life fairytale.

The bridesmaids were beautiful, although I was confused why they'd all chosen the exact same dress. My gut dropped when the flower girl entered, though. I was pissed off that another girl about my age got to be a part of the ceremony, in a prettier dress than mine, while I was stuck in the crowd. Jealousy coursed through me in a way that I'd never known; meanwhile, she didn't even seem to be enjoying the experience. I wanted to run into the aisle, shove her out of the way, steal her basket of petals, and show everyone that I could do it better.

Luckily, before I had any time to execute that horrible plan, everyone stood and turned to face the doors at the back of the church. I managed to peel my attention away from the girl I wanted to forcefully replace just in time to see the doors open to reveal the most stunning woman I had ever seen.

Her dress was made of satin and shined in a way that called out to me, begging me to touch it. The strapless neckline was daring for our southern state's typical dress codes, so it was completely unique to me. Rhinestone embellishments covered the bodice, and she had a full blown tiara holding her veil in place. I wanted to curtsy, convinced that I was in the presence of royalty for the first time in my life.

I'd met my soon-to-be-aunt, Sam, before but she had always come across as sort of plain, boring even. I didn't recognize her at all as the ethereal beauty seemingly floating down the aisle toward my uncle.

Later on, when my mother finally convinced me that the bride was truly Samantha, I was completely amazed, in awe of the dress and the magic it must contain to have transformed her into a real-life princess.

I've been obsessed with weddings ever since. Specifically the dresses and that magical feeling only the perfect wedding gown can inspire. Not so much the wedding itself. While other little girls might dream of finding their prince charming to marry one day, I've always been far more interested in the brides than the man they're walking down the aisle to. Father would rather I die than end up with a woman. *Can't win the support of his conservative Georgia voters if he's got a lesbian as his only child.*

Honestly, I'm not that torn up about it. I stopped believing in fairytales a long time ago. It's not like I'll be having a wedding of my own anytime soon.

The wedding dresses, though, I still want. I'm going to design them and inspire that sense of magic in others. I'm aware that magic isn't real, but that feeling of being special very much is. Every bride deserves to feel like the most beautiful woman in the world on their wedding day, and it's my dream to be the one who creates the gowns that make them believe it.

That's why I'm so excited to be studying to earn my degree in fashion with a minor in business. My parents just left after moving me in and taking a few staged photographs that were likely requested by my father's PR team.

I'm finally free of their fake bullshit and constant attempts to control every little detail of my life. They've put in a lot of money and effort to turn me into their idea of what a House of Representative's daughter should be, even if I know I'll never truly fit that description.

Thank fuck they don't care what I major in. My father thinks I'm only here to earn a "MRS degree," but that obviously isn't happening.

"Knock knock. Are we officially free?" Arthur asks as he

pushes open the door to my dorm room, looking around like my father might be hiding in the tiny space.

"It's real," I confirm, grinning conspiratorially at my best friend as he sits down at my desk, the only option other than the bed.

"About damn time," he exclaims. Arthur is the son of my father's campaign manager, and if I believed my father actually cared about other people enough to have friends, Arthur's dad would be his closest one. Our families have done everything together for as long as I can remember.

Thankfully, he's one of the few people I could stand in our posh private schools growing up, so I didn't mind always being around him. Art's straight and doesn't have anything about his sexual orientation to hide from his parents. He *is* hiding the fact that he's very liberal, though, and that's probably just as bad in the eyes of our fathers. Obviously, I am too, and we've been counting down the minutes until we could finally move out and be on our own.

We've always planned to go away to the same school, which our parents were thrilled about, but that's only because they want us to end up together. They've had this whole plan of how we'll get married and be some political power couple, and when my father retires, Arthur will replace him with his dad running his campaign.

That's not happening for so many reasons.

For now, though, we aren't ready to rock the boat. We're going to focus on earning degrees and enjoying the first true taste of freedom we've ever known.

"Have you heard from your roommate yet?" he asks, and I check my phone again before answering. She moved all of her stuff in yesterday, but texted me that she would be out all morning to give me space to move in. We haven't actually met in person, but Sage and I found each other in a social media group for freshmen needing roommates, and after talking a bit to determine that the other was normal enough, we agreed to pair up.

She posts a lot of inspirational quotes on her socials, and the few texts we've exchanged had far too many emojis and exclamation marks for my liking, but I'm sure that's just an online thing, no one is actually that happy all the time.

Arthur fills me in on how meeting his roommate went, and I go over my schedule for the hundredth time. The door opens once again, and I glance up, figuring Sage must finally be here. I'm mentally preparing to say hello to my new roommate when all of the air is sucked out of the room. My lungs stop working entirely when my gaze meets the greenest eyes I've ever seen. *Are they contacts? Are people actually born with jade green eyes?*

I saw her photo online, but the pretty girl I remember from the profile picture seems so dull compared to the radiant woman standing before me now.

Her long blonde hair is curled and a section is tied back with a light pink ribbon that matches the flowing sundress she's wearing. Her smile is dazzling, and I'm aware that she's talking, probably introducing herself as she looks between me and Arthur, but I can't focus on anything other than how soft and pink her lips look as they move to form the words. She bounces over to the side of my bed where I'm sitting, and I finally register sound as she says, "I'm a hugger if that's alright," before holding her arms open in my direction.

I have never once in my life described myself as a "hugger," but I scramble out of my bed like my ass is on fire because the most gorgeous woman I have ever seen is offering to wrap her arms around me, and *not* returning her hug right now sounds like the worst decision I could possibly make.

Sage pulls me in closer; she's shorter than I am by a few inches, but she manages to tuck me into her embrace in a way that's so warm and comforting that I'm afraid I might never let go. She smells like coconut sunscreen and lavender shampoo, and those scents should not work so well together, but on her, they do.

My heart drops when she starts to pull back, but instead of letting go, she casually grabs my hands in hers, holding eye contact as she continues to smile at me. "I'm so excited to finally meet you in person, Aspen. I just know we're going to be the best of friends. I'm so happy we're finally here, together!"

"Me too," I manage to agree, far too distracted that we're still holding hands to offer anything of value to this conversation.

She leans in a little closer and lowers her volume slightly, but not enough to make me think she doesn't want Arthur to hear. "I hope it isn't weird that I'm starting with this, but you're probably one of the prettiest girls I've ever seen, so I apologize in advance if you catch me staring," she says with a giggle.

"Are you into girls?" Arthur asks, sounding way too excited. Sage probably thinks he's creepy, but I know he's asking for my sake.

Before I even get a chance to hope that I could be so lucky, she's shaking her head. "Oh gosh no! Sorry honey, I wasn't hitting on you," she says with another laugh as she finally lets go of my hands and moves to sit on the edge of her bed. "I was just thinking about how easy rush is going to be for you."

"Rush?" I repeat back as a question, because I'm officially lost.

"Sorority recruitment. You are joining a sorority, right? I'm a third-generation AAA legacy, so I'll probably get a bid from them, but I'd bet even without letters of recommendation from alumni, you'll get bid offers from all of the top houses. Oh please tell me you are! We can request to be in the same rush group and visit all of the houses together. It'll be so much fun."

I hadn't intended to join a sorority.

I'm looking forward to being on my own for the first time. I'm sure I'll meet people in my classes, and I already have Arthur.

So do I even need more friends? As much as I still love dressing up and doing my hair and makeup to always feel like the most put-together version of myself, I hadn't envisioned joining a group of girls who always look like clones on social media.

But Sage is looking at me with those big emerald eyes like she wants nothing more in the world than to go through whatever recruitment is with me at her side. And I'm beginning to think it might physically pain me to disappoint her. *I'm so fucked.*

"Sure. Sounds like fun," I agree.

Arthur lets out a sound like he chokes on a laugh before coughing to cover it, and I turn to subtly glare at him to stay quiet, but of course, he doesn't listen. "Aspen is total sorority material," he agrees sarcastically.

Sage must not pick up on his tone, though, because her warm smile never falters. "I'll send you the sign up link! Oh, and you can borrow anything you'd like from me, or we can go shopping if you don't have things that work for the dress codes for each day."

Even though the process she's describing sounds kind of awful, I can't help but be excited. Her enthusiasm is contagious, and if she's there with me, how bad can it really be?

ACKNOWLEDGMENTS

Thank you so much to everyone who helped make this book possible!

Both covers were created by the very talented Rebecca at Story Styling Cover Designs and the amazing cover image was done by Michelle Lancaster. Copy edits were done by Brittany at Campfire Edits, Proofreading was done by Lindsey Middlemiss.

Character art drawn by Kierofoxen—thank you so much for all of the art you've already done, can't wait to get more!

Sensitivity feedback was done by Jonathan Samuels—Once again your unhinged comments were everything! I can't thank you enough for the feedback and entertainment!

The biggest shout out and thank you to my alpha/beta readers! Lys, Ronan, Charley, Jenny, Debbie, Elizabeth, Ashley, and Bryoni

Bec, hopefully you know how grateful I am to have you as one of my very best friends. I'm so glad that I get to do this author thing with you. Your feedback and emotional support means the world to me.

I'd also like to thank my very supportive husband who thought it was lame I put the same thanks in the first two books, so here's a new one. You're still awesome.

Thanks to my parents who've been very supportive, even if I hope they never actually read any of my books.

And to my kids, thanks for napping, going to bed on time, and letting mommy work, even after I quit my nursing job to stay home with you guys. I'll love you forever and always no matter what.

ALSO BY LEXI AMBER

<u>Lexi Amber</u>

Chicago Awakenings

Accidentally Joining His Cult *contemporary MM romance*

Accidentally Falling For My Best Friend *contemporary MM romance*

Accidentally Falling For Her *contemporary FF romance companion novella Preorder available Expected Fall 2025*

Accidentally Living With the Captain Preorder available Expected early 2026

<u>Co-authored with Bec Benson</u>

Love Without Labels

The Reality of Wanting Him contemporary MM romance OUT NOW

The Reality of Wanting My Bully Preorder available expected Dec 2025

www.ingramcontent.com/pod-product-compliance
Lightning Source LLC
Chambersburg PA
CBHW021028310726
48969CB00006B/1589